'I'm still not attracted to you,' she repeated.

Oh, but it was going to be fun tearing down her barriers and making her face the truth about the chemistry between them. Mitch grinned. Feeling happier, more optimistic and content than he had in a long time, Mitch looked deep into her eyes and ran his hands from her shoulders to her wrists.

Linking his fingertips intimately with hers, he asked softly, 'Then why are you trembling?' Why were their entire bodies still reverberating with excitement and desire?

Lauren tore her eyes away from his and stared at the open collar of his shirt. 'Because this whole idea of the two of us being together…because of a proposition put forward by my father—upsets me, that's why.'

Mitch knew the idea of dating—maybe even marrying—a woman he barely knew should have been disturbing to him, too. But now that he'd spent a little time with Lauren, it wasn't. Not at all. 'How come?' he asked.

'Because we're talking about the possibility of us one day getting married as calmly and logically as if it was a business deal, and it's not!' Lauren said emotionally, pushing him away.

Available in October 2003 from Silhouette Special Edition

Mercury Rising
by Christine Rimmer
(The Sons of Caitlin Bravo)

His Marriage Bonus
by Cathy Gillen Thacker
(The Deveraux Legacy)

The Cupcake Queen
by Patricia Coughlin

Willow in Bloom
by Victoria Pade
(The Coltons)

My Very Own Millionaire
by Pat Warren
(2-in-1)

The Woman for Dusty Conrad
by Tori Carrington

His Marriage Bonus

CATHY GILLEN THACKER

SILHOUETTE®
SPECIAL EDITION™

*First published in Great Britain 2003
Silhouette Books, Eton House, 18-24 Paradise Road,
Richmond, Surrey TW9 1SR*

© Cathy Gillen Thacker 2002

ISBN 0 373 16941 8

23-1003

*Printed and bound in Spain
by Litografia Rosés S.A., Barcelona*

CATHY GILLEN THACKER

married her childhood sweetheart and hasn't had a dull moment since. Why, you ask? Well, there were three kids, various pets, any number of vehicles, several moves across the country, his and her careers, and sundry other experiences. But mostly, there was love and friendship and laughter, and lots of experiences she wouldn't trade for the world.

You can find out more about Cathy and her books at www.cathygillenthacker.com, and you can write to her c/o Silhouette Books, 233 Broadway, Suite 1001, New York, NY 10297, USA.

SILHOUETTE®

is proud to present

the brand-new series featuring the wealthy Deveraux family, only from

CATHY GILLEN THACKER

THE DEVERAUX
LEGACY

The Deveraux Family: powerful, wealthy
—and looking for a lasting love!

Chapter One

"Don't you dare play innocent with me, Mitch Deveraux!" Lauren Heyward stormed the moment she entered Payton Heyward's office at Heyward Shipping Company. She leveled a slender, accusing finger Mitch's way. "I know what you and my father are trying to do! And it's not going to work!"

"And what, exactly, might that be?" Mitch Deveraux retorted dryly. He didn't have a clue what she was talking about, but he couldn't say he minded spending a little time alone with the young and beautiful shipping heiress. She was a sight to behold, in a fitted coral blazer, clinging white silk blouse and slim coral-plaid skirt that ended just an inch above her knees. The low-heeled pumps she wore were sensible but sexy enough to make the most of her trim, spectacular legs. And her beauty didn't end with a knockout figure. Her golden-brown hair looked soft and touchable as it fell to her shoulders. She had parted it on the side, and tucked it behind her ear. Mitch had never been much of a touchy-feely guy, but as he took in the delicate, aristocratic contours of her oval-shaped face, he found himself wanting to run his fingers through the golden-brown mane and experience the shimmering softness of her hair for himself.

Oblivious to the overwhelmingly sensual nature of his

thoughts, Lauren marched closer yet. "The two of you are trying to marry me off by proxy!" she charged as she inundated Mitch with an intoxicating patchouli perfume, and the clean, sexy smell of her skin and hair.

"Why would I want to do that?" Mitch deadpanned as their glances meshed and sexual electricity sizzled between them. He barely had a love life himself these days—he sure wasn't taking on the task of trying to manage anyone else's. Even if, up close, Lauren Heyward had the most beautiful dark brown eyes and softest lips he had ever seen, and was a very successful businesswoman in her own right with a professional savvy that reportedly rivaled his. In her personal life, Lauren Heyward's father had told him, Lauren was a flake who'd already weathered—and ended—two engagements.

Abruptly looking as taken with Mitch as he inexplicably was with her, Lauren looked deep into his eyes and seemed to consider him for a long moment before she said softly, "That's a very good question."

"And one I'll be happy to answer for you both," Payton Heyward interjected as he walked in and shut the door to the executive suite behind him. A folder of papers in his hand, Payton moved behind his desk. The silver-haired executive was dressed in a black suit, sage-green shirt and tie. Behind his wire-rimmed glasses, his brown eyes were direct, his manner both disciplined and imposing. "Why don't the two of you have a seat?" Payton directed, gesturing at the two chairs in front of his desk.

Lauren sat down—but only out of respect for her father. She had no patience whatsoever for what he was trying to do.

"I know dowries and arranged marriages have gone out of favor," Payton continued pragmatically as he also sat. "But I got to thinking the other day that maybe it's time they made a comeback."

In your dreams, Lauren thought fiercely, ignoring the oh-so-handsome man seated beside her.

"Especially in cases like yours, where you are both from wealthy families and are both unmarried as you reach your thirties," Payton continued.

"I'm only twenty-eight," Lauren said, trying to ignore the delicious scent of sandalwood and spice teasing her senses. Now was not the time for her to be thinking how incredibly virile and sexy Mitch Deveraux looked. Or consider how his solid six-foot-six-inch frame would match up with her slender five-foot-ten-inch body. Sometimes men as tall as Mitch seemed awkward and ill at ease in their own skin. Not Mitch Deveraux. He moved with a calm deliberateness that radiated both strength and control. And probably, Lauren thought recklessly, made love the very same way.

"Mitch is thirty," Payton retorted, giving Lauren a steady look that insisted she and Mitch would hear Payton out, whether they wanted to or not. "And twenty-eight is close enough," her father added firmly.

"I've also been married and divorced," Mitch pointed out.

Everyone in Charleston knew that, Lauren thought as she took in Mitch's short, dark brown hair and arresting deep blue eyes. Mitch's divorce from Jeannette Wycliffe had been both sudden and mysterious—to the point people were still speculating about the possible reasons for it, two years after it had become final.

"You're free now, and so is Lauren, and that's what matters," Payton countered. "Especially given the fact neither of you is getting any younger."

Lauren set her jaw and glared at her father. She had been under increasing pressure from him to do something about her single state before he did, and she resented it. "I'm not a spinster," she said. And felt Mitch's hot gaze slide over her from head to toe before returning with heart-stopping accuracy to her face.

"No, but you very well could be if you don't settle down and marry and have a family soon," Payton told her.

"I think we're jumping the gun here a bit," Mitch broke in peaceably.

Lauren would have been grateful to Mitch for that, had he not been hand-selected as her beau. Ignoring the unsettling way her senses stirred at his nearness, she said, "I agree."

Payton frowned. "I had a feeling you wouldn't have an open mind about this," he said.

Her father's feeling had been right. "Look, I've no doubt Mitch is a very nice person," Lauren said.

Reportedly, all the Deveraux were. Although she didn't know them that well, since she had gone to Charleston's all-girls schools from kindergarten on up, and they had entered the city's most renowned coed establishments.

"Not to mention he is very knowledgeable in the shipping business, too, since he is set to one day take over the Deveraux Shipping Company," Payton interjected.

"Then I'm sure Mitch has a lot in common with you, Dad, since you run our family shipping company," Lauren said patiently. "But Mitch doesn't have a lot in common with me. I work in the real estate business."

"Which makes it even more important that you marry someone capable of running Heyward Shipping when I'm no longer around," Payton countered.

"That won't be for years. And if and when it comes to that, I'm sure one of your vice presidents will be able to step into your shoes admirably," Lauren replied passionately.

"I want family running this company, Lauren. Family protecting your interests. And since there is no one else…" Payton leaned back in his chair and let his voice drift off.

Lauren could see that Mitch Deveraux was beginning to look interested in whatever her father was about to propose, but as far as she was concerned, this travesty had gone far enough. She vaulted out of her chair and began to pace her father's luxuriously appointed office restlessly. "I don't care how much sense it makes on paper. Or how the family business might stand to benefit from a relationship between Mitch and me. I'm still not going to date him." Lauren pointed at Mitch. *Not even if you think he's perfect for me.*

"Not even for one week, if at the end of the week you get the historic property you've been wanting ever since you were a kid?" Payton asked, smiling magnanimously. Ignoring her look of stunned amazement, her father continued bartering with her smoothly. "I bought 10 Gathering Street this morning, lock, stock and barrel. You do what I want, Lauren, and it's yours."

LAUREN'S HEART POUNDED as the news of what her father had done sank in. The two-story redbrick Victorian mansion at 10 Gathering Street had white trim and green shutters. With sixteen thousand square feet and twenty-four rooms, it was one of the largest homes in the historic district. Sadly, it had fallen into disrepair in recent years. Lauren had lamented the neglect, and wanted to take it on and restore it to its former glory for as long as she could recall. Two things had stopped her. It was way out of her price range, and it had not been on the market.

She regarded her father cautiously. "You own that property?" she repeated slowly.

"Yes. And I'm prepared to give it to you outright if you agree to spend every evening for one week dating Mitch Deveraux. Marry him at the end of that time, and I'll give you an unlimited budget to renovate and furnish it, too. Think of it, Lauren," Payton continued as he leaned toward her eagerly. "You'll be able to take that sad, neglected house and turn it into the showplace of your dreams.''

Lauren wanted to do that. She wasn't prepared to sell her soul, her body and her hand in marriage to accomplish it. She regarded her father grimly, almost afraid to ask for fear of what the answer might be. ''And what does Mitch get out of all this?''

To Lauren's chagrin, Mitch looked every bit as interested in the prize as she had been. ''I'd like to know that myself,'' Mitch said.

Payton shot Mitch a man-to-man glance before turning back to Lauren and speaking to both of them. ''If he agrees to spend every evening with you for one week, he'll get what he's been wanting. A merger between the Heyward and Deveraux shipping companies. The two of you have until 6:00 p.m. this evening to agree to my terms. Or there will be no deal.''

Although Mitch looked quite calm, Lauren had to struggle to keep control of her emotions as she regarded her father. ''I can't believe you are doing this to me!'' she fumed, folding her arms in front of her.

''I predicted you would feel that way,'' Payton countered as he stood and walked over to the minibar to pour himself a glass of springwater. But to Lauren's dismay, her outrage didn't change what her father was doing, or how he was doing it, one iota.

The hurts of the past came slamming back at Lauren. ''It's always business with you, above everyone and everything else, isn't it?'' she said to her father. She was so furious she was shaking.

''That's not true,'' Payton said, abruptly looking just as stricken and upset as Lauren felt.

''Isn't it?'' Lauren challenged bitterly. Tired of keeping her feelings to herself, she plunged on emotionally, ''The bottom line is you've always paid more attention to your business than you ever have to Mom and me, even when she was dying. Well, I can't forgive you for always putting your company's interests ahead of your family, Dad," she told him, her throat aching with the effort it took to speak at a normal level. "And I sure as hell can't forgive you for this!"

Ignoring the hurt look on her father's face, and the stunned look on Mitch's, she grabbed her handbag, turned on her heel and stormed out.

"SHE'S NOT THE ONLY ONE who is shocked by this proposal of yours," Mitch said in the silence that fell. He was damn near flabbergasted.

"I want my daughter to marry well," Payton Heyward said.

"But to a Deveraux?" Mitch countered, filled with the uneasy feeling that Heyward was withholding every bit as much information from Mitch and Lauren as he was telling. "As you pointed out to me six months ago when I first approached you with the idea of a merger, the Deveraux and the Heywards have a history of duking it out in the marketplace—in ever-inventive ways." Was this just another one of them? Mitch wondered. And if so, was Payton's daughter, Lauren, not only one hell of an actress but now an active participant in the competition between the two firms, albeit in an unexpectedly inventive way?

"Well, I thought it over, and you are right. Our two shipping businesses' continued battle for market share was unnecessarily sapping the energy and resources from us both. We should stop trying to outsell each other, agree to go after different areas of the marketplace and focus on simply increasing revenue in our own specifically targeted areas."

Mitch remembered the meeting—and his own disappointment and disillusionment afterward—well. "Right, and even after I finally managed to convince you that my proposal wasn't a trick to diminish your various accounts or overall sales, you still didn't want any part of a formal no-compete agreement, never mind a merger between our two firms.'' Nor, unfortunately, had Mitch's father. Mitch looked Payton straight in the eye. "You said competition was the lifeblood of business and that your ongoing contest with my father and me was what kept you and your sales force on their toes.''

"And that's still true,'' Payton said matter-of-factly. "But so is what you said. Maybe it's time we both looked at change. And the best way, the surest way, to do that is through you and Lauren. Don't you see?'' Payton returned to his desk and sat down, albeit a bit stiffly. "If you and Lauren marry and join our families and businesses through that marriage, it gives us an incentive to make the situation work fairly for both families and businesses. It's sort of like an insurance policy that both sides will do their best to see that you and Lauren are happy.''

"With one exception,'' Mitch corrected, his uneasiness only increasing as he looked Payton Heyward straight in the eye. "I never brought up the idea of either dating your daughter or marrying her. Furthermore, you just saw what Lauren's answer to your proposition is. She wasn't the least bit open to the idea.''

Payton waved a hand and countered confidently, "She's upset. She'll calm down once she's had an opportunity to mull it all over.''

Mitch wasn't so sure of that. Lauren had looked pretty certain of her feelings to him. "I'm not interested in having a woman forced to marry me for business reasons,'' Mitch said firmly. Being married for what he'd thought were all the right reasons, and having that not work out, had been hard enough. He didn't think he could weather another unhappy liaison, even if his emotions weren't involved this time because the marriage was strictly a matter of convenience.

"She won't be coerced into this if you play your cards

right and convince her to cooperate,'' Payton persuaded softly.

''And why would I want to do that?'' Mitch asked.

Payton smiled magnanimously. ''Because of the secret bonus in this for you,'' he said.

Secrets were trouble. Mitch knew that. And yet the more curious side of him couldn't keep from biting as he rose from his chair and began to pace. ''I'm listening,'' he said impatiently after a moment.

''If you can get Lauren to marry you, I will give you fifty-one percent of Heyward Shipping as dowry as well as the position of CEO during the transition period. I will control the other forty-nine percent until my death, and then that percentage will go to Lauren.''

''Which would leave me in control of the company,'' Mitch said. *And a huge chunk of the Deveraux-Heyward empire on his own.* The idea of that, of having his own shipping company to run even before his father retired and turned over the Deveraux empire to him, appealed to him immensely.

''Naturally I'd want to give you every incentive to make this arranged courtship and marriage of yours work,'' Payton continued, ''so if the marriage dissolves, your fifty-one percent of the company will revert to me, and eventually, Lauren's control.''

Mitch forced his attention to the problem at hand. ''Unfortunately,'' Mitch told Payton frankly, ''Lauren won't even go for the idea of us dating for one week. She'll never agree to the two of us marrying.'' Even if he wanted that, Mitch added silently to himself, and he didn't think that he did.

Payton eyed Mitch thoughtfully. ''That's why this part of our agreement must remain secret,'' Payton explained even more pragmatically. ''Lauren doesn't understand the shipping business and the enormous responsibility of running a huge company. She would not comprehend that I am only doing this to make sure that she and her financial interests are taken care of for the rest of her life. You, on the other hand, have already weathered a messy, ugly divorce. And no doubt know that passion is a poor basis for a marriage meant to last a lifetime.''

Mitch had already come to the same conclusion, and in fact, had been looking for a wife who would enhance rather than complicate his life. However, he wasn't sure an overemotional woman like Lauren was what he was looking for. He'd had in mind someone a lot more sedate and willing to follow his directions. On the other hand, a deal like this—with such a lucrative payoff—did not come along all that often. Mitch didn't want to pass it up. And that went double for the part of it that Payton had dared mention in Lauren's presence.

Already beginning to formulate a plan, Mitch checked his watch. ''You said I've got until six o'clock to decide about the merger?'' he asked casually.

Payton nodded. ''The deal requires you date my daughter for one week, starting tonight, every evening from 6:00 p.m. until midnight. I don't care what you do. Or how you spend your time. As long as you spend it together.''

Chapter Two

"I thought I might find you here," Mitch said as he stepped through the open front door at 10 Gathering Street and confronted Lauren, who was standing in the majestic front hall looking at the chandelier above her head. She had taken off her fitted coral blazer and looped it over the newel post of the sweeping staircase railing.

Lauren turned to regard him with a sweetly challenging look. "And I thought you might come after me."

"Because I found you irresistible?" he asked, mocking her wry tone to a tee.

"Because you found the business deal my father offered you irresistible," Lauren corrected, color filling her cheeks.

If only she knew what had been offered—in exchange for her hand in marriage—after she left.

"Don't you think that's a little like the case of the pot calling the kettle black?" Mitch questioned casually, shutting the heavy oak door behind him. He stepped closer, noting how snugly her sleeveless white silk blouse molded the fullness of her breasts and the slenderness of her torso, while revealing her well-toned arms and the sexy, rounded curves of her shoulders.

Lauren tilted her face up to his, looking all the more

outraged. "What do you mean?" she bit out in a low, clipped tone.

Mitch shrugged. "You're interested in the deal your father offered, too. Otherwise you wouldn't be here looking at the house and wondering just how bad it would be to date me for one week, if at the end of that time you owned this showplace."

Lauren shook her head indignantly. "Even if I agreed to that—which, by the way, *I have not*—I still wouldn't have the funds to fix it up."

Mitch had the strong feeling that now was not the time to bring up marriage and the huge financial bounty that would reap for both of them. Finding the interior of the house warm, he took off his suit jacket and looped it over the banister next to hers. "So you'll earn them with the sale of your existing home," he said, willing to do whatever was necessary to talk her into accepting the first part of her father's proposal.

Lauren's dark brown eyes flashed. "My house is already mortgaged to the hilt. I had to do that to underwrite the costs of restoring it to its former grandeur," she told him impatiently.

"So you'll wait a bit," Mitch said, loosening the knot of his slate-gray tie and the first two buttons on his starched dove-gray shirt, "and sell it for a profit then." Damn, it was warm in here! And rather musty-smelling, too.

Lauren strode across into the adjacent drawing room and went to one of the floor-length sash windows that fronted the house. She unlocked it and tried without much luck to push it up. "I'm successful at what I do, but I can't afford the upkeep, taxes and insurance on two multimillion-dollar properties."

Mitch joined her at the sill and easily raised the pane she had been unable to budge. "Surely you've got some money coming from a trust fund," he argued, as fresh spring air, redolent with the heady fragrance of flowers, poured into the room.

Lauren went to the next window and unlatched it. "It's all tied up in Heyward Shipping Company stock," she said as Mitch helped her lift that one, too. "I own forty-nine percent of the company, but I'm forbidden from selling a penny of it until I'm fifty. Or become an acting partner in the company, along with my father."

"That seems harsh," Mitch commiserated, as another draft of fresh air poured into the room. He and his siblings all had trusts from which they could draw forth on a yearly basis, regardless of what career they chose for themselves. And though they all preferred to support themselves with their own efforts, the money was still there for whatever they chose to use it for, even if it was nothing more than a financial safety net.

"It is harsh," Lauren concluded with a beleaguered sigh. "But then that's my father. He wants what he wants and he doesn't care what kind of machinations he has to go through to get it."

"And what he wants is you to be an active participant in the family company." Mitch understood that. His father had wanted the same thing from his children. Only Mitch had been interested in working alongside Tom, however. His younger brother, Gabe, had gone into medicine. His older brother, Chase, had started a magazine for men. And his baby sister, Amy, had started her own redecorating business.

"Right," Lauren said as she inspected the elaborate, composition-decorated brass and marble mantel. "But I have no interest in the shipping business."

That could be disastrous for the company she was inheriting. Especially given the rapid changes that were now happening in the centuries-old business. But figuring Lauren wouldn't be interested in the impact the Internet was having on the industry, any more than his father currently seemed to be, Mitch let the subject go. "How'd you get involved in real estate anyway?" Mitch asked as Lauren continued to inspect the intricate frieze carvings around the doors and windows.

"I like houses." Lauren ran her fingertips across the painted white paneling on the walls, disturbing a surprisingly thick layer of dust. "Love seeing what's inside them. And helping find the perfect owner for each house."

Mitch grinned as Lauren blew the dust off her hand. "Instead of the perfect house for each owner."

Lauren pivoted toward him, her eyes alight with a mixture of curiosity and pique. "And your distinction is…?" she prodded.

Mitch shrugged, and seeing no reason not to be forthright, said, "I get the feeling you care more about the homes than the people who buy them." There was a very real tenderness about her as she looked over the house and determined what it would need in the way of time and attention. It was as if she felt the people could fend for themselves—these lovely old houses couldn't—their very existence rested on continued loving care. Which, sad to say, some home owners and investors obviously were not motivated to give.

Lauren released a short, amused breath. "That's a very shrewd observation," she volleyed right back, holding his eyes. "And I'd probably be offended if it weren't so true."

Knowing she wasn't alone in her feelings of reverence for the historic district, but a little surprised she would be so candid about her emotions, nevertheless, Mitch asked, "Why do you feel that way?"

Lauren led the way back out into the hall, back past the library and the spacious and once-elegant formal dining room, to the kitchen. "Think about it," she said as she walked into a room with uneven floors, no appliances whatsoever and only the most rudimentary of metal sinks. She peered into the pantry, which housed several outdated cans of sardines, a bag of rotting onions and two empty mousetraps.

Holding her nose, Lauren plucked up the mesh bag and carried the seeping mess to the metal garbage can sitting just outside the back door. She dumped it inside, then went back to the sink to wash her hands. "Charleston was founded in 1670 and it's the oldest city between Virginia and Florida. The homes in the historic district have been here for several hundred years. They've weathered hurricanes and wars and all sorts of other calamities, and yet they are still standing, strong and proud. Homes like this are worth preserving."

"I agree with you there." Mitch opened a window, letting much-needed fresh air into the stuffy room, while Lauren knelt down to inspect the massive brick fireplace. "The historic section of Charleston is one of the most beautiful and memorable residential areas I've ever seen. And I've been in some of the finest homes up and down the East Coast. You didn't grow up here, though." Seeing she was about done, Mitch offered Lauren a hand up.

"No." Lauren smoothed her trim coral skirt over her hips. "My father wanted to live in the country. So we lived out at the family estate in Summerville, where he still resides on weekends."

Mitch knew the place—some forty-five minutes away. Payton Heyward's estate was a magnificent property, renowned for its beauty and historical significance. "But you have a double here in the city."

Lauren led the way down the hall to a series of small rooms that had once functioned as servants' quarters. "You've been doing your homework." She studied him with a mixture of suspicion and respect.

Mitch shrugged, turned and stepped back against the wall to let her pass in the very narrow hall. "You received a Carolopolis Award for the revitalization of that home when you were done with it. Everyone knew about it."

The historic town home, which was exactly two rooms across, upstairs and down, had been photographed and featured in the Charleston newspaper.

"What's so special about this house," Mitch continued, as Lauren smiled and led the way up the back staircase, "except for its size?"

Lauren slanted him a glance over her shoulder, her soft golden-brown hair brushing lightly against her pretty face. "It bothers me, the way it's been neglected. The family could have cared less about it," she continued as Mitch reached the second floor and began following her through a series of bedrooms, baths and sitting rooms, all seeming in equally bad condition. "They opened it to the public sporadically to raise enough money to keep on paying the taxes, but they didn't bother to take care of it in the process." Lauren paused to consider the floor-to-ceiling bookshelves in the massive upstairs library. "There's water damage all over the place, from leaks in both the plumbing and the roof. The floors, as you can see, need to be repaired and refinished. The kitchen is completely inadequate. And the whole house probably needs to be rewired from top to bottom."

"And yet," Mitch said as they headed on down the hall to the music slash ballroom, "you're willing to take it on."

Lauren turned to him with a smile as she walked through the spacious party room. "I could make several million selling it when I am finished."

Mitch had the feeling if she ever finished fixing it up and restoring it to its former glory, she would have so much invested in it, she wouldn't want to sell it. "Or you could turn it into a museum," he said.

"Or a bed-and-breakfast." Lauren opened the lid and fingered the chipped ivory keys on a badly neglected baby grand piano.

"Are you thinking about that?" Mitch grinned as her

noodling picked up speed and the familiar melody line of "Heart and Soul" filled the room.

He took over the bass and joined her in an impromptu duet of his childhood favorite. "I can't really see myself as an innkeeper," she admitted, making a face, as they continued to play on the hideously out-of-tune instrument. "I don't particularly like cleaning up after people. Tidying up after strangers is even worse. But you're right, I could make it a museum."

Mitch studied her as the song wound down to an end and they stepped away from the piano. "But you don't want to do that, either."

Lauren shrugged as she went to the window covered with moth-eaten velvet drapes. "A home this lovely deserves to be lived in. It's been roped off for far too long as it is."

She had a point there, Mitch knew. Still… "It's too large a place to live in alone," he said.

She gave him a look that let him know she had no intention of living the rest of her life alone. "I'll get married someday," she promised softly. She paused, a defiant gleam coming into her lovely dark brown eyes. "But I won't do it because my father has auctioned me off in exchange for some business merger."

Mitch leaned against the wall, facing her. "You'll marry for love."

Lauren lifted her slender shoulders in an indifferent shrug. "That's the only reason to marry." She paused, looking deep into his eyes. "But I can see you don't agree with me on that."

Mitch thought about what "love" had put him through. Feeling abruptly restless, he moved away from the wall, walked across the room. Hands braced on the frame on either side of him, he looked out into the spacious hallway, appreciating all over again how big and majestic this mansion really was, before turning back to face Lauren. "I think maybe your father is right,'' he said with all due seriousness. ''Maybe we'd all be better off if we approached marriage and relationships with the clear-headed approach we use on business deals.''

Lauren rolled her eyes as she breezed past him and continued down the hall, to the sweeping semicircular mahogany staircase that dominated the center of the house. ''You really want to date me, don't you?'' she mused.

Mitch caught up with her on the stairs. He wrapped his hand lightly on the railing as they made their descent. ''I really want the merger that will make Deveraux-Heyward shipping the most powerful firm on the entire eastern seaboard. And,'' he concluded as he reached the main level once again and turned to face her, ''if spending time with you for one week is what guarantees that, so be it.''

Silence fell between them as Lauren plucked her blazer off the railing and tugged it back on.

''We can do this, Lauren,'' Mitch insisted as he sat down on the fourth stair-step up. He clasped his hands between his spread knees. ''It's really not that much to ask.''

''Says you,'' Lauren retorted back as she paced to the front door and back. She leveled an accusing fingertip at Mitch. ''You haven't had my father trying to control your life in every way possible for the past twenty-eight years.''

Mitch shrugged, and still feeling overly warm, folded the cuffs back on his shirtsleeves, nearly to his elbows. ''From what I could tell, your father seems to love you very much.''

Still pacing, Lauren threw her hands up in exasperation. ''He does, which of course makes all his behind-the-scenes string-pulling on my behalf all that much worse.'' She paused, propped the back of one hand on her hip and looked straight at Mitch. ''It's like he doesn't believe in me to be able to make the right decisions on my own.''

''I'll be the first to admit that's unfair,'' Mitch commiserated quietly. "But you shouldn't let your pique with him about that keep you from owning this place and lavishing on it the tender loving care you know that it deserves and needs."

Abruptly, Lauren broke into a sweet-as-sugar, and just as impudent, grin. "Oh, you're good, Deveraux," she said. "Real good."

Mitch couldn't help it—he grinned back as he straightened. He drew nearer, finding himself still a good six inches taller than she was, despite the two-inch heels on her shoes. He looked down at Lauren, a little taken aback by the undercurrents of chemistry between them. "Does that mean I'm persuading you?"

"It means," Lauren delineated bluntly, with a take-no-prisoners look, "that I want to own 10 Gathering Street as much as you want the Deveraux-Heyward merger. So okay," she conceded on a reluctant sigh. "I'll date you every evening for one week. But I'll do so only on my terms."

"And those are?" Mitch braced himself for the demands to follow.

"It's strictly platonic." Lauren firmly ticked off her demands. "No kissing. No hand-holding. No fringe benefits of any kind."

Given the way she was looking at him—as though she just dared him to try anything the least bit romantic—it was all Mitch could do not to take her into his arms and kiss her senseless, then and there. "How about opening the door for you?" Finding his own pulse racing in what could only be anticipation, Mitch stalked her in deliberately predatory fashion.

Lauren stepped back, a slight look of alarm on her face. "No." She folded her arms in front of her tightly.

"You don't want me to pull up your chair," Mitch noted, pretending he couldn't imagine why not.

Lauren regarded him skeptically. "No."

"What about coats?" he asked lazily. "Should I help you on with your coat?"

Lauren flushed, the same soft hue as her blazer. "It's too warm for coats," she stated, digging in where she stood even more. "Besides, should I want to take one off, I can manage it on my own. And one more thing. I know my father and what he's banking on here, but you should know outright that no matter what else he offers me, our dating will not lead to marriage."

Even as he struggled over his own guilt over the secret dowry her father had already offered him, Mitch felt compelled to take on the role of devil's advocate. "Why are you so opposed to the idea of that?"

"I don't know." Lauren shrugged. "Maybe because it would be arranged?"

"Not if we decided on our own to wed," Mitch said.

Lauren stared at Mitch in mortification. "And why would we do that?"

"Because it makes sense," Mitch explained. "At least in a strictly business way." Able to see Lauren wasn't the least bit convinced, he explained, "The first tenet of business is to keep an open mind when trying to achieve your goals. It doesn't matter whether it's a short-term need or a long-term one. When a good idea is presented to you, you should make the most of it. Especially if it helps you meet your objective."

Lauren looked down her nose at him as she said dryly, "Let me guess. You think an arranged marriage is a good idea?"

Mitch paused, uncertain how much to reveal. The last thing he wanted to do was hurt Lauren, and he had a feeling that if she found out about the secret dowry he had been offered, she would be very hurt. "To tell you the truth," Mitch said eventually, "I've never really considered an arranged marriage before—" But now that he *was* thinking about it—with Lauren Heyward as his potential bride—an arrangement like that *could* work. Given the right circumstances and attitudes, of course.

"I haven't thought about it either," Lauren interrupted unhappily, "and with good reason—it's an outdated concept."

"But now that your father has brought it up I can see he's got a strong case for such a liaison," Mitch persisted. One that seemed a little more intriguing with every second he spent with Lauren Heyward. Seeing she was going to need a little more persuasion, he leaned closer and said softly, "Think about it. We have similar backgrounds. We both understand the shipping business because we grew up with it."

"But only one of us is actually *interested* in the shipping business."

"Even better," Mitch said emphatically. "Should we decide to marry one day, we won't be fighting over who gets to run it—I'll automatically have the honor. Plus a marriage-driven merger would allow us to expand and strengthen both our businesses, while still keeping both firms private and 'all-in-the-family' so to speak. Financially, it would be good for both of them."

Lauren went very still. "What about passion?"

Mitch had only been with Lauren a few minutes, and he was already fantasizing about what it would be like to make love with her. But sensing she wouldn't want to hear that, he merely smiled. "I think every marriage should have some."

"Exactly," Lauren replied with a mixture of satisfaction and relief. She looked at him in a way that seemed to imply on that score they weren't compatible at all.

He sized her up and then decided a level of truth was called for after all. "I am attracted to you, Lauren." He'd also never been able to resist a challenge—and the thought of taking her to bed and discovering all the ways to give her pleasure was very intriguing, indeed.

"Well, that's too bad," Lauren retorted with a haughty toss of her mane of golden-brown hair. "Because I am not in the least bit attracted to you!"

Fibber, Mitch thought. "Want to bet?" Mitch asked, and then did what he had been wanting to do since she had first stormed into—and out of—her father's office earlier in the afternoon. He took her in his arms, lowered his lips to hers and put her declaration of immunity to the test. She gasped as their mouths fused and he kissed her long and hard and deep. Until he felt the need pouring out of her, as surely as the desire and temper. Until she moaned softly and melted in his arms. His mouth tingling, his whole body aching with the yearning to make her his, Mitch reluctantly lifted his head.

"Okay," Lauren said breathlessly as he continued to hold her close, "maybe you are attractive." She braced her arms between the two of them, doing her best to keep them from touching above the waist. "But that doesn't mean I'm attracted to you, Mitch Deveraux."

Mitch smiled at the stubbornness of her complaint, and bent her backward from the waist, determined to make her face the truth, no matter what it took. "Kiss me again and then say that," Mitch challenged playfully, kissing the nape of her neck, the curve of her ear, before taking the softness of her lips and molding them to his. He kissed her again and again, persuading, tempting, until her body trembled even as it strained to be closer to his and her arms moved up to wreath his neck. And once he felt the soft surrender of her body, tasted the sweetness of her mouth, there was no stopping with just one kiss. Never mind one intended merely to prove a point.

Mitch's heart pounded in his chest. The rest of his body went rigid with desire. Knowing the only way to be close enough to her would be to take her to bed and make her his, he tugged her nearer yet. He hadn't wanted a woman as much as he wanted Lauren, since…well, maybe never.

He couldn't even say why, exactly. He just knew there was something special about her. Something special about *this*. And she knew it, too, Mitch thought. He could tell by the way she was kissing him back. Unfortunately, this wasn't the way he wanted her—on an ill-thought-out whim. Reluctantly, he drew back. Waited for her reaction. Which turned out to be every bit as predictable—self-protecting—as he thought it would be.

"I'm still not attracted to you," she repeated.

Oh, but it was going to be fun tearing down her barriers and making her face the truth about the chemistry between them. Mitch grinned. Feeling happier, more optimistic and content—than he had in a long time, Mitch looked deep into her eyes and ran his hands from her shoulders to her wrists.

Linking his fingertips intimately with hers, he asked softly, "Then why are you trembling?" Why were their entire bodies still reverberating with excitement and desire?

Lauren tore her eyes away from his and stared at the open collar of his shirt. "Because this whole idea of the two of us being together…because of a proposition put forward by my father—upsets me, that's why."

Mitch knew the idea of dating—maybe even marrying—a woman he barely knew should have been disturbing to him, too. But now that he'd spent a little time with Lauren, it wasn't. Not at all. "How come?" he asked.

"Because we're talking about the possibility of us one day getting married as calmly and logically as if it was a business deal, and it's not!" Lauren said emotionally, pushing him away.

"Maybe it should be," Mitch murmured back, and found he was beginning to agree with Payton Heyward more and more. The only mystery was why he'd never noticed Lauren Heyward before and sought her out on his own.

Lauren took a deep, bolstering breath. She let her hands fall to her sides as she looked into his eyes and squared off with him. "I want children, Mitch."

"I want them, too," Mitch said sincerely. So there was no problem there. If the kisses they had just shared were any indication, there wouldn't be a problem in the bedroom. The problem would be staying *out* of the bedroom.

Lauren pressed her right hand to her chest. "I want a marriage from the heart."

So had Mitch—once. But he had learned the hard way not to look for a passionate love affair to give him happiness. He clamped his lips together. "Infatuation fades."

Lauren narrowed her eyes at him. "Is that what happened with you and Jeannette Wycliffe?"

Mitch sighed, ran a hand through his hair. "Suffice it to say, we were two people who definitely never should have married."

"But you did get married."

Mitch nodded, reflecting soberly on what a gargantuan mistake that had been. "Because we let our hormones dictate our actions. When I marry again, it will be because I've thought it out thoroughly and rationally, and know it's a sound alliance that will infinitely benefit us both." That we'll be good together both in and out of bed.

Lauren rolled her eyes and looked at him askance. "It doesn't get any more romantic than that."

"I'm not looking for the romantic—I'm looking for the practical. And you should be, too," Mitch advised stoically. The way he saw it, a temporary liaison between them would be very advantageous. Should they prove compatible, in the bedroom and out, an eventual marriage would be even more beneficial to them both. But even if they didn't get along all that well or share the same goals and ideals, there wasn't much risk or cost to either of them in dating each other exclusively for a period of one week. He'd had business deals he'd worked months to achieve that had paid him far less in actual dividends than this merger would. And he wanted—needed—this merger. Both the Heyward and Deveraux shipping companies did.

"In fact," Mitch continued sincerely, "I think you should be grateful to your father for setting this up." He knew he was.

At that, Lauren just shook her head at Mitch and muttered something about him being about as romantic as a tree.

"What time are we supposed to do this again?" she asked with thinly veiled impatience.

"From 6:00 p.m. until midnight, every night, starting tonight," Mitch replied over the staccato tapping of her foot against the wood floor.

"Fine." Lauren sighed, doing nothing to mask her lack of enthusiasm for the evening ahead. She planted her hands on her hips. "Where do you want to meet?"

"I'll pick you up at your place." Mitch plucked his suit coat off the banister and headed for the door. "And you probably want to dress nicely," he added.

"Why?" Lauren regarded him warily.

"We're having dinner with my parents."

AND LAUREN HAD THOUGHT her day, already as eventful as all get-out, couldn't possibly get any worse. She held up a hand to stop Mitch's flight and stepped into the open portal in front of him. "Whoa! Why bring them into this?"

Mitch stood, his jacket slung over his shoulder. "Because I already had plans to see them. I can't cancel. My mom has been having a rough time."

Lauren's heart filled with empathy for Grace Deveraux. "I saw she had been fired from her job on *Rise and Shine, America!* How could they do that anyway? She was the best host they've ever had on that morning news show."

Mitch nodded. "We all thought so, too, but apparently

the network brass wanted to go with someone who would bring in younger viewers.''

"That's crazy. You can't teach experience."

"Exactly." Mitch continued out onto the front porch.

Silence fell between them as Lauren crossed the portal and shut the door behind her. "How is your mom?" she asked gently.

Abruptly, Mitch's blue eyes became troubled. "We're not sure. She seems fine on the surface, but…she has to be hurting at the way she was dismissed from her job. Anyway, we're taking turns sort of circling the wagons and making sure she has plenty of moral support. Tonight is my night, and my father is joining us."

That was interesting, considering Grace and Tom had been divorced for thirteen years. "Are the two of them thinking of getting back together?"

Mitch shrugged.

Even though he didn't come right out and say so, Lauren could tell by the look on Mitch's face that he wished they would.

"They've both been dating other people since the divorce," he said.

"And now?"

"No one special, on either side, from what I can tell. But I don't know a lot about their personal lives." Mitch regarded Lauren casually. "What about your dad? Is he seeing anyone?"

"He hasn't dated at all since my mom died eleven years ago. He says he already had the love of his life. Which makes it worse, you know," Lauren related with a beleaguered sigh, "because the two of them had an arranged marriage. They didn't know each other from Adam when the two of them got together."

"But they fell in love."

"Yes, they did. Although my mom and I always—

always—came second to his business,'' Lauren reflected with more bitterness than she would have liked.

Mitch looked at Lauren sternly. ''Just because he cares about his company doesn't mean he doesn't care about you.''

That just showed what little Mitch knew, Lauren thought. Her father never did anything that didn't somehow positively impact his business. Hence, Payton's trying to fix her up with the son of his fiercest business rival. Payton Heyward was always thinking ahead. Always trying to make more money. Or become more successful yet. And while Lauren applauded her dad's ambition, she did not like the way he had—with Mitch's help—tried to include her love life in Payton and Mitch's plans for a merger between the Heyward-Deveraux shipping companies. But since this was the only way she was going to get the mansion she had wanted to refurbish for most of her adult life, Lauren knew she had to either bow out or cooperate. And for the sake of this lovely old home, she was going to cooperate—for a week anyway.

''So—'' Lauren dug the toe of her shoe into the brick and mortar floor of the porch, then looked up at Mitch ''—which one of us is going to tell my father we're taking him up on his deal?''

''I'll call him, if you'd like,'' Mitch said.

Lauren nodded. Bad enough her father had won this round of machinations. She didn't want to hear the victory in his voice when he realized it. Because although she had agreed to date Mitch Deveraux for one week—against her better judgment—there was absolutely no way she was marrying him, no matter how much her father wanted it, or how wonderfully Mitch kissed!

Chapter Three

"I thought you said you were bringing a date tonight," Grace Deveraux said to Mitch as he walked into the family's Charleston mansion several hours later.

Mitch looked at his mother. Thanks to her career as a television newswoman, she had one of the most widely recognizable faces in the entire country. She couldn't go anywhere without being recognized, which was why she was currently staying with Tom Deveraux in the home they had shared before their divorce, some thirteen years ago. It was the only way she could get any privacy in the wake of her very public firing.

Not that his mother had let the catastrophe get her down—her short and fluffy blond hair was as youthfully and impeccably arranged as always, her blue eyes lively, her trim figure clothed in a stylish silk pantsuit.

Mitch smiled, glad to see his mother looking so well. The idiots who had pronounced her "too old" to do her job might not know it yet, but Grace would land on her feet yet. And Mitch and the rest of the Deveraux clan would be there to applaud her when it happened.

Mitch accepted a glass of wine from his dad. "Lauren called and said she was running a little behind schedule and would just meet me here." Mitch hadn't been pleased to get the message from his secretary. He had the feeling it was just one of many excuses Lauren would offer up over the coming week to avoid spending even one more second than she absolutely had to with him. But since he hadn't known where Lauren was when she called, and she hadn't been answering her cell phone, he'd had no choice but to do as she had asked, and arrive without her.

"Lauren who?" his father asked as he sat down kitty-corner from Grace and Mitch.

Mitch figured now was as good a time as any to lay the bomb on his parents. "Lauren Heyward."

Tom Deveraux frowned. Mitch wondered if it was his imagination or had the gray at his father's temples recently become more pronounced?

"You know the rule about climbing into bed with the competition," Tom said.

"Tom!" Grace chided, a flush coming into her pretty cheeks.

"Mitch knows what I mean," Tom said, raking a hand through his closely cropped dark brown hair. "I wasn't speaking literally. Although now that we've brought it up, that better not be the case, either." Tom leveled a warning look at Mitch, his brown eyes darkening all the more. "There's nothing more potentially damaging than pillow talk, when it comes to industrial espionage."

The last thing Mitch wanted to be imagining was his head next to Lauren's as they exchanged teasing quips and soft words of love and lust after making love. He didn't want to think about her lying naked beneath him, either, her slender arms and long sexy legs wrapped around him. His relationship with her was too potentially beneficial to both of them to risk ruining with casual sex. If things went his way, he could make his mark with this deal with Payton Heyward, and Lauren would own the historical home of her dreams. And that was as far as Mitch was prepared to take it at this time, despite Payton Heyward's very interesting offer. Or his own desire for Lauren.

''Lauren doesn't work for her father,'' Mitch said, putting his own uneasiness about Payton Heyward's unprecedented actions aside. ''Furthermore, she has zero interest in his company.''

''Doesn't matter,'' Tom said gruffly. ''She's still an heiress to our biggest rival. And could inadvertently end up passing information to her father about what we're doing at Deveraux Shipping Company.''

Mitch had no intention of letting Lauren know anything she shouldn't. He would also keep a very close eye on her. ''The competition between Payton Heyward's company and ours isn't the biggest threat to our continued prosperity, Dad. The Web-based exchanges on the Internet are.''

''Those companies are a fad.''

Mitch knew a lot of top businessmen thought so, given all the dot-com firms that had already gone under. He didn't agree. He felt it was one of the fastest growing markets and would continue to be for some time. ''They also offer faster bookings at cheaper prices.'' And that was a problem, Mitch thought.

''Most big deals are made over a meal and closed with a handshake. That's always been the case and always will be.'' It was the really big deals, not the unpredictable little shipments, Tom Deveraux was interested in locking up.

In the past, those big deals had kept the Deveraux and Heyward shipping companies on top. But Mitch knew there was more money to be made by pursuing lots of smaller customers, too. They just needed a cost-effective way to do it. ''I still want to use this year's expansion money to put up our own Web site and start doing business that way as well,'' he said.

Tom gave him a look that reminded Mitch just who was CEO of the Deveraux Shipping Company. ''And I want to invest in more container ships.''

They would have more ships at their disposal if they merged with Heyward Shipping, Mitch thought. Because

Payton Heyward had just added two new state-of-the-art vessels to his fleet. And then they could still add an e-commerce component to their business, too, without over-mortgaging the firm, without worrying whether Payton was going to edge out Tom on an upcoming deal with a cus-tomer or vice versa. But he sensed he was going to have a hard time convincing his father to put his own uneasiness and suspicion aside and merge companies with Payton Heyward.

"When did the two of you start dating?" Tom asked.

"Tonight's our first date," Mitch said. "And you might as well know there are going to be six others this week as well."

Grace looked over with a raised eyebrow. "Cleared your calendars, did you, dear?"

Briefly, Mitch laid out the deal that had been offered to Lauren and him by Payton Heyward, while Lauren was present. He did not tell them about the dowry Payton had promised after she left in a huff. As he had expected, his parents were as shocked as he had been.

"Forget for a moment the fact that I would never agree to a merger between our two companies," Tom said when Mitch had finished. "This whole idea of an arranged court-ship is crazy! I'm surprised you even agreed to hear Payton out, never mind agreed to follow this cockeyed plan of his."

Grace nodded her agreement as she swiftly took Tom's side in this. "Are you sure you know what you're doing here, Mitch?"

Mitch knew he could convince his father a merger be-tween the two powerhouses was the right way to go, once he had Payton Heyward firmly in his corner and all the details worked out. His business case was that strong. But he would have to wait for the right time to do that and, unfortunately, now was not the right time. It was victory enough that he had even been able to broach the topic with his father, given his father's insistence they keep their firm private and family-owned, despite all business indicators to the contrary. "Look, all Lauren and I agreed to do was spend time with each other every evening for one week so she can get this mansion that she wants and I can talk merger with her father. The way we see it, what we're doing is not any different than schmoozing a client to close a deal."

"It's a heck of a lot different," Grace interjected firmly. She looked at Mitch as if he had just sold his soul. "It's always a mistake to date someone for the wrong reasons."

"It's only a week," Mitch said impatiently. Although he hadn't actually ruled out the idea of eventually marrying Lauren, he hadn't ruled it in, either. He figured he would just have to wait and see how things developed. But if those kisses they had shared this afternoon were any indication of the fireworks yet to happen between them, he'd definitely be thinking about it by the end of the week.

"You tell yourself it's only a week, now," Grace said. "But you're just marking time until you get what you really want. Peoples' feelings are involved here, and things have a way of getting complicated when you least expect them to."

No kidding, Mitch thought, recalling how fast and unexpectedly his previous marriage had gotten ugly and come to an end. He'd thought he'd known Jeannette, too. He'd thought they could make each other happy forever. And look how wrong he had been.

"I agree. You shouldn't be spending time alone with a woman unless you're genuinely interested in her," Tom said. "I don't care what prize was offered to you in return. To do otherwise usually ends up with someone being hurt. And you're better than that."

"Who says I'm not genuinely interested in Lauren?" Mitch stated angrily, resenting the implication that he was in some way cold-bloodedly using Lauren, when that wasn't the case at all. They hadn't pursued this deal. Her father had presented them with the arrangement, as well as the prizes. He and Lauren had just opted to take Payton Heyward up on his offer.

"Are you telling us you find her attractive?" Grace asked.

Attractive wasn't the half of it, Mitch thought, thinking back to the way his senses stirred whenever he was close to her. And the way she kissed! He'd never felt lips as soft or sensual, or wanted anyone so much so fast... Deciding there was no harm in being honest with his parents about that much, especially because it would make him look better in their eyes, Mitch said, "Yes."

Grace and Tom groaned in unison. "Even worse," Tom said.

Grace agreed. "Now I know someone is going to get hurt."

Mitch rolled his eyes. With this family of his, sometimes you just couldn't win.

The doorbell rang. Theresa Owens, the family's housekeeper, swept through the foyer to get it and ushered Lauren in. She looked breathtakingly beautiful in a sleeveless black dress that had embroidered flowers along the hem. Her golden-brown hair was loose and tousled, and pink tinged her cheeks. She had a bottle of wine in her hands and fortunately not an inkling about how Mitch's father felt about Mitch consorting with the "competition."

"Sorry I'm late," Lauren said as everyone stood to greet her.

Mitch glanced at his watch and saw it was indeed ten minutes after six o'clock. He grimaced, wondering what Payton's rules were about that. He'd hate to be disqualified on a technicality before they'd even really started.

"I ran into Daisy Templeton," Lauren continued breathlessly, and handed the bottle of wine to Grace. "She's starting a search for her biological parents. And she knows

I've done a lot with birth records to better understand some of the complicated real estate transactions that have occurred on some of the properties I've bought and sold. You know, sometimes a property was supposed to go to an heir, only the heir died, and then it ended up with a second cousin, so what originally started out as a Smith-family holding suddenly became a Donahue property or a Calhoun. Anyway, I got hung up, giving her some advice on the best way to proceed.''

Grace suddenly looked very pale as she handed the wine to Tom and eased her way into a chair.

"Why would she want to do that?" Tom asked calmly, putting the wine on the bar. "I mean, we've all known for years that Daisy was adopted, but I always thought Daisy was very happy with the Templeton family."

"Then you're the only one," Mitch murmured.

Tom shot him a reprimanding look.

Mitch shrugged. "You don't get as wild as Daisy's been without some reason," Mitch said. "Frankly, I don't think she's ever felt she really belonged with the Templetons."

"Of course she belongs with the Templetons," Tom said sharply. He gave Mitch an impatient look. "They adopted her, didn't they?"

"If you'll excuse me—I—" Grace stood abruptly and put her hand to the back of her neck as if she had one of her tension headaches coming on. "I forgot I had a previous engagement this evening," she murmured as everyone turned to her in surprise. "I'm so sorry, Mitch, Lauren. I won't be able to have dinner with you after all." She turned on her heel and walked toward the door with all the careful poise of an actress leaving the stage.

"Grace—" Tom started after his ex-wife.

Grace put up a hand to halt him, but did not turn around. Tom stopped in his tracks, and his broad shoulders slumped dejectedly, as he watched her disappear up the stairs.

Mitch looked at his father. "What was that about?" Clearly, his mother was annoyed with his father. Grace hadn't even looked at Tom as she had made her excuses.

"I don't know," Tom said in a too-vague way that made Mitch think his father most certainly did.

"I hope it wasn't something I said." Lauren pressed a hand to her chest. She looked stricken.

"Of course not," Tom and Mitch reassured in unison.

"Mom just…she's been this way since she returned from New York," Mitch explained. Things would be going along smoothly, and then his mother would suddenly look his father in the eye and end up walking out of the room, visibly distressed. They all assumed it had something to do with her being fired, that she was just feeling very tense and emotional in the wake of her public humiliation.

"I think we should take Grace at her word," Tom said, going over to open the bottle of wine that Lauren had brought as a gift. "And accept that she had another invitation she forgot about and intends to honor."

If you say so, Mitch thought. But he wasn't buying it. Not for a red-hot minute.

DINNER WAS SERVED shortly thereafter. Mitch urged Lauren to talk about her career in acquiring and renovating historic properties for resale, which she did happily. He also asked her a few questions about her experiences with the family shipping business, and learned, along with his father, that Lauren never set foot in the executive offices if she could help it, and she usually could.

When Lauren excused herself to run out to the kitchen to get Theresa's recipe for hummingbird cake, Mitch looked at Tom. "See? She's not exactly Mata Hari."

"How do you know?" Tom retorted grimly, looking as if he was all too willing to place Lauren in the ranks of the notorious World War I spy. "Just because she acts

innocent in the ways of the business doesn't mean you
aren't the one being set up here.''

Like the real Mata Hari, Lauren was sexy and beautiful,
maybe even a tad mysterious. But Mitch couldn't see Lauren seducing him for information. ''What do you mean?''
Mitch demanded.

''Payton Heyward has never been interested in taking
his company beyond the Heyward family.''

Mitch regarded his father pragmatically and pointed out
the obvious motivation, ''Until now, Payton Heyward was
probably hoping Lauren would marry and produce a child
so Payton and Lauren would not be the last of the blood-
line. But since that hasn't happened, Payton's decided to
take matters into his own hands, and secure her financial
future, and the Heyward family legacy in the shipping industry, in another way. Through a merger with us.'' As far
as Mitch was concerned, businesswise Payton's actions
made perfect sense. Personally, it was risky. If the situation
backfired in any way, or Lauren learned of the dowry Payton had secretly offered on her behalf, Lauren might not
ever forgive her father. Or Mitch. And therein lay the real
risk.

Tom's jaw hardened. He looked not the least bit ap-
peased. ''Look, call me suspicious if you will, but I've
been around this business for a very long time. If Payton
Heyward is suddenly wanting to merge with us, if he is
really even wanting to consider it, then there's a damn
good reason.''

Mitch looked at his father warily. ''You think they're
in trouble, financially, and he's looking to bail out through
us?'' Mitch asked uneasily, realizing his father might have
a point. Payton Heyward had recently bought those extra
container ships. And as yet the scuttlebutt was the ships
weren't fully booked. That had to be putting a strain on
the Heyward-company finances.

Tom shrugged, abruptly looking as unsure as Mitch felt

about the situation. "I don't know what's going on there. I'm not sure I want to know," Tom replied unhappily, sighing before leaning forward urgently once again. "And by the way, what I've told you about climbing into bed with the competition goes both ways. Don't be pumping Lauren for information, either. It would be unethical."

"I'm more principled than that," Mitch said, beginning to get angry now. He loved his father with all his heart. But he loathed the way Tom kept treating him when it came to the family business, like a student who still needed schooling, lots of it. Tom didn't treat his other children that way. But then his other children weren't involved in the family business.

"I'm going to go out for a while," Tom said, getting up from the dining-room table abruptly. "I need to clear my head."

Mitch nodded and watched his father go.

"WHERE'S YOUR FATHER?" Lauren asked when she returned several minutes later, handwritten recipe in hand.

"He went out for a while," Mitch said.

"Meaning we're on our own for the rest of the evening," Lauren supposed, looking no happier about that than Mitch felt.

"It would appear so." Mitch glanced at his watch, saw nearly two hours had passed. *Only four hours and two and a half minutes to go.*

"So now what?" Lauren said, suddenly beginning to look as restless as Mitch felt.

Mitch shrugged and got up from the table. "I don't know. We'll figure out some way to kill the rest of the evening." Without getting extraordinarily close.

"Such as…?" Lauren slipped the recipe into her handbag, then waited for Mitch to fill in the blanks.

"I don't know." Mitch shrugged again. All the things Mitch would normally want to do with a woman on a first date were pretty much out, given the unusual circumstances of their pairing. Too late, he realized he should have treated this date like a business deal and come up with more of an agenda ahead of time. "We could go to one of the clubs and listen to music, or, uh, maybe go to a very long movie," Mitch suggested. Walking on the beach was out, as was anything else even quasiromantic until he'd had a little time to decide whether he could persuade Lauren to forget about her rules.

"Anything, just so long as we're not alone," Lauren qualified, narrowing her eyes at him.

"Right," Mitch replied.

Lauren inclined her head at Mitch and grinned. Abruptly looking like the mischievous playgirl he knew she wasn't, she sauntered closer and teasingly tugged at the knot of his tie. "Ah, Mitch." She batted her eyelashes at him coquettishly. "If I didn't know better, I'd think you were afraid to be alone with me."

She could be Mata Hari for all you know.

Mitch shifted his weight uncomfortably as Lauren came closer yet and wreathed both her arms around his neck. She stood on tiptoe, pressed her slender curves close to him. Then looked deep into his eyes and whispered in a soft teasing voice that sent the blood rushing like a riptide to the lower half of his body. "What's the matter, Mitch? Afraid I might seduce you into doing something against your will?"

Chapter Four

"Don't we both wish that were the case," Mitch said, tightening his arms around Lauren's waist, holding her closer yet, so their bodies were all but intertwined. "But not a chance," he murmured, looking deep into her eyes. "Because I *never* do anything I don't want to do."

Gazing into his eyes, listening to the conviction in his low voice, Lauren could believe him.

The phone rang. Mitch leaned back just enough to be able to reach into the breast pocket of his suit coat and extract his cell phone. He checked the caller ID screen, pushed the button. Frowning, he held the phone to his ear. "Yeah, Jack, what's up? ...I don't know. Well, if he's not answering...yeah... I'll be right there." Mitch ended the connection and slid his cell phone back into his suit jacket. He released Lauren with a beleaguered sigh, the sexual electricity of moments before forgotten. "We've got to go. There's trouble at the docks."

Lauren picked up her handbag from the floor next to the sofa. "What kind of trouble?" she asked, sincerely interested.

Mitch looked at her with sudden wariness. "Problem with a shipment," he said vaguely, after a moment, looking strangely loath to confide anything in her at all. "The company attorney, Jack Granger, can't find my father—

he's not picking up his cell phone—so I've got to handle the situation.''

Lauren wondered if that was all Mitch was upset about. Somehow, it seemed like more than just that worrying him. "Does this happen a lot?" she asked casually as they walked outside to his car, wanting somehow to help him feel better about whatever was going on, even if it was just by talking about it.

Mitch tensed as they reached the passenger side. "Lately, more than I'd like to admit," he said, making no move to open the car door for her. "What about what happened just now?" Mitch backed her up against the side of the Lexus and caged her there with his arms, one hand planted on either side of her. "Does that happen often?" All too aware of the sudden pounding of her heart, Lauren leaned back against the metal, putting as much distance as she could—which wasn't much—between herself and his strong, hard body. Flushing self-consciously despite herself, she asked, "Does what happen often?"

Mitch favored Lauren with a challenging half smile she found even more disturbing than the way he was holding her captive. "Do you tease men about seducing them?" he queried in a low, inherently seductive tone.

Lauren's neck and shoulders drew taut as a bow, even as she defiantly lifted her chin. "I'm not a flirt, if that's what you're asking," she stated plainly.

Mitch shifted so his feet were braced slightly apart, his knees nudging hers. "You were doing a pretty good job of it," he observed, giving her a narrow-eyed glance.

To both our surprise, Lauren thought, aware she had never before teased a man in such a wanton manner. She couldn't even say why she had done it exactly. She'd just felt Mitch pulling away from her in a way he hadn't earlier in the day. And she'd wanted to goad him back into the reckless good cheer and impulsive sexuality that had so marked their encounter earlier in the day. She had wanted this week of dating to be something she didn't have to think about or consider. She had wanted it to mean nothing more than a reckless, meaningless fling that was forgotten almost as soon as it happened. And the only way she had known how to accomplish that was to keep the chemistry flowing between them—to the point it overrode all common sense and customary judgment. Too late, she saw what a mistake that had been. She wasn't an impulsive person, and neither was Mitch. "Just giving you a hard time," she said lightly.

Mitch quirked an eyebrow and looked down before returning his probing gaze to hers. "You did that, all right."

Lauren's jaw dropped in shock. She was flooded with embarrassment. "Mitch!"

Ignoring her censure, he cupped her face in his hands and rubbed his thumb across her lower lip in a way that had her heating with desire from head to toe. Looking at her, Mitch warned softly and seriously, "Don't play with fire, Lauren. Not unless you want to get burned."

LAUREN WAS SILENT during the drive to the docks. As much as she loathed the scolding way he had done it, Mitch had been right to warn her away from any disingenuous behavior. She had been prodding him unnecessarily, in a way she had instinctively known he wouldn't appreciate. She wasn't sure why. Except that, deep down, she was angry he had seemed, on some level, to be holding her at arm's length this evening, after coming on to her so strongly that afternoon. And also angry that he hadn't told her father what he could do with his proposition from the get-go, but instead had helped talk her into it! Not that she'd been a hard sell, Lauren admitted ruefully to herself. She had wanted to turn that mansion into the beautiful showplace it should be for so long. To be able to do that and call it her own home, too, well, it would be a dream come true. She was still going to have to figure out how to sell enough property to be able to pay for the renovations, of course, because there was no way she was marrying Mitch to get the money to do that. But she figured she would solve that problem over time.

Meantime, all she had to do was keep Mitch at arm's length during their dates for the rest of the week. Given the way they had just ticked each other off without really even trying, she was pretty sure she could do that. She just had to keep him wanting the same thing. Given the vaguely irked look on his face, that too seemed like a done deal.

Jack Granger was waiting for them in his office when they arrived at the Deveraux Shipping Company. The company attorney looked ruggedly handsome in a button-down white dress shirt with the sleeves rolled up. He had loosened his tie and unbuttoned the first two buttons of his shirt.

Jack took one look at Lauren, then turned to Mitch and, looking much more weary and disillusioned than a successful, career-driven bachelor in his early thirties should, said grimly, "Damn it, Mitch. You know how your father feels about consorting with the enemy. How could you have brought Lauren Heyward here? Tonight, of all nights!"

BESIDE HIM, Mitch felt Lauren take a step back. Her shock was every bit as palpable as his own anger. Jack Granger had worked for the firm for years. First as a dockworker, summers while he was in high school, later as an intern. Now he was the company attorney, and, as a personal favor to the Deveraux clan, the legal expert the entire family relied on for advice. Jack had recommended the lawyer who handled Mitch's divorce for him.

Consequently, Jack knew things about what had gone on between Mitch and Jeannette that no one else in the world knew—save Jeannette, Mitch and their two attorneys. But that didn't mean Jack could chastise Mitch when it came to company business. On the executive level, they were on equal footing. Mitch looked out for the continued growth of the company. Jack enforced existing contracts, even when those contracts were handshake deals. As CEO and president of DSC, Tom Deveraux presided over them both. And it was Tom both wanted to please.

"Excuse me?" Lauren stammered to Jack.

Mitch held up a hand, letting Lauren know it was all right, he could handle this. He turned to Jack. "My father knows I'm seeing Lauren tonight."

Jack grimaced at Mitch and raked a hand through his dark blond hair. "I doubt Tom would approve of you bringing her here when we're in the middle of a crisis."

No helping it, Mitch thought. He wasn't about to bow out on his date with Lauren and lose his chance at merging the two most powerful shipping companies on the entire eastern seaboard. Not even if Lauren's being here made Jack uncomfortable. "Like I said, Jack, my father knows Lauren is with me," Mitch repeated evenly, letting Jack know with a glance the decision had been made. A decision for which Mitch was fully accountable. Mitch sat in one of the two armchairs in front of Jack's desk and signaled for Lauren to do the same. "Now, what's up?"

Jack sighed and took a seat behind a desk littered with contracts. He leaned back in the leather chair, rested his elbows on the chair arms and steepled his hands in front of him. "There's been a delay with the five hundred luxury cars we were supposed to ship to Miami tonight. Only half of them arrived," he confided, concerned. "LC Motors insists we wait for the rest of them before taking off. Meanwhile, we've got containers of perishable foods on the ship that need to go out as scheduled tonight."

What a mess, Mitch thought. He was glad Jack had called him in to help handle it. "Have you tried putting the rest of the cars on a different ship?" Mitch asked.

Jack nodded. "Nothing's available for five days. Everything else is booked solid."

Mitch slanted a sidelong look at Lauren. To his chagrin—he would have much preferred she had been bored or distracted—she looked as tense and concerned and attentive as he and Jack. "Those shipments can't be moved around?" Mitch asked.

"No." Jack frowned again. "It's all cargo from regular clientele."

Realizing it was going to be a long evening, Mitch stood. Preparing to head for his office, he took off his suit jacket, unbuttoned his collar, and loosened the knot of his tie. "Let me see what I can do."

Jack gave Lauren a considering look, which seemed to warn her from doing anything that would hurt the Deveraux or the company they owned, as she rose to accompany Mitch down the hall. "I'll keep trying to get in touch with your dad," Jack said before they left.

Lauren and Mitch walked down the hall the short distance to his office. "Tough break," she murmured sympathetically as Mitch opened the door to his own suite of offices and turned on the lights.

"Yes, it is," Mitch agreed. The question was, how to fix the situation without giving either Lauren—or by extension, her father—a chance to take advantage or betray him, and prove his father and Jack Granger right about her, and her motivation, after all.

Lauren sat down and waited patiently while Mitch worked the phones. To Mitch's chagrin, he noted uneasily that though he gave her some old *Business Week* and *Fortune* magazines to flip through, Lauren secretly appeared to be hanging on to every word he said, even as she turned the pages and pretended to read the material in front of her. Were Jack and his dad right? Mitch wondered as he made yet another call. Was Lauren with him simply to uncover anything that would give her dad the edge in the ongoing competition between the two firms? Or was he right? Mitch wondered. And this was all simple coincidence, albeit an unfortunate one. Problems were a dime a dozen in any business. And missed shipments happened all the time. Generally not, however, when he was "contracted by gentleman's agreement" to have the daughter of his fiercest competitor, and a savvy businesswoman in her own right, with him.

Half an hour later, Jack came back in. "Any luck?" he asked Mitch hopefully as soon as Mitch hung up the telephone.

Mitch shook his head, displeased to report, "LC Motors and Specialty Foods are both threatening to take their business to one of the Web-based exchanges on the Internet to find alternate transportation if we don't do as they want."

If possible, Jack looked even grimmer. "So what are you going to do?" he asked.

Mitch shrugged. "The only thing I can. Order the ship to get under way immediately, with whatever cargo is on it. And then talk to Payton Heyward. See if he's got a ship we can use for the rest of the cars as soon as they arrive. We ship a lot for both LC Motors and Specialty Foods. We can't afford to lose either's business. And that means keeping to the contracted schedule as close as possible."

Jack shot another long considering look at Lauren before turning back to Mitch.

Mitch knew what Jack was thinking. Jack was thinking he shouldn't be giving any business to a competitor. Had Mitch not wanted to merge firms with Payton Heyward, he would have agreed. He would have found some other company to handle the cargo rather than do anything to strengthen their chief rival. But he did want to merge firms with Payton, and this was the surest, quickest way to prove that the two powerhouse shipping companies could work together in ways that would benefit—and empower—both.

"You can't do this on your own," Jack warned humor-

lessly at last. "Your father is going to have to sign off on
it."

"If you can find him, I'll be glad to turn this problem
over to him," Mitch promised. "Until then, I'm going to
use my executive powers, as second in command, to do
what I have to do to solve the problem." And the first
order of business was to get the loaded ship under way.
The second was to find Payton Heyward and get him to
cooperate with Mitch in a way Payton had never joined
forces with Mitch's father.

Mitch studied Jack. "Are you with me or not?" he
asked.

Jack nodded reluctantly. "I'm with you," he said. "I
just hope you know what you're doing. 'Cause if you
don't, and this backfires on us in any way, there's going
to be hell to pay."

"DO YOU HAVE PROBLEMS like this all the time?" Lauren
asked as they drove the short distance to the penthouse
apartment where Payton stayed during the week, in lieu of
commuting back and forth between Charleston and his
Summerville estate.

"Unfortunately, nowadays, we do," Mitch explained,
trying not to get too used to having Lauren's soothing,
perfumed presence in the car beside him. He turned to look
at her as they waited at a red light, and explained, "It used
to be that a shipping company established a regular clientele—these were all usually handshake deals—and then
the two stuck together, through good times and bad. If
there was unusual weather or some other calamity, it
wasn't a problem. Chiefly because there was nowhere else
to turn. Now if something goes wrong, a customer can just
switch on his computer, go to one of the auction sites on
the Web, post his needs. The customer will start getting
bids immediately and will usually find an alternate shipper
within twenty-four hours."

Lauren frowned, looking, Mitch thought, more troubled than someone should who had no interest at all in the family business. "But your family's company doesn't do that," Lauren supposed slowly, her soft tone as sympathetic as her pretty, dark brown eyes.

"No, and neither does your father's," Mitch said as the traffic light changed, and he pressed his foot down on the accelerator again. "And that's beginning to cost us both. And it's a shame. We should both be doing business on the Web as well as the old-fashioned way."

Lauren raked her teeth across her lower lip. "Why don't you do that if it's something you need to be doing to stay competitive?"

Mitch sighed as he turned into the parking lot and guided his Lexus into a visitor space. "I can't speak for your father," he said as he cut the engine and turned to Lauren. "But we haven't done so yet chiefly because all our container ships are filled to capacity, as is."

"Then why worry about it?" Lauren asked, getting out of the car before Mitch could get around to help her.

Mitch took her elbow as they headed toward the building entrance. "Because the way the shipping business is conducted is changing, Lauren, and both our companies need to change, too—at least stay ahead of the curve. Otherwise, five years from now both could find themselves out of business."

Lauren said hello to the uniformed doorman and headed for the elevators at the other end of the elegant marble-floored lobby. "If you merge, will you force some of the auction sites to fold?" she asked.

"No." Mitch stepped into the elevator behind her, taking in the appealing perfection of her skin. "Although statistically about half will fail on their own, anyway, due to poor plans, etcetera. But we will make ourselves stronger, bigger, more competitive. And that's what both Deveraux and Heyward shipping companies need to do if we're to keep growing,'' he said, looking deep into her eyes and trying to determine once again if he could trust her as much as his gut told him he could.

"I guess you're right,'' Lauren commiserated as she leaned against the railing that lined the back of the elevator and looked up at him. "Whether we like it or not, business—any kind of business—is tough. To stay on top, you really have to be on your toes all the time, not just between the hours of nine to five.''

Like now? Mitch wondered, excruciatingly aware this problem had conveniently happened during the hours of his first arranged date with Lauren, at a time when his father was oddly, and unusually, out of touch with the office.

His instincts kept telling him it was all just a coincidence.

Bitter experience, and his involvement with his ex, told him to be on guard for something more complex and deviously underhanded.

"WHY WOULD I HELP bail you out?'' Payton asked, after he had let them both into his apartment. He looked just as suspicious as Mitch felt when Mitch had first learned of the problem.

Excruciatingly aware that although the two of them were tentatively discussing a merger, they were still chief competitors, and not in any way bound to do favors for each other that would hamper their own capacity to do business, Mitch looked Payton straight in the eye. "Because Deveraux Shipping Company will pay you to ship those cars as soon as they arrive at dawn tomorrow morning. And I know you have more shipping capacity than you need right now, thanks to the purchase of those brand-new, state-of-the-art container ships you bought last spring.''

Payton studied Mitch with something akin to respect

while Lauren waited nervously nearby. "We'll get the full fee?" Payton ascertained.

Mitch nodded, knowing now was where it would get particularly tricky, and said, "Minus a ten percent referral fee, of course." After all, he reasoned practically, Deveraux Shipping had to make something on the deal. Given how thin their profit margins were these days, the lost revenue was going to be hard enough to absorb as it was.

Payton sipped the vanilla-flavored protein shake he had been preparing when they arrived. Despite the way he was dressed—in a golf shirt and slacks—he remained the hard-edged businessman. "That's highway robbery," he growled.

"It's also business you wouldn't have if I weren't putting it in your lap." Mitch took a drink of his own smoothie and found it disgustingly bland and chalky. With effort, he kept from grimacing, even as he noticed Lauren had simply put hers aside. But then, maybe she'd had one of these vitamin-laced health concoctions before. "You don't have long to decide," Mitch continued. "If you can't help me, I'll go to the next shipping company on my list."

Lauren crossed her legs and continued to watch the byplay between the two men. She might say she hadn't the least enthusiasm for the family business, but there was no doubt she had understood and latched on to every word that was being said, both here and earlier, in the Deveraux offices, Mitch noticed. Which meant he was going to have to be more careful than he had expected, because the merger hadn't happened yet. And might not happen, if at any point during the week Lauren changed her mind and refused to keep her deal with him. Or Mitch failed to convince his own father it was what they needed to do, not just to survive, but to grow.

"Then you will have lost this chance to pick up the extra revenue," Mitch continued, glancing at his watch, knowing that like it or not, his time was running out. He was going to have to call both LC Motors and Specialty Foods shortly and tell them what was to be done.

Payton Heyward grinned in a way that said he appreciated Mitch's aggressiveness in solving this problem. "One of my ships just came in this morning. I'll have them send it over to your docks."

The two men shook on the deal. Payton consulted the clock above the mantel. It was eleven. He narrowed his eyes at Mitch and Lauren thoughtfully. "I thought the two of you were supposed to be on a date this evening."

"We were. Are," Mitch said.

Lauren nodded, her affection for her father shining through now as clearly as her pique with him had earlier that day. "Wherever Mitch goes, I go," she parried. "At least between the hours of six and midnight."

Payton harrumphed, looking less than happy about the detour their date had taken, despite the additional business it had brought his company. "Then get back to it," Payton advised, showing them to the door. "You two have wasted enough time on business, when you should have been courting, as it is."

"Well, that went a lot easier than I thought it would," Lauren remarked as they headed back out to Mitch's car. She turned to Mitch with a sexy smile. "I half expected him to tell you no, and then get on the phone and steal the extra business out from under you." She paused, shook her head, sighed. "I don't know what's happened to him, but he hasn't been as aggressive at going after business lately as he has been in the past."

Maybe there were reasons for that, the same reasons that were suddenly prompting Payton Heyward to consider a merger. Uneasily, Mitch realized his father was probably right on the money about one thing. Payton Heyward hadn't told Mitch everything, just as he hadn't told his own daughter everything. Hence, it was up to Mitch to use whatever means necessary to discover what was going on behind the scenes, and make certain that Payton wasn't using Mitch and the Deveraux Shipping Company to bail him out of a messy financial situation or quietly failing business. The last thing Mitch wanted to do was drive his own family company into ruin because he had failed to investigate the obvious.

Oblivious to the grim, suspicious direction of Mitch's thoughts, Lauren continued, "Take tonight for instance. Since it's a weeknight, and he's here in the city, my father'd normally be out courting a major client and showing him the sites. Instead, according to his doorman, he was home all evening, alone. That's unlike him, Mitch."

"Maybe he's just getting older. And can't keep up the same pace he used to."

"Maybe." Lauren sounded unconvinced.

They lapsed into silence until they arrived at the Deveraux mansion. Lauren's car was parked on the street right where she'd left it before dinner with his father. "I'll follow you home," Mitch said.

Lauren consulted her watch. "We still have another forty-five minutes."

"So we'll have coffee at your place," Mitch said with a shrug. "Unless you'd rather go somewhere else. There's a gourmet coffee shop up on King Street that's open until midnight—"

"No. My place will be fine."

Lauren led the way, and five minutes later they arrived at the double house Lauren owned. The stuccoed brick town-house style villa was two rooms wide on both floors and surrounded by palmetto trees and overlooked South Battery. And that evening, as always, the view of the water beyond the seawall was staggeringly beautiful. Moonlight shimmered on the water—ships, some moving gracefully across the water, some at anchor—were visible in the distance.

Mitch inhaled the tangy scent of saltwater as Lauren led

the way up the brick sidewalk, across her welcoming porch, and let them inside. The interior of her home was decorated with floral fabrics and antiques.

As soon as Lauren walked in, she went to her answering machine and pressed the button to retrieve her messages. The first two were from clients, confirming or changing dates to view houses. The third was enough to stop Mitch in his tracks.

"Hi, Lauren. Ron Ingalls calling you back. First, just let me say I think it's great what you're trying to do for your father. I'm not sure it's going to be possible—the guy's no pushover. But sure, I'd be glad to help you try and get what you want. I'm actually going to be in South Carolina on Wednesday, so maybe the two of us can meet then. In the meantime, I'll try and find the information you need tomorrow and get back to you. Later." *Click.*

"I wasn't aware you knew Ron," Mitch said mildly.

Lauren turned to Mitch, her expression happy but relaxed. "He and my dad go way back," Lauren replied, looking as innocent as a newborn babe. "My dad always gets his new container ships from Ingalls Shipbuilding in Newport News, Virginia. You've met him, too, I guess."

Mitch nodded. The forty-year-old executive was an accomplished businessman and a very affable guy. Mitch or his father played golf with Ron whenever Ron was in town, and usually managed to work in some business out on the greens, too. "We've bought a couple ships from him. Although we also get ships from a company in Maine, and another one in Connecticut." Unlike Heyward Shipping Company, DSC preferred not to rely on just one supplier.

"Hmm. Well." Lauren looked as if she could have cared less about that. She smiled at Mitch casually, the only sign of her inner restlessness the light tapping of her fingers against her thigh. "Did you want some coffee?"

I'd rather sit here and talk about what it is exactly that

Ron is going to do for you and your dad. Had Ron been referring to Mitch on the phone, or some other guy who was no pushover? There was no doubt Ron's allegiance would be to the Heywards before the Deveraux, and it bothered Mitch to think that Lauren could be conspiring with her father to pull something over on Mitch and his father. "That would be great," Mitch said, doing his best to keep his suspicions to himself.

Lauren smiled again, even more warmly. "The kitchen's back this way, if you want to come with me."

"Mind if I stay in here and turn on the news?" Mitch asked. He needed more information—the kind Lauren was not going to give him, and he wanted something to cover the sound of him looking around.

For a second, Lauren looked both taken aback and hurt that he would prefer the company of the television to her, and Mitch felt even more guilty about what he had to do next. But that didn't change his decision. He had been a chump once where a beautiful woman was concerned. He wasn't going to ignore the early warning signs again. This time he was going to find out for sure what kind of woman he was dealing with before he got further involved.

"I missed the weather earlier and I want to know if I should get my car washed tomorrow," Mitch fibbed.

Lauren rolled her eyes. Looking very annoyed, she muttered, "Suit yourself," and then turned to exit the room. Mitch waited until she had rounded the corner, then switched on the TV and headed for the antique secretary where the phone was. The polished cherry-wood surface was bare except for a pad of paper and pen, and a leather-bound address book—which was filled with addresses and phone numbers of shipping-industry people, as well as countless other Charleston heavy hitters and real estate-industry people.

Of course, that in itself could mean nothing, Mitch reassured himself as he picked up the phone and scrolled

through the list of incoming phone calls on Lauren's caller
ID. It was who had called her recently, and how many
times, that was going to tell him what he really wanted to
know.

LAUREN TOOK HER TIME in the kitchen. She just didn't
understand it. One minute Mitch was warm and person-
able, exactly the kind of guy she'd like to get involved
with. And the next he was all business, as emotionally
remote as could be.

Not that she shouldn't have expected as much, she
scolded herself firmly. The fact Mitch Deveraux had even
agreed to date her for the sake of a merger should have
told her what kind of man he was deep down. The kind
who put business first, always. The kind she had always
sworn she would avoid.

If she didn't want the mansion at 10 Gathering Street
so very much…

But she did.

So she had to get through this date, and six more, Lauren told herself firmly, looking at her watch. Luckily, she
only had ten more minutes to go. She filled two coffee
cups, put them on a silver serving tray along with cream
and sugar and headed back into the living room. As she
had expected, Mitch was sitting on the sofa, his eyes glued
to the TV.

For the next ten minutes they sat and sipped coffee and
made such inane conversation she knew she'd be hard put
to recall any of it even half an hour later. Promptly at the
stroke of midnight, he stood and prepared to go. Without
making the slightest attempt to kiss her good-night, he
thanked her politely for the coffee and headed for the door.
"I'll see you tomorrow night at six."

Wondering what had happened to the man who hadn't
hesitated to put the moves on her earlier in the day, Lauren
watched Mitch Deveraux stroll down the front walk to his

car. She told herself she should be relieved that Mitch suddenly wanted to take a step back and proceed a hell of a lot more cautiously, as well. But she wasn't. It didn't matter that it was a sure way to get hurt when the week came inevitably to an end. She didn't care that setting herself up that way was foolish. She had wanted another hot, reckless, impetuous kiss. Or two, or three. The question was—why hadn't he?

Chapter Five

As soon as he got to the office the next morning, Mitch telephoned Harlan Decker, the burly ex-cop-turned-PI who verified the resumes and work histories of potential employees and also investigated any theft or vandalism at the docks. "I've got some phone numbers I need identified ASAP. Think you could do that for me?"

"No problem," Harlan said. "Just fax them over and I'll get right on it."

Mitch hung up, sent the fax and dialed Ron Ingalls. The CEO of the Newport News, Virginia, shipbuilder was a little harder to get hold of, but eventually he got on the line. "Hey, Mitch, how are you?"

"Fine, Ron. Thanks. Listen, DSC is considering adding another container ship or two to our fleet before the end of the year, and I wondered if I could get a look at your latest price list and projected inventory and availability dates."

"Be happy to send that to you," Ron said. "In fact, I can bring it to you myself a little later in the week—I'm going to be in Charleston to play golf and meet with another customer."

"Sounds good." Mitch welcomed the chance to look Ron in the eye and discover if he was in any way involved in an attempt to sabotage the Deveraux Shipping Company. They set a time and place. Ten minutes later, Harlan Decker called back with the results of his search. "One number belongs to Southern Specialties bakery, another to Bob Blum."

"The owner of The Golf Emporium," Mitch affirmed.

"Right. And one for Robert Kellogg, Jon King, Annette Barnes and Susan Gordon."

Mitch relaxed. Those were all prominent people in Charleston who had nothing to do with the shipping industry and were probably calling for social reasons.

"Another for Jeannette Wycliffe."

"Whoa." His body rigid with tension, Mitch leaned forward in his chair and rested his elbows on his desk. "Are you sure about that?"

"That the number belongs to your ex-wife," Harlan said, not about to pull any punches. "Yes."

That wasn't good, Mitch thought. Especially since he had never known Lauren and Jeannette to be friends, and, given the acrimonious nature of their divorce, Jeannette would not possibly have one good thing to say about him to Lauren.

"And then there's one for Ron Ingalls in Newport News, Virginia," Harlan continued pragmatically. "His home number."

Interesting, Mitch thought, unsure what to make of that.

"That's it," Harlan concluded. "Except for Payton Heyward's number for the apartment in the city, as well as his office."

Nothing suspicious in that, unless she was helping him with some business angle she did not want Mitch to know anything about.

Without preface, his father's warning about the inadvisability of climbing into bed with the competition came back to haunt Mitch.

"Anything else you want me to do?" Harlan asked.

Mitch thought briefly of having both Lauren and her

father investigated, then nixed the idea. If there was anything nefarious to be found, he was going to discover it himself.

He headed down the hall after disconnecting with Harlan, saw his father's office was still empty—unusual for midmorning—and went a little farther down the hall to Jack Granger's office. "Have you seen my father this morning?"

Appearing as tense and preoccupied as Mitch felt, Jack looked up from the stack of contracts on his desk. "He's not here," Jack replied. "I had an e-mail from him late last night. He said he was going to get away for a few days."

"Did you tell him about what happened last night with the Specialty Foods-LC Motors shipment to Miami?" Aware his father might be ticked off at the way Mitch had handled the situation, Mitch had been intending to do that himself in person as soon as his father got in.

Jack shrugged. "I e-mailed your father the information, but I don't know that he's reading his mail. He left the impression that he would be pretty much out of contact for the next day or two."

"And in the meantime...?" Mitch asked.

Jack went back to sifting through the papers on his desk. "You and I are to handle things as per usual while he's gone."

The only problem was, his father was never gone. Since the divorce, the business had become even more important to Tom Deveraux. He rarely took a vacation and worked long hours every day. And often entertained clients and made more handshake deals in the evening and on the weekends.

"I'm sure it will be fine," Jack continued, giving Mitch a steady look. If Jack had any reservations about the situation, Mitch noted, Jack wasn't about to reveal them.

Finally, Jack said, "You handle all the executive decisions. I'll take care of any legal issues that come up."

On the surface, it was a workable agreement. However, there were several things Mitch did not get. "I don't understand why he e-mailed you and not me," Mitch said, wondering why his father seemed to sometimes confide more in the company's attorney than in his own family members. Did he find their capacity for understanding lacking? Or were there private legal problems he was involved in?

Jack shrugged and continued watching Mitch with lawyerly impassiveness. "Maybe he did e-mail you and it just hasn't arrived yet," he suggested finally.

That was bull, Mitch thought, and they both knew it. Unfortunately, it was also all the information he was likely to get out of Jack, since what little his father had told Jack had obviously been in confidence.

Mitch heard footsteps behind him. He turned and saw Lauren striding down the hall that linked the executive offices of DSC. Her golden-brown hair was loose and shining, the ends swinging softly against her shoulders. She was dressed in a trim black business suit and red blouse. Mitch didn't think he had ever seen her look so pretty as she did at that moment—his heart raced at just the sight of her.

She smiled as she neared him, in a drift of tantalizing perfume. "Got a minute?" she asked.

Jack said a polite hello to Lauren and frowned at Mitch. Mitch knew what Jack was thinking—that Mitch was consorting with the competition. Given what Mitch had just found out about the phone calls Lauren had been receiving at her home lately, he wasn't so sure Jack and his dad weren't right. On the other hand...what was that old saying? Mitch wondered. *Keep your friends close, and your enemies closer? Whichever one Lauren was, he knew he wanted her by his side.*

"I always have time for you." Mitch told Lauren as he cupped a hand beneath her elbow and ushered her down the hall into his own office. He shut the door behind them, relishing the chance to spend some unscheduled time with her, instead of just the required dates. "What's up?"

Lauren sat down in one of the chairs in front of his desk and crossed her legs at the knee. Leaning forward, she clasped her hands around her bent knee. "Your mother called me this morning and asked me to help her find a house of her own to buy. I wasn't sure how you'd feel about that, so I wanted to run it by you first."

Mitch sat on the edge of his desk closest to Lauren and braced his hands on either side of him. "I don't think it's a conflict of interest, if that's what you're asking," he said, looking down at her.

Lauren compressed her lips before cautioning matter-of-factly, "This process is probably going to take a while, and that might be awkward when we stop seeing each other at the end of the week."

Mitch lifted a curious eyebrow. "Who says we're going to stop seeing each other?" He grinned speculatively.

Lauren's shoulders stiffened. She rose and, her back ramrod straight, moved away from him. "There will no longer be a need."

Speak for yourself. Mitch could already see himself needing to be with her often, even when it was no longer required of both of them. Mitch straightened, too. "If we can deal with a week of dating, I'm sure we can deal with that," he said casually.

Lauren smiled in obvious relief. "That's what I was hoping you'd say." Holding her purse in front of her like a shield, she moved for the door, looking more than ready to tackle her day. "Well, I'm off to meet your mother for breakfast, then."

"Mind if I tag along?" Mitch asked, striding ahead to open the door for Lauren. He didn't know if his mother was aware Tom had run off to parts unknown for a few days. But if she wasn't, he figured he should be the one to tell her.

"Not at all," Lauren said. "But we'll need to take separate cars."

"No problem," Mitch said.

WHEN THEY ARRIVED at the downtown restaurant, Grace was beautifully dressed, but her eyes were puffy and she didn't look as if she'd had much sleep. Mitch's worry about his mother instantly increased. He kissed her cheek and helped her with a chair.

"This is a surprise." Grace beamed up at Mitch, looking as happy as always to be able to spend time with one of her children.

"I can't stay long," Mitch qualified as he seated himself between Lauren and his mother. With his father out of town he'd have double the workload. "But I wanted to hear all about your plans," Mitch told his mother seriously. "I didn't realize you were looking to buy a place of your own quite so soon."

Grace took a delicate sip of her tea. "I thought I might as well get on with it. I've already instructed my attorney in New York City to put my apartment there up for sale."

Mitch stirred sugar into his coffee. "You don't want to go back?"

"No. I'm tired of living away from my family, Mitch. My children are all settled in Charleston, so this is where I want to be, too."

Mitch believed that. He also sensed there was more. "Is it hard for you, living in the same house with Dad?"

Grace arranged the bangs of her short blond hair with her fingertips. "He's been very accommodating about everything."

Mitch knew an evasion when he heard one. He also recognized trouble brewing when he saw it. He studied his mother intently. "The two of you didn't have an argument, did you?"

Grace swallowed abruptly, even as she held his eyes. "Why would you think that?"

Aware Lauren was watching the byplay with interest, Mitch shrugged and continued his conversation with his mother. "What does Dad think of you buying your own place?"

Grace leaned back as the waiter brought their breakfasts, then cut into her fruit with more than usual enthusiasm. "First of all, I don't need his permission or approval, Mitch. We're divorced. Second, I haven't had a chance to tell him."

Mitch added salt to his eggs. "You didn't see him last night?"

Grace shook her head. "He wasn't there when I got home."

"And this morning?" Mitch pressed.

Grace lifted her shoulders in an indolent shrug. "He wasn't there when I went down for breakfast. Theresa said she hadn't seen him since early last evening."

At that revelation, Mitch swore silently to himself. He had hoped his father would have talked about the reasons for his disappearing act with his mother instead of leaving her as perplexed and puzzled as everyone else, save maybe Jack Granger.

Grace looked at Mitch steadily. "You know something about what your father's up to, don't you? And you're trying to tell me."

Mitch slanted a look at Lauren before he answered. Like him, Lauren seemed concerned about his mother. Finally, Mitch turned back to Grace and reluctantly revealed what he knew. "Jack Granger said he got an e-mail from Dad. Dad's decided to take a few days off. I'm not sure where."

"I think I have an idea," Grace muttered.

Mitch studied the veiled anger and jealousy on Grace's face. "There's no other woman, Mom."

"You can't possibly know that," Grace retorted stiffly.

What could Mitch say to that? His mother was right. His father was as capable as any man of having a love affair.

Giving Mitch a look that stated plainly that this part of the conversation was over, Grace looked at Lauren. "Now, about these houses you want to show me this morning. Where do you suggest we begin?"

MITCH MET LAUREN at her home promptly at six, as per the terms of their agreement with her father. The fundraiser they were scheduled to attend at a downtown hotel wasn't scheduled to start for another hour and a half. Mitch had gone home to shower and shave, prior to their date, but Lauren was still in the business clothes she'd had on earlier in the day. "So how did it go with my mother?" Mitch asked as a visibly distracted Lauren motioned for him to follow and then led the way up the wide staircase of her elegantly appointed home, to the study on the second floor.

"It was a typical first attempt looking for the perfect house to settle in, when money and time are no object." Lauren moved a large stack of several heavy real estate books from the damask sofa so he could sit down.

Trying not to get too caught in the view of Lauren's legs—which looked sensational in the translucent black stockings she wore—Mitch loosened his tie, sat back against the cushions and asked, "What's she looking for?"

"She's not sure—which is part of the dilemma." Lauren plucked the pages coming out of her printer and glanced through them thoughtfully. "A house in the historic district would be more protected from hurricanes, but a house on the beach also holds a lot of appeal for her. She's going to take her time and study the listings I gave her and we're going to go out again tomorrow morning and view the properties she wants to see. And if none of those work for her, I'm preparing another batch, too. I'm confident we'll eventually hit on what she wants." Lauren paused to study the guarded expression on Mitch's face. "You're not very happy about what she's doing, are you?" she guessed softly.

Mitch shrugged, knowing this was too important a subject to pretend otherwise. "I admit, I'd like to see my mother and father living under the same roof a little longer."

"Does she usually stay with your dad when she's in Charleston?" She slanted him an interested glance that was sexy as all get-out. Lauren sat back down in front of the computer and scrolled through other properties, printing out specs on some, bypassing others.

Trying to keep his mind on the conversation at hand instead of where he'd like the evening with Lauren to lead—the bedroom down the hall—Mitch sat back and explained, "Initially, after the divorce, my mom tried staying in a hotel when she came back to Charleston on holiday. But that quickly became a problem because she was constantly being recognized and approached by fans of the morning show, which makes it hard for her to have any privacy or get any rest. So Dad suggested that she stay at the house when she comes to see us, and Dad goes to a hotel. He was going to do that this time but she convinced him it would be more practical if the two of them both stayed in the mansion this time, since she hasn't yet figured out where she is going to live or what she is going to do next."

"That's very modern of them." Lauren switched off her computer and printer, stood. "I've dealt with a lot of divorced couples in my line of business—most of them aren't that civil or understanding of each other's situations."

Mitch nodded, wondering how it was Lauren could still look and smell so darn good after what had to have been a very full workday. "The problem is they're old-fashioned people and there's still some chemistry between them. It makes it hard for them to be under the same roof and not be together."

She walked over to the floor-to-ceiling cabinets and plucked out a folder emblazoned with the name of her real estate firm. She slanted him an intrigued glance as she slid the papers she'd just printed out, into the folder. "You think the two of them would rather be sharing the same bedroom?"

Mitch nodded, wondering even as he did why it was that he could talk to Lauren so easily. "Of course, whether or not that's ever going to happen again remains to be seen," he said.

"What about you and your ex-wife?" Lauren took the folder back and laid it, front and center, on her desk. She came around to stand before him, bracing her hands on either side of her. "Do you ever see her?"

Where had that question come from? Mitch wondered, even as he noted the way her trim black skirt pulled snugly across her abdomen, hips and thighs. "No," Mitch replied, shifting his gaze back to Lauren's face. "Do you?"

"Sometimes," Lauren replied with an easygoing shrug. "Jeannette Wycliffe is the best events planner in Charleston. She's also doing my father's black-tie birthday party later this week, which, I guess, because of the terms of our agreement with him, you are going to have to attend as my date."

Well, one mystery solved, Mitch thought with relief. Maybe the rest of the phone calls would have equally innocent explanations. At least Mitch hoped that was the case, because he was beginning to see he could be seriously interested in a woman like Lauren, which was a possibility he hadn't really been open to before they had gotten acquainted and started dating. "When is the party?" Mitch asked.

Looking distracted, Lauren shrugged out of her tailored black blazer and toed off her low-heeled black pumps. "Friday evening, at the Summerwinds Hotel downtown."

Dry-mouthed, Mitch watched her unbutton her red blouse and pull the hem of her shirt out of the waistband of her black skirt. As she slipped off her blouse and revealed a formfitting opaque spaghetti-strap camisole beneath, he wondered just how far she was going to go with this unexpected disrobing. With effort, he returned his gaze to her face. Finding himself too restless to sit, he rolled to his feet and began to pace. "How many people are going to be there?" he said.

"Close to five hundred."

Mitch shoved his hands into the pockets of his trousers. "That's a pretty big birthday party."

Lauren shrugged and continued talking to Mitch as she crossed the hall in her stocking feet to her bedroom. "For him, it's just another opportunity to do business."

Mitch followed her as far as the doorway to the bedroom.

He noted she didn't look particularly happy about that as she rummaged through her wardrobe, until she found what she was looking for—a sheer black chiffon blouse with some sort of embroidery across the hem, wristbands and collar.

"As much as I'm loath to admit it—" Lauren sighed, shooting Mitch another somewhat distracted glance as she slipped the blouse off the padded-satin hanger "—my father never does anything without it somehow being related to furthering his own business goals or agenda."

Mitch continued to lounge in her bedroom doorway. He watched in complete fascination as Lauren slipped the blouse over her opaque black tank top, instantly transforming the outfit from business attire to evening wear. He wondered if she had any idea how she was inflaming his desire with the ongoing transformation that was so inherently innocent and matter-of-fact, and yet at the same time so damn seductive it would have done justice to Mata Hari. Mitch swallowed around the tightness in his throat.

"And your father's agenda is what right now?" Mitch asked, deciding this sleuthing behind the scenes could work both ways.

Lauren sorted through her earrings, finally selecting a pair of diamond-studded gold hoops and a matching choker from the velvet-lined jewelry case on her bureau. "I have to say that right now his top priority is probably to get me married advantageously, in a way that also very much profits his business."

Payton Heyward had said the same.

But the question remained—why did Payton want the merger now? What was driving his urgency behind the scenes? Because Mitch had come to agree with his father on one thing—there was something else going on in the background that Payton wanted kept from Mitch and everyone else. The only question was—was Lauren in on the secret, or out of the loop?

"Has your father always wanted you to marry someone in the shipping industry?" Mitch asked casually, watching as Lauren took off the small onyx studs in her ears and slipped in the hoops.

"No." Lauren met Mitch's eyes and continued with a candor that caught Mitch unawares—as much as her day-to-evening transformation had. "He wanted me to marry someone wealthy, of course. He felt it was the only way I'd know for certain I was being married for me and not my money." Lauren paused as she wrestled with the back clasp of her necklace. "I'm not sure that logic follows, though."

Mitch stepped in to help Lauren with the necklace.

"Why not?" he asked as she held her hair off her nape and his fingertips brushed the silky soft skin beneath.

"Because I think people who've grown up having money are more frantic about the idea of losing it," Lauren said unhappily.

Was that what was going on with her father? Mitch wondered as he stepped back once again and watched Lauren run a brush through her hair, then twist the glossy length of it up onto the back of her head and hold it in place with a pretty clip.

Was that the reason Payton Heyward was suddenly so gung ho about the idea of a Deveraux-Heyward merger and marriage? Mitch wondered. Because Payton had overextended his own finances with the purchase of those two new containers ships and was in a panic about what to do about it?

"People get used to a certain lifestyle. They don't want to give that up for something less," Lauren said as she went to the shoe rack in her closet.

"So they'll do anything to maintain their lifestyle," Mitch guessed, still enjoying the view a lot more than he knew he should. Trying hard not to notice how very pretty she looked, or how seductive and pleasurable it was watching her get geared up for their evening ahead, he braced a shoulder against the portal and crossed his arms in front of him.

"Like marry someone they don't really love," Mitch continued.

Lauren shook her head, agreeing. "Or sell a historic home that has been in their family for generations just to get a quick million or two or three to fritter away. Of course, even worse than that, is seeing a person destroy a beautiful home with sheer neglect," Lauren stated grimly as she braced herself against the closet frame and slipped on a pair of black evening sandals.

"Would you do it?" Mitch asked casually, deciding to use her distraction to his advantage.

"What?" Lauren went into the bathroom and grabbed her toothbrush.

"Marry for money." Mitch moved so he could still see her.

Lauren turned and made a face at him. "I thought I'd made my feelings for that clear the day we agreed to this farce of a courtship." Lauren uncapped the toothpaste and layered it on her brush.

"You could have just been playing hard to get—to raise my interest."

Lauren rolled her eyes, then brushed, rinsed and spit. "Is that what it would take to get you interested?" she asked, blotting her lips with a towel.

Mitch shrugged, taking the banter to an even more disarming level. "It's a well-known fact in Charleston that I like a challenge." Was that what she was trying to do—play hard to get? Because if so, Mitch was loath to admit, it was working. He was interested. Very interested.

"It's also well known that you don't like lost causes. I'm a lost cause, Mitch." Lauren put a bottle of mouthwash to her lips, swished some around and spit again. Her expression turning pensive, she blotted her lips on a pale pink hand towel and reached for a lipstick on the bathroom counter. She turned her complete attention to her reflection. "I don't know what's gotten into my father lately. Maybe it's the fact that I'm closing in on thirty and he's going to be fifty-four later this week. But I'm hoping when he sees that you and I don't work out, he'll just get forget this idea about arranging a marriage between the two of us and concentrate on the merger."

As Mitch watched her apply her lipstick with easy, practiced strokes, he told himself he was not emotionally involved enough to be disappointed about her lack of interest in the situation. "And you wouldn't mind that?" Mitch ascertained carefully.

She gave him a strange look, and demanded, innocently enough, "Why should it matter to me whether you two merge businesses or not? I'm not involved in that in any way."

Mitch shrugged. "You'd stand to benefit or lose financially, depending on the outcome."

Lauren sighed and recapped her lipstick with a snap.

When she turned back to him, Mitch asked, "Why are you giving me that look?"

Lauren gave him a look of choirgirl innocence as she swept past him once again. "What look?"

As if she didn't know, Mitch thought, frustrated she would select this moment to clam up. "The one that says you're disappointed in me," he explained. When it was possible it should be the other way around.

She shrugged, abruptly looking as wary of him as he felt of her. "I'm just trying to figure out what kind of man you are."

"A talented businessman." Mitch smiled.

"Besides that," Lauren qualified.

Mitch stared at her in confusion as she spritzed on some perfume. He'd thought if anyone could understand the importance of making something of yourself instead of resting on the family laurels and living off a trust account, it would have been a successful, career-oriented heiress like Lauren. In fact, he was willing to bet if asked to define herself, she would say that she was one of the city's premier real estate brokers.

"What else is there?" he asked, wondering what it was exactly that Lauren wanted from him—aside from possibly bailing her father out of whatever financial or business trouble Payton Heyward had gotten himself in.

Lauren rolled her eyes and shook her head. "Exactly." She sighed.

LEAVE IT TO HER, Lauren thought as she led the way back downstairs, to be looking for a Renaissance man where none was to be found. Still, she wanted to know more about Mitch. Even if he was loath to tell her. "Pretend you're writing an ad about yourself for the personal section of the newspaper." She gathered up her purse and stepped out onto the front porch. "What would it say?"

"I have no idea," Mitch replied dryly as she turned around and locked up behind them. "Since I neither find nor advertise for dates that way." One hand braced on the brick just above her head, his body lightly, protectively caging hers, he peered down at her mischievously in the muted evening light. "Do you?"

Lauren flushed at the wicked gleam in his eyes and stepped out from under the sheltering warmth of his arm. She shot him an equally provoking glance. "I haven't had to since I meet so many people in my line of work. And you didn't answer my question. What would you say in an ad about yourself if you were trying to get a date?"

"Career-oriented man seeks career-oriented woman."

"Who...?" Lauren prodded when he didn't immediately go on.

To her mounting frustration, Mitch shrugged and offered nothing more.

"Cooks, sews, swims. What would you like any prospective date to do?" Lauren nudged as they moved off the porch and sauntered down the walk, side by side.

Mitch regarded her with mock solemnity. "Not ask too many questions."

Lauren felt like stamping her foot. "I'm serious!"

"So am I." Mitch paused to unlock and open his car door. He grinned, looking handsome and sexy as ever in his slate-gray suit and matching tie. "This is a ridiculous conversation we're having."

"Only because you don't know yourself or what you want," Lauren retorted as she lowered herself gracefully into the passenger seat.

"Now, that," Mitch said, leisurely shutting the door, circling around the Lexus and climbing behind the wheel, "is just not true. I know exactly what I want," he told her confidently. And then he put his arms around her, hauled her close and kissed her.

Chapter Six

"This was not part of any bargain we made," Lauren said as soon as she could come up for air.

"Well, then it should be," Mitch murmured, and then he lowered his head and kissed her again.

And the kiss felt like a test. One, Lauren thought as she sank even deeper into the steamy embrace, she was destined to fail. She had seen Mitch watching her as she got ready to go out. Felt his hot blue gaze caressing first her legs, then her hips, her face, even her hair. The only part of her he hadn't surveyed with much interest was her upper torso, but he was making up for that now, she realized, as his hands circled her ribs, climbing higher still. Taking her to a pleasure-filled heaven unlike anything she had experienced.

Mitch had wanted to see firsthand just how far Lauren was willing to go for her father and the family business and the historic mansion she wanted. If the heat of the kisses she was giving back to him were any indication, pretty far. He hadn't expected making out with her to feel so real. Having her snuggled against him this way, in equal parts wonder and surrender, her lips pressed erotically to his, her arms wreathed around his neck, her breasts swelling to fill his palms, felt right. It felt like something he should pursue. But not here, Mitch realized reluctantly as his lower body pulsed and hardened, and her nipples beaded beneath the layers of silk and chiffon. Not when they were sitting in his car in front of her home, in plain view of anyone who passed by, and he was feeling so simultaneously unsure of her and recklessly drawn to her.

The first time he made love to Lauren—and he was beginning to see that would happen before the week was up—was going to be private. Personal. And about as far from any spying or business deals or arranged courtships as he could get them. When it happened, it would mean something, and not simply be a way to a desired result.

Reluctantly, he let the kiss trail to an end. And drew back. "As much as I want to," he murmured, gently pushing the hair away from her cheek, "we can't do this."

Lauren drew a shuddering breath. The misty longing left her eyes as abruptly as it had appeared. "You're right," she said coolly as she moved away from him and returned to her side of the car. "Our situation is too complicated as it is. Plus—" she focused all her attention on fastening her seat belt, then stared straight ahead "—in case you've forgotten, we have a set agenda this evening. The two of us are due at the literacy fund-raiser as we speak. And I don't want to be late."

Nice save, Mitch thought. *Too bad I don't believe a word of it.* "I guess you're right," Mitch drawled as he put his key in the ignition and started the car. He looked past Lauren, making sure the way was clear as he guided the Lexus onto the street. "We wouldn't want to set tongues wagging by coming in all disheveled, and late, to boot. Not unless we want to endure a lot of teasing from my family."

The color in Lauren's cheeks increased, as did the dread in her dark brown eyes. "They're going to be there?"

Mitch nodded. "Everyone except my dad, who's out of town, and my brother Chase and his wife, Bridgett, who are still on their honeymoon." He looked at Lauren and noted with relief she was finally beginning to relax just a little bit again. Although he doubted she would forgive him anytime soon for the no-holds-barred way he had just kissed her. "What about your dad?" Mitch asked.

Lauren sighed, some of the light going out of her eyes. "He usually goes to this—everyone who's anyone in Charleston does—but he e-mailed me that he was too tired to attend tonight, so I'll be representing our family," she stated matter-of-factly.

Mitch didn't know whether to be relieved he wouldn't be spending the evening under Payton Heyward's watchful eyes, or sorry he wouldn't have the chance to relate to him.

"It's for a good cause," Mitch said eventually as they left the city and headed out toward the ocean.

"Yes, it is," Lauren agreed, tugging her skirt lower, toward her knees. She turned her attention to the marsh grasses waving in the spring breeze on either side of the raised highway. "Have you signed up to collect books yet?"

Mitch frowned as they drove across the causeway toward the towns that had sprung up close to the beach. He slanted a quick glance at Lauren. "Isn't that done by volunteers?"

"Right. Which is why we have to *volunteer,*" Lauren explained.

Mitch maneuvered his car through the considerable traffic. "I think I'd rather just give a sizable donation.... What?" he said when she said nothing in response, just gave him one of those looks that suggested he rethink his position, pronto. "It's a better use of my time to bring in the bucks so that I can make the sizable donations to charity that I do."

Lauren just shook her head. "Well, this year you may have to roll up your sleeves and wade into the thick of things like the rest of us hands-on types,'' she said autocratically.

Wondering how she figured that, Mitch drove up to the gatehouse that bordered the hotel property. He held up his invitation and was waved through the entrance by the uniformed guard. ''And why is that?'' He mocked her know-it-all tone.

Lauren grinned. ''Because I've already volunteered to drive one of the pick-up vans one night this week.''

Well, that's one way to spend a date, Mitch thought as he pulled up in front of the magnificent beachfront hotel where the event was being held, and parked his car in the lot, adjacent to the beige-stucco building. No sooner had they bypassed the fountain in front and begun to ascend the steps than they met his sister, Amy, and brother Gabe coming back out of the hotel. They headed straight for Mitch and Lauren.

''Bad news,'' Amy said, the seriousness in her turquoise eyes belying her status as the baby of the family. ''Jeannette Wycliffe planned the gala tonight and she's here. Thus far, Gabe and I have managed to avoid her, and we suggest you do the same.''

Mitch frowned at the mention of his ex-wife. He knew Amy wouldn't have brought her up in front of Lauren unless there were a problem brewing—a big one! ''I can handle Jeannette,'' Mitch said firmly, wishing he didn't have to nevertheless. ''It's Mom I'm worried about.''

Lauren touched Mitch's arm lightly. She looked up at him with a concern that had nothing to do with any embarrassment Lauren might experience from a possible brouhaha. ''Jeannette wouldn't be unpleasant to your mother, would she?''

Amy, Gabe and Mitch looked at each other—no one knew quite how to answer Lauren. ''It's more like what Mom might say to Jeannette, if she gets the chance,'' Gabe told Lauren with the same gentle, tactful manner he used on his patients over at the hospital.

Amy brushed her long dark hair off her shoulders and explained reluctantly. "Mom's still furious over the hell Jeannette put Mitch through when they were getting divorced."

Grace had also promised to give Jeannette a piece of her mind if she ever saw her again, Mitch recalled. None of them wanted that to happen, especially here, especially tonight, when the occasion was supposed to be about helping kids learn to read.

As involved in helping others as always, Gabe said, "Let's make a pact. If anyone sees Jeannette heading for Mom, or vice versa, that person'll cut 'em off at the pass and make sure no contact is made between those two. Deal?"

Everyone nodded—including Lauren, Mitch noted. "Where is Mom?" Mitch asked, glancing around at the well-dressed crowd pouring into the hotel.

"She said she'd meet us here," Amy said, "so Gabe and I thought we'd wait out here for her and escort her inside."

Daisy Templeton came up to join them. She was wearing a demure lilac-colored tea-length sheath, and she carried a camera in her hand. "Hi, guys," Daisy said.

For someone who had reportedly just been kicked out of her seventh college in five years, Daisy was remarkably cheerful, Mitch thought. Daisy stepped back, tilted her head slightly and regarded Mitch with a critical eye. "Say, you've got a pretty good chest. Nice broad shoulders. How'd you feel about taking your shirt off for me?"

Mitch laughed uneasily, knowing Daisy wasn't so much coming on to him as making the usual spectacle of herself. "I don't think so."

"Gabe?"

Gabe shook his head. "Not this time."

Daisy snapped her fingers. "Aw, shucks. I had a feeling you two guys would say that. And you're so good-looking, too. Well, I'll just have to keep searching for a more co-operative model." She moved off through the throng of people gathering in front of the hotel.

Lauren, Mitch, Gabe and Amy looked at each other.

"She was kidding, wasn't she?" Amy said finally.

"I'm not sure." Lauren bit her lower lip. "With Daisy, you never know. Maybe we better keep an eye on her, too. I'd hate to see her get in any more trouble with her parents here tonight." Lauren nodded in the direction of a tense-looking older couple going into the hotel lobby. Fortunately, Richard and Charlotte Templeton were blissfully unaware of what their youngest daughter was up to now.

"How did you and Daisy get to know each other?" Mitch asked Lauren.

Lauren edged closer to Mitch. "We've volunteered at some of the same charity events, from the time Daisy was a teenager." Worry crept into Lauren's dark brown eyes. "She was cute and cheerful and ready to help in whatever way she was needed, but also pretty wild even then. Her parents weren't very tolerant. They were constantly scolding and reprimanding her."

"That can't have been very pleasant," Amy said.

"It wasn't," Lauren admitted, her eyes once again turning to Mitch. "I've got to say, my heart really went out to Daisy. I think she's sweet, beneath the rebel exterior. I think she's just—I don't know, I don't want to say un-loved, but—" Abruptly, some of the color left Lauren's face. "Oh, no—" she murmured as a laughing Daisy finally found what she'd been looking for in front of the fountain. Grinning broadly, her camera still in hand, Daisy knelt in front of an extraordinarily good-looking young man who'd already taken off his jacket and tie, and was working—quite happily—on his shirt.

"Oh, man," Mitch echoed Lauren's sentiments as he

wrapped an arm around Lauren's shoulders and took in the scene. "This is not a good idea. Not at all…"

"Come on, show me some beefcake!" Daisy teased, dancing around the hunk and snapping photos from various angles as she went.

The young man tossed off his shirt and thrust out his chest.

"A hundred bucks if you'll get in the water!" Daisy said.

Behind her, a hotel employee threaded his way through the crowds of onlookers to Daisy's side. Ignoring the cars continuing to pull up, and the prominent citizens there to attend the fund-raiser piling out onto the curb, he told Daisy sternly, "Miss! You can't do this!"

"Want to bet?" Daisy waggled her eyebrows at him and grinned as another limo drew up. Grace Deveraux got out, looking lovely as ever in a glittering red gown. Spotting the four of them, Mitch's mother waved and walked over to join them.

"You're creating a spectacle!" the employee continued scolding Daisy Templeton sternly.

"No, a spectacle would be if Cal here actually got in the fountain and splashed around!" Daisy said.

Looking as anxious to please the beautiful twenty-three-year-old Daisy as Daisy was to have her way, Cal waded into the fountain, shoes, pants and all, and stood beneath the spray. Daisy hooted with laughter, kicked off her shoes, and before anyone could do more than draw a breath, waded right in after him, taking action shot after shot. And that was when it happened, when both her parents came striding out of the hotel lobby, horrified looks on both their faces.

"Daisy, for heaven's sake," Charlotte Templeton gasped, a hand to her chest.

Richard Templeton shared his wife's displeasure as he said tightly, "Get out of that fountain right now."

"What do you think you're doing?" a pale-faced Charlotte demanded of her daughter.

Daisy shrugged. "You told me I needed to get a job if I wasn't going to be in school! So I got a freelance assignment. If I can come up with something eye-catching enough, my photo will appear on the cover of *Charleston Nights* magazine."

"I don't care. This is quite inappropriate!" Charlotte Templeton said.

"No," Daisy said, whirling on both her parents furiously as she stepped out of the water, onto the cement.. "I'm inappropriate, Mother! And let's face it, in your and Father's eyes, I always have been!"

Bravo, Mitch thought. Because it was true. And—from what little he had observed—it was also something that should have been said years ago. Before Daisy decided she was unappreciated and unloved.

"We're going home—now!" Richard Templeton took Daisy by the arm. Charlotte Templeton rushed after them. Together, the three marched toward the curb. The young man—now as red-faced as Daisy—climbed out of the fountain and retrieved his clothes. The Templetons limo appeared like magic.

"Some spectacle, hmm?" Mitch said to his mother, guessing from the look on Grace's face that she disapproved mightily of Daisy's antics, as well.

Beside Mitch, Lauren frowned. And like Mitch, her attention remained glued on the Templeton family as they climbed into their limousine.

As much as Mitch sympathized with the irrepressible Daisy, who seemed like a duck out of water whenever she was around her stick-in-the-mud parents, he had to concede that Daisy had brought on the latest calamity herself.

"Daisy really is old enough to know better," Lauren murmured. "I mean, surely she could have found a less embarrassing time and place to take the tantalizing photos she wanted.''

''It's not her fault,'' Grace said, surprising them all by siding with Daisy after such a flamboyant display. ''Her parents never should have adopted her. They should've known—under the circumstances that...well—''

Everyone gave Mitch's mother an odd look before Grace could finish whatever it was she was about to say. ''I'm sure they were only doing their best to give Daisy the best life possible,'' he said. ''And you have to admit that financially, anyway, Daisy hasn't lacked for anything.''

''Except perhaps acceptance and understanding,'' Lauren murmured.

''If Daisy would just meet her parents halfway and behave even half as circumspectly as her older sister, Iris, things would probably go a whole lot better for her,'' Mitch continued matter-of-factly.

''On the other hand,'' Lauren interjected, taking the opposite tack, ''for a while, Daisy's brother, Connor, was pretty outrageous, too, when he was her age. So maybe Daisy is just following in his footsteps.''

Abruptly, Grace looked as if she'd had quite enough of the discussion. She put a hand to her forehead. ''If you all will excuse me, I'm going inside and say hello to everyone else,'' she said. ''I haven't been to one of these charity events in Charleston in ages.''

''We'll go with you, Mom,'' Amy said as she and Gabe moved to flank Grace on both sides.

''Sorry about that,'' Mitch said to Lauren as the two of them lagged behind deliberately. ''Mom's not usually prone to emotional outbursts but she's been a little edgy since she got back to Charleston.''

''Understandably so,'' Lauren replied with a respect Mitch appreciated. Lauren slipped her arm in Mitch's as they ascended the steps. ''It must be hard for her having to face everyone tonight so soon after getting canned by the network.''

''I think she just wanted to get it over with,'' Mitch said, relieved that Lauren intuitively understood the Deveraux family dynamics. ''She knew she was going to have to make a public appearance here in Charleston sooner or later. And it's for a good cause. The money raised tonight will help a lot of kids learn to love books as much as everyone here does.''

THE NEXT FEW HOURS passed quickly. Mitch and Lauren managed to have a lot of fun, while at the same time interacting with the rest of his family and their many other friends. But because of the social nature of the event, she and Mitch didn't get any time alone. As the party neared an end, Mitch was approached by colleagues in the shipping business. Amy and Gabe became equally distracted. And it was then that Grace apparently decided to make a beeline for Mitch's ex-wife, Jeannette Wycliffe. Lauren cut her off at the pass, as planned. Seconds later, Grace was surrounded by a TV crew from a local station, there to film a small bit for the late news.

Leaving Grace to hold court, Lauren eased away as unobtrusively as possible. And nearly bumped noses with Mitch's ex. ''Nice save,'' Jeannette Wycliffe noted.

Lauren tensed as she faced the statuesque beauty in the floor-length dress. ''What do you mean?''

Jeannette's hazel-green eyes glowed with an unhappy light. ''Grace Deveraux was going to give me a piece of her mind about my now-defunct marriage to her son. You cleverly stepped in and stopped her.''

Lauren didn't know why exactly, but she had the feeling Jeannette would have relished such an emotional scene, if only for the embarrassment it would have caused Mitch, and indeed the whole Deveraux clan.

For all their sakes, Lauren did her best to inject calm

into the potentially explosive situation. "It wouldn't benefit any of us to talk about anything but the wonderful cause we are celebrating tonight," Lauren said tactfully, looking around them. The ballroom had been turned into a whimsical children's library, complete with faux stacks and cozy reading nooks and a yellow brick road that paved the way from buffet tables to volunteer sign-up stations. The waitstaff were dressed as characters from favorite children's books. Some were from classic tales—like *Mother Goose, The Hardy Boys,* and *The Wizard of Oz.* Others were more modern. Life-size portraits of kids reading were stationed strategically around the room. The centerpieces were made of balloons. Linens and napkins were crayon colors. Jeannette's assistants were costumed like turn-of-the-century librarians, complete with old-fashioned eyeglasses.

Lauren turned back to Jeannette and continued with respect, "You've done a really incredible job here tonight with the party." That was no surprise, of course. Jeannette Wycliffe was best known for her excellent work. She was also very beautiful, although there was a brittleness in the dark-haired woman's demeanor that hadn't been there before her marriage to Mitch. She looked, Lauren thought, like someone who'd been very dissatisfied by life.

"Thank you," Jeannette returned just as quietly, finally pulling herself together, too. "Your father's birthday party is coming together very well also, I might add."

Lauren smiled, still glad she had hired Jeannette to plan and oversee it. She and her father might have their differences, but she wanted only the best for Payton, as he did for her. "We're really looking forward to it."

Jeannette nodded. And then, just when Lauren thought they were going to be able to end their conversation on that pleasant, professional note, Jeannette caught her arm before Lauren could turn away.

"Look, Lauren, I know we're not friends, but I saw you

come in with Mitch. And I just have to say it,'' Jeannette said, her voice quivering emotionally. ''I think dating him is a big mistake. Take it from me—he won't make you happy.''

Caught off guard by the raw hurt in Jeannette's tone, Lauren said just as quietly, ''You don't know that.''

''I wish I didn't,'' Jeannette said miserably. ''But the sad fact of the matter is that Mitch Deveraux doesn't care about what anyone else wants. When it comes to him, it's all about him and his goals. Goals he would do anything to achieve.''

A chill went down Lauren's spine at the certainty in Jeannette's eyes.

Lauren stared at her, not knowing what to say that would benefit either of them at that point.

She took a step back, felt a warm, strong hand closing around her elbow. She looked up to see Mitch standing beside her. He nodded at his ex-wife. ''Jeannette.''

Jeannette smiled back at Mitch tightly. ''Mitch.''

''If you'll excuse us.''

''Certainly.''

Mitch eased Lauren away. His expression was impassive, his body rigid with tension and something else that might have been disapproval. Clearly, he hadn't wanted Lauren and Jeannette trading notes on him. ''Ready to leave?'' he asked crisply.

Lauren glanced across the ballroom and saw that Gabe and Amy Deveraux were already escorting Grace out, as well. Deciding they had all done enough to advance the cause of literacy for one night, Lauren breathed a sigh of relief. ''Absolutely.''

Mitch waited until they were driving away from the hotel before finally asking, ''What did Jeannette say to you?''

''She doesn't think we should be dating.''

''No surprise there,'' Mitch sighed as he drove past the guardhouse and then, instead of following the rest of the cars toward the main highway, turned the Lexus onto a side street, away from the congested main thoroughfare. "If she can't have me, she doesn't want anyone else to, either."

"So I take it this means Jeannette didn't want the divorce," Lauren guessed as they bumped along on a roughly paved lane fronting some beach houses.

Lauren knew it was none of her business, but she couldn't help it. She was more curious now than ever about the reasons for the end of Mitch's marriage, as well as the reasons behind Jeannette Wycliffe's anxiety tonight. Jeannette was an accomplished career woman in her own right. Lauren had never seen her looking so uneasy or upset before, but she had clearly been both tonight.

"You could say that." Mitch turned again so they were driving over a narrow one-lane bridge through an even more remote area of marsh grass and water marked with signs that read, Breach Inlet. Deadly Currents. No Swimming. No Wading.

Lauren swallowed as Mitch's car bumped along even harder. They reached the other side of the bridge and hit solid ground again. A steep slope of big boulders and a narrow strip of beach separated them from the water below.

"But you did want the divorce?" Lauren asked. She felt herself tense when another Danger sign came into view.

"Yes." Mitch swore, slowing even more as the car pulled hard to the right.

"Why?" Lauren asked. She watched Mitch stop the car on the berm, well out of harm's way, and cut the engine.

"Because she lied to me," he said.

Chapter Seven

"A big lie, or a casual itty-bitty one?" Lauren asked as Mitch switched on the emergency flashers.

Mitch turned to Lauren. "Is there a difference?" He wished she wouldn't ask these questions, but he also knew her well enough by now to realize there was going to be no dissuading her. Hence, they might as well just get it over with.

"Well—" Lauren drew back slightly to give him room to maneuver, as he reached past her to open the glove compartment "—if Jeannette was throwing you a surprise party and didn't want you to know and told a few fibs to cover her tracks, that would be one thing."

Yes, Mitch thought, it would have been. Unhappily, it wasn't the case. Mitch grabbed the flashlight. Abruptly feeling way too confined, he got out of the car and moved around to inspect the tires on the passenger side of the car. Lauren followed suit. As he had feared, the right front had a flat.

Aware Lauren was still waiting for an answer, he said, "It was a big lie."

"And that's all you're going to tell me," Lauren ascertained, sounding disappointed.

"I don't talk about this," he said.

"Maybe you should."

Which was, Mitch thought, exactly what his mother and sister had said when he had refused to tell them. "It won't change what happened," he stated gruffly, already circling around to the trunk.

"But it might make you feel better about it," Lauren said, turning to face him. "Because right now you still seem pretty ticked off, and it's been—what—a year since the two of you divorced?"

"Two," Mitch corrected, handing over the flashlight to her. And Lauren was right—he was still pretty peeved about it, whenever he thought about it, which wasn't often. "For you to understand," Mitch said finally, still looking for a way out of a conversation this personal, as he jerked off his tie, tossed it inside the car and rolled up his sleeves, "I'd have to go way back."

Lauren smiled. "I don't mind."

"Don't you want me to call you a cab?"

"You could. But it would probably take forever for them to get out here this time of night. I can wait till you put on the spare. Which, unless I miss my guess, is exactly what you were just getting prepared to do."

"True. But our date is over in roughly—" Mitch glanced at his watch "—seven minutes, anyway."

Lauren smiled, looking all the more determined. "Good effort for a way out, but I don't think so. I'd rather stay, lend a hand if necessary, and hear your side of the breakup. Because obviously your brief run-in with Jeannette annoyed the heck out of you, even if you'd like to pretend it didn't."

Mitch studied Lauren for a moment, thinking. He could tell by the gentle, compassionate way she was looking at him she was sincerely interested in him and wanted to help him get over whatever he'd been through. He also knew he did trust her to be discreet about something like this. He couldn't say why exactly, when the circumstances of their getting together had created a lot of questions in his mind. He just knew on a gut level that whatever he told her in confidence about his romantic past would remain just between the two of them.

"How did you get involved with her anyway?" Lauren asked as Mitch opened the trunk and took out an emergency road kit.

"It was at one of those charity events. I had just started attending them on behalf of the company. And as usual, Jeannette had done an incredible job. I complimented her and we got to talking. One thing led to another and we started dating."

"How old were you then?" Lauren watched as Mitch set up the spotlight so it illuminated the entire side of the car, then went to the passenger compartment and set the emergency brake.

"Twenty-five and so was she." Mitch went back to the trunk and removed the jack and the wheel wrench.

"You were both pretty young, then."

Some of the old bitterness came back to haunt him as he recalled how completely Jeannette had betrayed him. "Looking back now, I can see how cleverly she stage-managed every detail of our courtship, but all I really knew then was that it was exciting and she seemed to want everything that I wanted." Mitch hunkered down beside the car. "Especially the stable family life and the kids."

"But she didn't."

"No," Mitch said as he blocked the front and back of diagonally opposite tires with two blocks, to keep the car from shifting while he worked on it. "And I blame myself for that because we didn't once sit down in a businesslike manner and go over everything point by point."

Lauren shrugged and shook her head so her golden-brown hair was blowing away from her face instead of into her eyes. "It probably wouldn't have gone over too well if you had—it's not very romantic."

Mitch circled around to the front of the car again. "I'm

beginning to think romance has no place in relationships," he said as he returned to the flat and used a wrench to loosen the lug nuts.

Lauren edged closer, still studying him intently. "You really mean that?"

Mitch glanced up at her. If he didn't know better, he would think Lauren was really interested in him in a man-woman way that had nothing to do with the deal they'd made with her dad or the rewards they would both reap at the end. "I really do," he said softly.

"So, back to your story." Lauren leaned against a boulder. "When did the two of you decide to get married?" she asked.

"A year to the day after we started dating."

"I remember the wedding." Lauren smiled. "It was some blowout according to the write-up it received on the society page."

Mitch slipped the jack under the axle, next to the flat. "Jeannette went all out with the arrangements," he said, as he positioned the handle on the jack. "It took her just two months to pull everything together."

"Did she continue working after you were married?"

"No." Mitch turned the jack handle clockwise until the tire cleared the ground. "She wanted to concentrate on our life together."

"When did the deception occur?" Lauren asked, moving back slightly so he'd have plenty of room to work.

Mitch grimaced, remembering. "Almost immediately." The next was even harder for Mitch to admit because it demonstrated how big a fool he had been. "For nearly two years she made a great show of trying to get pregnant. She had me convinced that she wanted to have our baby more than anything in the world."

"And you bought it."

Mitch removed the lug nuts. "Hook, line and sinker."

"How did you discover she didn't really want this?"

"I was worried because she hadn't conceived." Mitch lifted the wheel off and set it on the ground. "And I wanted us to go to a specialist, to make sure everything was in working order."

"But she didn't."

"No," Mitch said as he headed back to the trunk to get the spare tire. "She argued for more time, said if we just relaxed it would happen. In the meantime, she began looking for a big house in the historic district and she started throwing a lot of very big, elaborate parties. She was trying to emulate my aunt Winnifred's lifestyle and, frankly, I wasn't all that enthusiastic about it," Mitch confessed, positioning the spare tire on the wheel. "I like a party as much as the next guy, but for me, work comes first. Anyway, I could see Jeannette was getting really frustrated with me and the situation. And I knew it wasn't going to get any better until we knew the truth. So I pulled all kinds of strings and made an appointment with a fertility expert."

"Jeannette wasn't happy about that."

Mitch frowned. "No. Not at all. She canceled and rescheduled at the last minute several times. Eventually," Mitch sighed as he tightened the lug nuts, using a crisscross pattern, until they were equally snug. "I just made an appointment, picked her up for what she thought was a lunch date and took her to the doctor's office. And it was as we were walking into the doctor's office that she finally took me aside and told me the truth." Mitch grimaced as he turned and looked Lauren straight in the eye. "She'd had her tubes tied six weeks before we walked down the aisle. And she'd been afraid to tell me. She said she knew the two of us didn't really need children to be happy. She cited my aunt Winnifred as an example, because Winnifred had never had kids and was quite happy, as well as one of the most popular hostesses in the city."

Lauren looked as shocked as Mitch had felt at the time. "You must have been devastated," she whispered, upset.

"As well as furious," Mitch conceded, using the jack to lower the vehicle back to the ground. Pausing, he turned to Lauren. "I felt like such a chump. Looking back, I can see there were signs from the very first that she wasn't being as truthful with me as she should have been, but like a fool I ignored them."

Still looking a bit stricken, Lauren regarded Mitch with all the sympathy and understanding he ever could have wished for. "Did Jeannette ever plan to tell you?"

"No." Mitch removed the jack and wheel blocks. "And she was hurt and angry I'd forced her hand."

"You must have been pretty hurt, too."

Mitch nodded, knowing he had never felt as betrayed as he had then. "When I thought about all the lies she'd told me, the level of deception Jeannette had perpetrated, I knew I couldn't stay married to her a second longer. So I asked for an immediate divorce."

"And she gave you one."

"Not for almost a year, even though we were living apart," Mitch said. "And that's when it began to get really ugly behind the scenes. Jeannette couldn't—wouldn't—believe it was over as far as I was concerned. She said if I had ever really loved her, I could get past it. She even offered to try to have her tubal ligation reversed if I would do my part and allow her to have what she really wanted too, which was to become the leading social hostess in the city."

"You said no," Lauren guessed, looking as if she agreed with his decision one hundred percent.

Mitch shrugged and carried the jack, wheel wrench and jack handle back to his trunk. "I'd fallen in love with this image she'd created for me, not the real Jeannette. Once I saw who she was, there was no pretending we'd ever have a viable marriage. So I threatened to sue her for fraud if she didn't give me what I wanted—which was a quick divorce with no financial settlement—we both walked out of the marriage with exactly what we walked in. She finally relented, only because she wanted to land another rich husband and she knew her chances of that would be diminished if the truth ever got out.''

"No wonder your family has no affection for Jeannette," Lauren murmured as Mitch returned for the flat tire. "After the way she led you on about giving you a child…''

"They don't know about any of that." Mitch returned the tire to the trunk, too. "I never told them.''

Lauren rose gracefully to her feet. "Why not?''

"Bad enough I'd been snared by a fortune hunter.'' Mitch reached into the emergency kit for a packet containing disposable cleaning cloth and ripped it open. "I had no desire to add to my humiliation.''

"But you told me," Lauren said, standing up to face him. "You're not sorry you confided in me, are you?''

"No," Mitch said. And it was true. He wasn't. Because something right had come out of it. He felt as if he'd been purged of the awful bitterness he had been carrying around inside himself for so long.

Lauren smiled, looking relieved. "Did the experience put you off marriage forever?''

"No." Mitch scrubbed the grime off his hands. Then deciding he needed a second cleaning cloth if he was to do the job right, broke open another packet. "But if I were to marry again, I'd go about it in a much more organized, businesslike fashion.''

Lauren gave him a streetwise look that said, *Here we go again*. "By doing what?" she asked as Mitch decided against switching off the spotlight and tossing it in the trunk just yet. Wanting a moment to enjoy the sea air and the quiet moonlit evening before they finished packing up, he leaned against the car and folded his arms in front of him.

"For starters, I'd pick someone from a similar background, who understands that money and social standing are not the key to happiness." *Someone like you, Lauren.* "And then I'd insist we talk about all the important things, like family, first. I would want whomever I marry to want kids as much as I do. And, this time I'd insist on a prenuptial agreement. I'd want a detailed contract about how the money should be split up if and when the marriage dissolved."

"Isn't that a little cold-blooded?" Lauren moved so she was standing directly in front of him. Her heels planted firmly on the pavement beneath her, she splayed her hands on her hips. "I mean, you're practically *predicting* that the marriage won't work out."

Mitch studied Lauren's upturned face. Despite the long day and even longer evening, she was as lovely as ever. He studied the windswept disarray of her golden-brown hair, the flushed color in her cheeks, the sparkle in her dark brown eyes. "That's what I thought the first time. That's why I didn't ask for one. Now," he said, carefully underscoring every word, "I would."

Lauren arched her delicate eyebrows in pointed disagreement. "Well, I wouldn't."

"Then you'd be a fool," Mitch said, refusing to pull his punches just to protect her feelings. "Because if you did marry and it didn't last, you could very well lose the mansion at 10 Gathering Street you've been working so hard to own, as well as a big chunk of any money or stock you have now."

A pulse throbbed in Lauren's neck as she regarded him in silence, clearly wanting to trust his judgment on the matter but not quite able to. "Marriage isn't a business arrangement, Mitch," she said heatedly at last.

Mitch shrugged his shoulders uncaringly. "If you ask

me,'' he returned gruffly, ''it should be.'' Business was safe. Romance wasn't.

Lauren shook her head, her disappointment in him plain. ''Speaking of business,'' she said, her voice turning light, ''our date was over almost half an hour ago.''

Mitch did his best to contain his disappointment. There, for a while, he had been hoping this arranged courtship of theirs would lead to something even better than the financial rewards they had both been promised for participating. ''I guess I better get you home then,'' he said at last.

''I guess you better,'' Lauren agreed, already turning away.

They drove back to her place in silence. Mitch wondered what Lauren was thinking, but she remained moody and distant and gave him no clue.

''I don't suppose we could subtract the extra hour tonight from the date tomorrow,'' Lauren said as Mitch parked at the curb.

Mitch shook his head. Assured of her attention, he turned to her and continued, ''It's not in the oral contract we made with your father. I think the overtime is on us.''

Lauren wrinkled her nose in aggravation. ''I really wish my father hadn't put us in such a straitjacket in terms of this dating business. Even though I know full well why he felt he had to.''

Warning bells went off in Mitch's head at the combination of regret and wistfulness in Lauren's low voice. Was she getting ready to confide in him, too? Or just thinking about the things she would still rather he not know? he wondered as he walked her to her front door. ''Why?''

Lauren shrugged and seemed to pull back just as they reached the porch. ''It's just the way my dad is,'' she stated, suddenly getting a faraway look in her eyes. ''He's very protective of the people he loves. He always sheltered me when I was a kid. When my mother died of an aneurysm when I was eighteen, he became even more vigilant.''

Mitch and his siblings had been given free rein at an early age—fostering independence in their children was one of the many things their parents had done right. "That must be difficult for you,'' Mitch empathized.

Lauren's pouty lower lip curled ruefully as she studied the toe of her shoe. "He says he just wants to see I'm taken care of in case anything ever happens to him. But unfortunately,'' she finished unhappily as she plucked her house keys from her handbag, "to him that means he wants to make all my decisions for me, right down to choosing my husband and setting the terms of my marriage.''

Ouch, Mitch thought, understanding full well why Lauren would be peeved about that. "I agree your father's off the mark in what he's trying to do, in hooking the two of us up together permanently. I mean, if we wanted to marry for business reasons, it would be one thing. We're responsible adults. We're free to do what we choose. But to have someone decide that for us—well,'' he finished wryly, "let's just say it's not a recommended strategy for any parent to pursue.''

"Even if my father's heart is in the right place and his business reasons are solid?'' Lauren questioned curiously.

"Even then,'' Mitch affirmed.

Lauren tilted her head to the side and evaluated Mitch thoughtfully a moment longer. "What about you, Mitch?'' she asked lightly. "Where is your heart? Is it in the right place, too?''

Mitch had to say this for her—Lauren didn't mince words when it came to examining his motives. And he admired her for it. Even as he refused to let her imply what was or wasn't behind his actions. "I admit I undertook this week-long venture for purely capitalistic reasons,'' he said. "But you should know that's changed. I am interested in you." Even though he couldn't yet trust her in every respect. Otherwise, he wouldn't have told her everything he had tonight. He wouldn't have opened up his heart to her.

For a moment Lauren didn't seem to breathe or move. Then she collected herself and shrugged her slender shoulders. "I'm afraid, under the circumstances, Mitch, that I can't be interested in you," she said just as frankly. "Not that way. Our private agendas are just too diverse."

Disappointment unlike anything he'd ever felt washed through Mitch. "The kisses you gave me earlier say differently," Mitch pointed out.

Before he could take her in his arms again, Lauren levered a hand against his chest, preventing an instant replay of the same. "Combining romance with business was a mistake," she told him coolly. "Now, if you'll excuse me, I've got an early morning."

So did Mitch. For once, it didn't matter. He knew where he wanted to be, and that was right here with Lauren. But, having been reared a gentleman, he graciously took the hint, accepted her time-out and let the evening end. "Tomorrow then?" he said, knowing he would make the most of that date, too, and every one after.

Lauren nodded.

"Any idea what you want to do?" Mitch asked. Suddenly, the week Payton Heyward had arbitrarily decided upon was not nearly long enough. Maybe because Mitch was no longer simply marking time with Lauren.

Lauren sent him a brisk, officious smile that should have discouraged Mitch completely. It didn't.

"How about I e-mail you by around four-thirty or so tomorrow afternoon?" she said. "By then, one of us should have a plan."

Chapter Eight

"I'm glad we could get together," Mitch told Ron Ingalls the next day as they met for lunch at a popular seafood place. Mitch had been in business long enough to know there was no limit to the information that could be garnered via small talk in a relaxed setting.

"I am, too." Ron looked trim and fit as always as he paused to place his order with the waiter and then handed over a notebook emblazoned with the Ingalls Shipbuilding, Inc., logo. The CEO smiled at Mitch as he began his pitch. "In addition to the details you requested, I've also enclosed information on a container ship that is nearing completion. It was built to spec for someone else but it's top of the line."

Mitch scanned the specifications with interest, noting that the ship was indeed state of the art. "When is it going to be ready?"

"A few weeks." Ron steepled his hands together and leaned forward energetically. "To be perfectly honest, I'd be willing to make a deal on it."

Mitch would have liked to purchase it. But until his father and he agreed on how to use that year's expansion money, Mitch realized with disappointment, it would not be possible.

Deciding to work the conversation around to the real

reason for the business lunch—his desire to know why
there had been so many phone calls between Lauren and
Ron Ingalls of late—Mitch put the folder down and asked
casually, "Have you offered the ship to Payton Heyward?"

"No."

This was a surprise, since Payton Heyward bought ships
only from Ingalls's operation and the Deveraux bought
them from several different companies. "Why not?"
Mitch asked flatly.

Ron hesitated uncomfortably, then still appearing wary
of revealing too much, said reluctantly, "Because Payton
Heyward's the one who changed his mind about buying
the ship."

Mitch didn't have to feign concern. This was a very
disturbing development because it could mean that he and
his father's hunch about Payton Heyward being in some
kind of trouble was right on the money. "That's unusual,
isn't it?" Mitch asked casually as he broke open a warm
roll.

"Very," Ron conceded. "In all the time I've been selling his company ships, he's never canceled an order for a
vessel until now."

Mitch sat back in his chair as the waiter placed their
plates in front of them. "Did he say why?"

Ron shrugged. "He said that he thought he might have
overextended the company a bit. He bought two ships from
us last spring. To add a third was maybe expanding a little
too fast. So he forfeited the deposit and canceled the order."

"That's too bad." Mitch cut into his crabmeat-stuffed
sea trout.

"Yes, it is." Ron acknowledged sympathetically. "But
I understand. Better to walk away now than get himself in
bigger trouble later."

Especially when you might have found a way to bail

yourself out financially through a merger—and maybe even a marriage—to another company, Mitch thought sardonically. Deciding he didn't know Ron well enough to be able to judge whether or not the shipbuilder was involved in any ruse the Heywards might be perpetrating on the Deveraux, Mitch kept the small talk firmly on track. "How does Ron like the ships he did buy?"

Ron brightened at the opportunity to continue his sales pitch. "He loves 'em. In fact, I'm playing golf with him later today."

Score one for Payton. "Is his daughter joining you?" Mitch asked casually.

Ron appeared surprised by the question. "Lauren? No. She's not really all that wild about the sport, although she can wield a pretty mean club when she has a mind to."

Mitch had no doubt of that. If Lauren played golf with anywhere near the expertise she sold real estate *or* kissed, she was likely to be an ace on the greens. "Then you've played with her before," Mitch presumed, taking a bite of perfectly prepared asparagus.

"Oh, yes." Ron grinned with what appeared to be genuine affection. "Occasionally she tags along on one of our golf and business outings just because her father asks her, but I can always tell her heart isn't really in it, that she'd rather be somewhere else, doing something—anything—else."

Which could mean, Mitch thought, that Lauren was being strong-armed into helping her father.

Then again, it could also mean that she was so truly disinterested in the family shipping business that her father had decided to do an end run around her. Without any knowledge on her part whatsoever.

"I gather you know her?" Ron asked.

Mitch nodded and revealed a little more. "We've been getting acquainted socially," he said honestly. "She's showing some houses to my mother, trying to help her find a place here in Charleston.''

Ron signaled the waiter for some coffee. "Well, if anyone can do it, Lauren can."

Mitch paused as their plates were cleared away, dessert menus handed out, two orders of the restaurant's famous pecan-rum pie placed. "Has she ever sold you any property?"

Ron nodded as the waiter filled their coffee cups. "She helped me find a vacation home down at Hilton Head on one of the golf courses. The negotiations were complicated—it required great subtlety and skill on her part to get me what I wanted at the price I wanted to pay, and it wasn't even her territory or area of expertise. But her father had asked her to help me out, so she hung in there like a trooper, driving back and forth as necessary until the deal was done. When it was all over, she told me I was going to owe her a pretty big favor. Sure enough—" Ron grinned, remembering "—not too long ago she called me to collect."

Mitch wanted to believe Lauren was innocent of any skulduggery behind the scenes. But if "the favor" wasn't connected to the shipbuilding business, what could Lauren have wanted from Ron? She didn't seem to need any more clients herself.

Mitch waited, but to his frustration no further information was forthcoming. "Were you able to help her out?" he asked eventually.

Ron sipped his coffee, a concerned look on his face. "I've been trying. I haven't been able to manage what she wants me to do for her father quite yet. But there's still time for me to pull it off. Now, back to that container ship I've got in inventory, and the deal I'd like to propose to you…"

"HAVE YOU HEARD from my father yet?" Mitch asked Jack Granger as soon as he got back to the office. He wanted to run Ron Ingalls's proposed deal by Tom—the figures on the container ship were that good. And although it could be part of a complicated ruse to win the ongoing competition between the Heyward and Deveraux shipping firms, it could also be exactly what it appeared to be—a real bargain, and exactly what the Deveraux Shipping Company needed to expand its business. Until Mitch knew for sure, or had at least run the proposal by his father and gotten his opinion on the situation, Mitch wasn't closing any doors.

Jack shook his head, his expression abruptly becoming closed and unreadable. "Nothing since yesterday morning's e-mail," Jack murmured as he busied himself with the papers on his desk.

"This isn't like him," Mitch said, walking farther into Jack's office and shutting the door behind him.

Jack leaned back in his chair and folded his hands behind his head. "It has been a long time since your dad's taken any vacation. Maybe he just needed a break," Jack said.

Mitch disagreed. Something had to be wrong for his father to take off like that and remain incommunicado. And to his mounting frustration, he had the feeling the firm's attorney knew more about what that reason might be than Mitch did. Feeling more stymied than ever, Mitch returned to his office and checked his e-mail. On it was a note from Lauren, replying to his e-mail earlier that morning. It read:

Mitch,
   Thanks for suggesting such a nice restaurant, but a bit of a personal emergency has come up, so our date tonight is going to be more like a work session. Wear old clothes and meet me at my house at six. I'll explain then and provide dinner.

                                                             Lauren

Mitch stared at the computer screen, wondering what the emergency was, and if it related to either her family's business or his, or even to the golf date her father was having with Ron Ingalls that very moment. Knowing the only way to find out would be to spend as much time as possible with her, learning as much as possible, Mitch hurried through the rest of his own business agenda. Like it or not, he was going to have to continue investigating Lauren—and her father, too. Something was driving the urgency behind Payton's actions. He had to find out what it was. Only then would he know whether he was free to pursue Lauren the way he wanted to pursue her—which was full out, with nothing and no one standing in their way.

By five o'clock, a cold front had moved in from the north, dropping the temperature twenty degrees. The skies were dark and the air was scented with impending rain. Trying not to view it as a sign of a disastrous evening ahead, Mitch went home to change and then headed over to Lauren's.

He arrived a little before six. He wasn't surprised to see that parked cars lined both sides of the street—that was usually the case in the historic district. He was stunned to see the tall wrought-iron gate that blocked her driveway was closed and locked, her car nowhere in sight. This meant she probably was going to be late for their date again.

Determined to be on time even if she wasn't, Mitch drove on. Finally finding a space nearly two blocks from her house, he parked and headed back in the direction from which he'd come. As he walked, it began to rain, lightly at first, then more heavily. Cursing his lack of either umbrella or jacket, he hurried on. And that was when he saw Lauren.

Despite her admonition that he dress casually, she was still wearing a sexy mint-green business suit that made the most of her slender, curvaceous figure. She had her back to him and her arms were full of packages, including a cardboard gift box some five feet long. A cell phone pressed to her ear, she was talking in a light flirtatious voice as she struggled to put her packages down on the stoop without dropping them. Telling himself he was doing them both a favor if he could exonerate her from any charges of wrongdoing by eavesdropping, Mitch ducked under the canopy of a large shade tree.

"...I know this isn't the way you usually operate..." Lauren's voice floated out to him. "But the utmost secrecy is important for obvious reasons until I tell you otherwise." She listened intently to the person on the other end of the connection. "Yes. Absolutely. I agree with you entirely. No one must know that we've been in contact with each other because then they'd know immediately what we're up to."

I wish I knew, Mitch thought.

"Yes, I agree," Lauren continued in a crisp, businesslike tone. "You and I are going to have to coordinate this precisely for maximum effect. I don't have all the details yet, but as soon as I can pin down the arrangements on this end, I'll let you know and we can go from there." She laughed softly. "I really appreciate what you're going to do for us, and I know my father will, too. He's convinced this will really help business. Now, don't underestimate yourself, Lance. Everyone knows you're the best in your field. All right. Yes. I'll talk to you soon. Bye."

She turned slightly and caught sight of Mitch lingering beneath the trees next to the sidewalk. Startled, she pressed a hand to her chest. "I didn't hear you come up," she said, looking all flushed.

Wondering who the hell "Lance" was and about his secret connection to Lauren, Mitch pushed away from the trunk of the tree and walked through the rain to her front porch.

Years of practice helped him keep his tumultuous emotions well hidden as he smiled at her and explained casually, "I didn't want to interrupt." He helped her with her packages while she unlocked the front door. "Your call seemed important." *As did whatever skulduggery you were trying to arrange.*

"It was." Looking both relaxed and relieved, Lauren led the way inside. "I've been trying to get hold of that person for days now."

Again, Mitch waited for Lauren to tell him more. Again, to his frustration, Lauren didn't elaborate.

A distracted look on her face, she picked up the long cardboard box that upon closer inspection bore the words The Golf Emporium, opened it and pulled out a putter. "What do you think?" She slipped off her jacket, revealing an ivory silk shell and a single strand of pearls, and gave the golf club a few practice swings. "Do you think my dad is going to like this? I had it made specially for him—for his birthday."

Mitch tore his eyes from the swiveling motion of her hips as she perfected her stance. He turned his eyes to the silky skin and well-toned muscle on her bare arms. "He should love it." *As well as whatever else it is you are doing for him behind the scenes.*

"I hope so." Lauren sighed. She turned to Mitch, an earnest look on her face as she stepped out of her shoes and walked around in her stocking feet. "He's a very difficult man to buy for." She cupped her hands around the club and looked up at Mitch. "I mean, he already has everything he wants. Or almost everything."

Wondering what it was about her that made him want to haul her into his arms and kiss her whenever he was near her, Mitch folded his arms in front of him and replied,

"Everything except you involved in the family shipping company."

Or are you already working to accomplish this in a very clever, clandestine way? Mitch wondered uneasily. Lauren seemed so sweet and guileless in unguarded moments like this, that he didn't want to think it was true. But on the other hand...he'd been a chump once with his ex-wife, ignoring the signs of potential trouble there. He didn't want to make the same mistake again with Lauren.

"My father knows I'm not cut out to run the company," Lauren said as she put the golf club back in its box. Abruptly, resentment burned like fire in her dark brown eyes. "That's why he wants me to marry someone like you. So if and when he does decide to retire someday he'll have someone in the family to watch out for my financial interests."

Or even run the company for you, Mitch thought, wondering once again if Payton Heyward's offer of a secret dowry was on the up-and-up. Did Lauren really not know about it? And if not, what business-related secret meant to please her father was she busy arranging with Lance? Had she learned Heyward Shipping was in trouble and was trying to simultaneously save it and bail Payton out without having to resort to marrying Mitch? That, Mitch thought, would at least make sense and square with everything he already thought he knew about Lauren.

Still regarding him thoughtfully, Lauren bit into her lower lip. "You know, you're really kind of wet," Lauren said, fingering his soggy sweatshirt. "And you look like you feel absolutely miserable."

Mitch did, but not for the reasons she was thinking.

"Why don't you take off your sweatshirt and I'll throw it in the dryer for a few minutes," Lauren suggested cheerfully.

Figuring the distraction would help keep her off her guard, Mitch tugged it obediently over his head.

Lauren gave his chest the once-over and grinned, as if at some private joke.

"What?" Mitch asked as he cradled his damp shirt in his hands.

Lauren's lips took on a mischievous curve. "I should have known the T-shirt underneath your sweatshirt was going to be gray, too, given how much you seem to like that particular color."

"Give me a break." Mitch picked up her light mood. "Do you know how many gray shirts there are in South Carolina?" *As well as guys with the first name of Lance?*

"Lots." Lauren gave him a flirtatious glance then set her cell phone down on the table and slipped into the guest bath tucked beneath the stairs. She came back out and handed him a towel. "But there are lots of other colors, too." Lauren took his sweatshirt and carried it back to the kitchen. She opened a folding door, revealing a washer and dryer, stacked one on top of the other. "I bet you don't have any," she teased.

"I have black and white T-shirts." As Mitch ran the towel over his hair, it was all he could do not to cast a look over his shoulder at the cell phone still lying on the table. "Navy blue, too."

"But your favorite is gray." Lauren switched on the dryer and turned back to him.

"You got me there," Mitch admitted, admiring the way her golden-brown hair fetchingly framed her oval face before falling softly to her shoulders. "So what's happening?" Mitch leaned against the kitchen counter, surveying her indolently. He wondered if there was any way he could check out her cell phone and see if it was a model that listed previous calls made and received, too. "What was the personal emergency you talked about in your e-mail?" *Was that in any way connected to Lance?*

"I had some bad news." Lauren fiddled with an earring and tucked her hair behind her ear. "I got the estimates from the electric and plumbing contractors today. It's going to cost an arm and a leg to get 10 Gathering Street in livable shape again. There's no way I can do it without my father's funds."

Mitch shrugged. "You pretty much knew that going in, didn't you?" Which was what made even messing with the renovation such a bad business move, in his estimation. She would never get back out what she put into it.

Lauren made a face as she led the way back into the foyer and up the stairs to the second floor. "Let's just say I had hoped otherwise. Anyway," she said as she went straight to her closet and pulled out several large suitcases and an oversize canvas laundry bag. "I think I've come up with a way to get the funds."

Mitch bypassed her antique four-poster bed, with the mountain of pillows and lavender silk Jacquard coverlet. "And that's what—marry me?"

The stubborn look returned to Lauren's face as she opened a suitcase and began methodically transferring the contents of her dresser drawers into it. "Get real. No, I'm not going to let my father manipulate me into marriage. I'm going to rent my place out and move into 10 Gathering Street tonight. That way, my mortgage here will be taken care of and I can put any money I earn into renovations."

Not sure what he could do at this point except keep her company, Mitch sat down on the edge of her bed. "But it's a mess over there." Regardless of what she might or might not be trying to do to him and his company, Mitch hated to think of Lauren living in a mansion with drafty rooms, a leaky roof and decades of ground-in dirt. Adding a construction mess would make it even worse. "If you do it a room at a time, it'll take years," he continued, thinking of the twenty-four-room mansion.

"I've got time." Lauren shut one drawer and opened another.

"And you're going to have to find somebody to rent

this place.'' Which was a shame, Mitch thought, tearing his eyes from the flimsy transparent-lace undergarments in her hands, because this warm and cozy residence—or someplace like it—was where she should be.

Finished, Lauren went over to the closet and brought out a filled shoe rack. ''I already have.'' She began stuffing her shoes into the cloth laundry bag.

That was fast, Mitch thought. And though he didn't agree with what Lauren was doing, he did admire the way she was taking charge of her destiny. He went over to help her with a second shoe rack. ''Who?''

''Your mother. And, by the way, she's moving in tonight, which is why we have to hurry and get my clothes out of here.''

Mitch abruptly stopped what he was doing. He straightened and looked over at her. ''You're kidding.''

''Nope.'' Lauren began taking clothes on hangers out of the closet, too, and laying them on the chaise. ''We went out looking at property again this morning and she just didn't like anything she saw, so Grace said to heck with it, she was just going to rent a place until she could find what she wanted. I told her I thought it was a good idea. And I thought her idea to rent my place was even better.''

Mitch did his best to ignore the tantalizing scent of Lauren's perfume. ''My mother suggested that?''

''No,'' Lauren announced proudly. ''I did. But Grace readily agreed. Her only stipulation was that she be able to move in tonight because she just can't spend one more night under the same roof as your father, and I said okay.''

Mitch stared at Lauren, not sure what to say to that. ''The last I saw, they were getting along well enough, all things considered.'' At least until his father had gone out of town without any warning or explanation.

Lauren paused long enough to give Mitch a compassionate glance. ''Apparently sharing space again has been a little more difficult than either your mother or father thought it was going to be," she stated gently. "And since Tom won't hear of Grace moving to a hotel, and Grace doesn't want Tom moving to one again, never mind making up excuses to be out of town and out of touch, this is the best solution. Besides, your mother thinks she'll be happier in her own place again. Until that happens, this is a good solution."

Mitch had the feeling the situation was even more complicated than his mother was admitting, either to Lauren or to him. For one thing, his father could have come up with a legitimate business trip, if he just wanted time to himself. Instead, Tom had opted to go off without a word of explanation to anyone in the family. If his normally businesslike father was reacting this emotionally to whatever it was, it meant there was big trouble brewing below the surface. The kind his mother seemed to bracing for, too.

Unfortunately, because his parents refused to confide in him, Mitch was as powerless to help either of his parents now as he had been when he was in his teens and they had split up. Reluctantly, he turned his attention to Lauren and the problems she was setting herself up for. "What about when my mother moves out?" he asked.

Lauren shrugged. "Then I'll lease it out again, to someone else."

Reminded of the seemingly impetuous way his mother had moved out on the family years ago, Mitch said quietly, "I don't approve of any of this. I want you to change your mind and tell my mom the 'lease' is off."

Lauren's eyes flashed. "It's not up to you to approve or disapprove of anything I do, Mitch, any more than it is my father's," she told him heatedly. "I am my own woman."

Mitch wasn't disagreeing with that—Lauren was her own woman and then some. That didn't mean he intended to let her ride roughshod over him and his feelings the way his ex-wife had. Mitch gave her a stern look. "I mean it,

Lauren,'' he warned, closing the distance between them autocratically. ''I won't have you meddling in my family's affairs.''

Lauren arched an eyebrow at him. ''And how are you going to stop me?''

''Like this,'' Mitch said, deciding it was past time they had turned their attention where it should be—to the two of them! Grabbing her by the waist, he tugged her toward him so swiftly she barely had time to gasp her indignation before he fit their bodies together like two interlocking pieces of a puzzle, tunneled a hand through her hair, tilted her head back and lifted her lips to his.

Their mouths met in an explosion of heat and passion, their tongues mating in an erotic dance that was sexier and more enticingly erotic than anything he had ever experienced. He kissed her again, a kiss brimming with an emotion and hunger he hadn't known he possessed. Lauren moaned, a soft helpless little sound in the back of her throat that sent his senses swimming. Loving the way she felt against him, all soft and warm and womanly, Mitch pressed her hips against his, deepening the kiss even more, wanting her to feel, and to need, exactly the way he was. Her mouth was pliant beneath his, warm and sexy, her body soft, supple, surrendering. And then all restraint faded. She whispered his name. Their kisses turned even hotter, more explicit. Groaning, he slid his hands beneath the hem of her blouse, to the silky skin beneath. She surged against him, and his hands moved higher still, over the slenderness of her ribs, to her lace-covered breasts. Still kissing her rapaciously, he caressed her through the fabric, feeling her nipples tighten beneath his palms. Lauren made another soft, mewling sound of pleasure. And still it wasn't enough. Would never be enough until she understood just how much he wanted her, how right this felt.…

This hadn't been part of the deal they'd made. Lauren knew that. And yet, as Mitch rained kisses across her throat, behind her ear, and captured her lips once again, she couldn't seem to stop. Any more than she could not respond to the voluptuousness of his kiss or the feel of his hot, hard body next to hers. She knew they'd come together for all the wrong reasons. This was an arranged courtship, for heaven's sake! An extension of a business deal! And yet she wanted him. Oh, how she wanted him.

Not just like this…

Not just kissing, with his hands on her body and his arousal pressed up hard against her. But naked. In her bed. Stretched out overtop her. Taking her. Making her his, for now, for forever. And it was that thought, more than anything, of the two of them joined together hotly, passionately, irrevocably, that swiftly had Lauren gasping and coming up for air.

She stared at Mitch, still breathing hard—still wanting him so much! He stared back.

And that was when the doorbell rang.

Mitch tensed, sighed, swore.

Lauren used his distraction to put her hands on his chest and ease away. "Saved by the bell," she said lightly as his incredibly talented hands slipped once more to the outside of her blouse. And then away.

"Temporarily, anyway," Mitch murmured, letting her know with a long glance that their kisses were not over. Not anywhere near over, interruption or not.

Her face flaming, her heart still pounding, Lauren smoothed her clothing as best she was able over her tingling body and dashed down the steps. Mitch was right behind her. Grateful for the interruption—for who knew what romantic foolhardiness it had prevented!—Lauren swung open the door and found Mitch's mother on the doorstep with her suitcases, ready to move in.

Chapter Nine

Grace took one look at Mitch, and said, "I can tell you don't approve of this arrangement."

Mitch shrugged. "If you want my opinion, I think you and Dad are both behaving impulsively."

Lauren moved between the two. "And I think you, Mitch Deveraux, are taking your mother's moving in here a little too seriously," she said, glaring at him on his mother's—and her own—behalf.

"After all, it's only a temporary arrangement," Grace said.

Temporary arrangements could do a lot of damage, Mitch thought as he picked up his mother's suitcases and carried them just inside the door. Take his week of dating Lauren, for instance. He'd thought that would be a snap, but here it was, only Wednesday, the third night into their bargain, and already he was in way over his head. Fighting feelings of desire and need that surpassed anything he had ever felt before. Despite the fact he wasn't sure yet that he should even trust her, at least when it came to their family shipping businesses.

"What about your relationship with Dad?" Mitch demanded of his mother as he set the suitcases out of their way.

Grace dropped her handbag onto the secretary next to Lauren's front door. "What about it?"

"I thought the two of you were trying to be friends again," Mitch reminded her. What had happened to that?

Grace stiffened with tension as she pivoted back to Mitch. "We were—are."

"Then…?" Mitch asked, wishing more than anything his mother would let him help her find her way back to his father so their family could be healed—and whole—again in a way it hadn't been since Grace and Tom's divorce.

A flicker of hurt crossed Grace's face. "It's not as easy as it seems." She folded her arms defiantly. "There are things you don't understand."

Mitch released a long-held breath and continued to fight for patience. "Then tell me so I can," he demanded brusquely, knowing no problem ever got solved unless the person or persons struggling with it wanted to solve it.

Grace was silent. Finally, she touched a hand to her elegantly done blond hair in a classic evasive gesture and said, "I think you need to worry about your own love life and forget about mine."

At this point, thanks to Lauren's meddling, his was even worse. Mitch glared at Lauren. "You're going to help her do this even though I think it's a mistake?" he asked, making no effort to hide his resentment.

Lauren nodded, refusing to back down.

"Fine." Mitch threw up his hands in frustration, turned his back on both women and stalked out the door. Just because *they* were making a gargantuan mistake that was damn near guaranteed to further his parents' continued estrangement when they finally had a real chance to get back together again, did not mean *he* had to be part of it.

Lauren followed him as far as the edge of the porch and lounged against a pillar. She waited until he was halfway down the sidewalk before drawling, "Forgetting something?"

Mitch sighed, barely able to contain his restlessness as he swung back around to face her. "What?" he barked out.

Lauren gave him a smart smile. "Our date."

AN HOUR AND A HALF LATER, Lauren had had enough. "How long are you going to continue to sulk?" she asked Mitch as they carried her belongings into 10 Gathering Street. It had stopped raining and the air was clean and fresh.

Mitch shifted the box of her belongings in his arms as she led the way up the once-elegant front staircase. "I'm not sulking."

"Okay, then.." Lauren carried her portable stereo and case of compact discs into the bedroom and bath suite she had selected as her temporary quarters, and put them on the floor next to the portable TV she'd brought. "How long are you going to show your disapproval?"

Mitch set the box of toiletries and towels down next to her suitcases. He straightened and looked her over from head to toe, taking in the snug-fitting jeans and lemon-yellow V-necked sweater she had changed into, before shifting his gaze to her face once again. "I can't help feeling how I feel."

Lauren opened one of the folding chairs she had carted inside for her, and another for him. "Maybe we better talk about this," she said sitting down and gesturing for him to do the same.

Mitch turned his around and sat down, folding his arms across the back. "I don't think you understand how much my brothers and sister and I want my parents to get back together so our family can be whole again."

"You're wrong about that," Lauren corrected softly. All she had to do was look at the sadness in Mitch's eyes, or hear the anguish in his voice when he talked about his parents' divorce and the animosity that had followed. "I lost my mom when I was a kid, remember? There's no way I'm getting her back. And yet there's a part of me, even now, that still yearns to have both a mother and a father again." It had been nearly twelve years since her mother had died, and yet holidays were still rough for her and her father, Lauren recollected sadly. Maybe because they served as a reminder of all they had lost and would never have again.

Mitch sighed and shoved a hand through the short, straight layers of his dark brown hair. "Then you should know how important it is to keep my mom and dad under the same roof so they can work out their problems, face-to-face, and at the very least try and become good friends again instead of just not-quite-so-bad enemies," he chided.

Lauren took exception to his stern tone. Her slender shoulders stiffening as restlessness overcame her once again, she stood. "And you should know that right now anyway, the experience has turned out to be too intense for your mother," she said, leading the way back down to the car.

Mitch paused, searched her face as Lauren opened the trunk once again to remove the last of her belongings. "My mom said that to you?" Mitch ascertained.

Lauren nodded, filling Mitch's arms with clothing. "Apparently, your father called her last night, and she and your father—well, it was a difficult conversation. When she arrived to look at houses this morning, she was still pretty upset over whatever it was they'd said to each other."

"Did she tell you anything else?" Mitch asked.

Lauren shrugged, picked up two shopping bags full of shoes and closed her trunk. "Just that there were some things your mom didn't think she and your father would ever be able to talk about. And she thought it might be best to try to limit the time they spent together for a while, because living together had turned out to be too difficult for them after all.''

Mitch blew out an aggravated breath, and the two of them headed up the stairs side by side once again. ''I'm sorry we put you in the middle of all this.''

''Look, it's just the way things are,'' Lauren said as they set down the last of her things. ''We can deal with it, and they can, too. Now, about dinner.'' Lauren straightened. ''I forgot to bring any dishes with me. And I don't have any groceries in here yet, either. So is takeout okay?''

''Sure,'' Mitch said, looking relaxed and agreeable once again. He paused to brush a tendril of hair from her face. ''But why don't we eat at my place.''

Lauren hesitated and stepped back a pace, her skin already tingling from the brief, casual touch. Seeing where Mitch lived and slept would only deepen the growing intimacy between them. And that was a proposition, given the arranged nature of their relationship, that seemed more dangerous every day. On the other hand, she was curious. Not to mention hungry and tired and in need of a place to put her feet up. Plus, they still had several hours to kill before this third date would be over. ''Okay,'' Lauren conceded, already looking around for her cell phone and house key. ''But I want to be back here by midnight.''

Mitch frowned. ''Where are you going to sleep?'' he asked, his deep blue eyes radiating concern. ''You don't have a bed or any furniture here.''

''Good point.'' She'd been so anxious to lease her home so she could afford to start making repairs on the mansion, she'd forgotten all about that. ''I'll have to go buy a sleeping bag, I guess.'' Either that or sleep in the guest room at her father's city apartment and endure all his questions about how things were going with her and Mitch.

''You could stay at my place,'' Mitch said quietly.

Lauren lifted her head. At her surprised look, Mitch continued affably, "I'm serious. I've got a sofa bed in my study. You could sleep there or...in my bed."

Lauren thought about the sexy kiss they had shared earlier, when they were arguing. If his mother hadn't arrived and interrupted just in the nick of time, who knew where that would have led? To her bed? "Wouldn't you like that," Lauren murmured.

"Hey..." Mitch lifted his hands in a lazy gesture of self-defense, mischief sparkling in his eyes. "I meant alone, but if you'd prefer it otherwise, I could deal with that," he teased with a sexy smile.

"I'll just bet you could," Lauren retorted dryly. She gave him a quelling look, determined to put *that* fantasy to rest. "But I'm sleeping alone tonight no matter what house I'm in." She couldn't let herself forget how and why they had happened to end up spending every night together, even if she was enjoying Mitch's company. Besides, she had the oddest feeling he didn't quite trust her, though she didn't have the slightest clue why not. She knew their fathers had been fierce competitors over the years, often struggling to land the same big accounts. But that had never affected her or Mitch.

Mitch regarded her with quiet acceptance, whatever he was thinking now a mystery to her. "So how about it?" he asked seriously, his offer still good.

What he was saying made sense, Lauren admitted to herself reluctantly. It was certainly easier than checking in or out of a hotel. "Okay, but just for tonight," she cautioned. Tomorrow, she would get a refrigerator and maybe rent some furniture—a sofa, a bed, coffee table and chairs and have them all delivered to 10 Gathering Place so she could start living there and transforming it into the dream home she knew it could be.

Mitch smiled, his mood suddenly lighter, too. "Pack a bag then and we'll be on our way."

"I WAS RIGHT," Lauren crowed victoriously as the two of them walked into his fifth-floor condominium in the large square building overlooking an upscale Mount Pleasant shopping arboretum. She had won the impulsive bet they'd made on the drive over. "You do have a very monochromatic color scheme." She looked around, admiring the elegance of his surroundings, even as she lamented the lack of other colors in his life. "Slate-gray carpet, pale gray walls, silvery-gray leather sofas and chairs. Even your kitchen counters are granite, and the floor tile is gray, too." She knew gray was his favorite color—that was obvious, even his car was gray—but this was taking it to an extreme.

Mitch merely grinned at her and taunted, "You haven't looked at the bedroom or my study yet."

Lauren's pulse kicked up another notch. "Are you saying those are different colors?"

Mitch merely shrugged and smiled at her in a way that raised her awareness of him—and the stakes—even higher. "You want to know, you're going to have to find out for yourself."

Lauren knew it was dangerous, going into the bedroom of a single man on the prowl, but she couldn't resist. She had to know. So she went down the hall, past a bathroom decorated in tones of silver and white, to the large master bedroom. The furniture in there was sleek and modern, in a shiny lacquer black, but the carpet, bedspread, vertical blinds were all—*you guessed it*—gray. Aware the room carried the faint lingering fragrance of his after-shave lotion, she moved into the master bath. It had a double shower with glass doors and a white whirlpool tub big enough for two. The ceramic-tile floor was white as well, but the wallpaper was an elegant gray foil.

She also noted, quite without wanting to, that there were no female clothes hanging in the closet, no cosmetics or perfume or hair spray on his countertops. She didn't know why that would matter to her, since she wasn't the jealous type and they didn't have any real hold on each other, either, but somehow it did.

Looking very pleased she had opted to go to his place for a change, Mitch took Lauren's hand and led her back through the bedroom to the study on the opposite side of the hallway. "No gray here," he said with a grin of purely male satisfaction. And he was right. The pine floor was so dark it was almost black, the walls were covered with floor-to-ceiling bookshelves and cabinets in the same hue. The desk that sat in the middle was enormous. And also quite valuable.

Forgetting for a moment about their bet—that said the loser footed the bill on their already purchased take-out dinner—she ran her hand across the silky smooth grain. "This is an antique," she said, impressed.

Mitch sat down on the edge of the massive mahogany desk. "It belonged to my great-grandfather," he said.

And it was obvious to Lauren it had been lovingly cared for ever since.

"My dad gave it to me when I graduated from college. I think he wanted me to put it in my office down at Deveraux Shipping, but I loved it so much I wanted it in my home, so—" Mitch patted the surface fondly "—here it is."

"It's lovely." Lauren edged closer yet, so her thigh brushed his knee.

"And the one piece of furniture I have that I'm truly attached to," Mitch admitted. Lacing an arm around her waist, he pulled her between his spread legs and onto his lap.

"And you know why?" Lauren retorted, telling herself it wouldn't hurt anything to sit there, her bottom nestled against the apex of his braced legs, just for a second. "Because the piece has history."

"As well as a lot of sentimental value," Mitch said

as he laced both arms around her waist and settled her closer yet.

Lauren grinned. Maybe she and Mitch had more in common than they knew. Who would've thought? "Now if we could just get you to live in the historic district, too…" she teased.

"Hey—" Mitch planted a palm against his chest in self-defense "—my condo's in a good location, near a lot of restaurants and stores, and it's appreciating nicely. I should be able to sell it in a few years and make a tidy sum, and in the meantime, there's no grass or routine maintenance to worry about. That's all done for me."

Lauren turned her head slightly to the side as she studied the handsome visage of his face. "You could have that done for you if you owned a house," she pointed out softly, loving the warmth and strength of him.

"I suppose." Mitch gently traced the curve of her cheekbone with his thumb. "But I'd have to arrange it."

"And you don't even want to bother with that," Lauren guessed, wishing he would kiss her again, even though she knew they shouldn't.

"Right." Mitch paused, his hand still lightly cupping her face, and looked deep into her eyes.

Without wanting to, Lauren noted his hesitation and wariness matched her own.

"Why do you look so unhappy for me?" he asked after a moment, obviously mistaking her ambivalent feelings about their situation for disapproval of his ultramodern, ultrasingle lifestyle.

"I just can't imagine not living in a place that meant a lot to me," Lauren fibbed, telling herself her falling spirits had nothing to do with the way she and Mitch had met, and the very wrong reasons they were together—even now. "And with the personal budget you must have for such things" she babbled on, working hard to hide her true feelings, "I don't understand why you don't live in a place that's both beautiful and of historic importance.'' Like it mattered where he lived, she thought, as long as he loved her and wanted her for her. Which, unfortunately, hadn't happened. And might not ever happen thanks to her father and his meddling, Lauren thought sadly.

"My condo's nice-looking," Mitch defended himself, a perplexed expression on his face.

"You know what I mean." Lauren slid off his lap and began to pace again. "Charleston is a city that's so rich in history," she said, feeling more restless and disgruntled with their predicament than ever. "You should be celebrating that, reveling in it."

Mitch continued to study her curiously as he stood, too. He picked up a paperweight from his desk and shifted it idly from hand to hand. "When did you get so interested in the history of the homes around here?"

Lauren smiled fondly, recalling. "It was one of my mother's passions. She used to put our home in Summerville up for tour every spring and fall. And she'd bring me into Charleston to enjoy the historic-home tours they have here, too."

"You must miss her," Mitch said as he put the paperweight back down, the gentle empathy in his eyes like a balm to her senses.

"I do." Lauren swallowed around the growing knot of emotion in her throat. "I don't think my dad's ever gotten over losing her. Which is, of course, part of the problem," Lauren continued candidly. "My father's loneliness is the reason he's so determined that I not live out the rest of my life alone. He wants me to have a mate I can count on. A partner. Protector. He just doesn't understand that something that intimate and personal can't simply be arranged like any other business deal."

"Maybe you should be finding your father a mate, then," Mitch said.

"I would if I believed deals like that worked," Lauren

returned just as lightly, holding Mitch's intent blue gaze with effort. "Unfortunately, I don't, so...there's no point in wasting our time on something that's bound, by its very nature, to fail anyway."

The way Mitch looked at her then gave her the feeling that he not only understood what she was feeling, but that he also understood her like no one had ever understood her before.

Sentiments like that, however, were as dangerous as they were seductive, Lauren reminded herself sternly. If she let herself have them too often she'd forget what a mutually beneficial business arrangement this was, at the core, and begin to think of it as an actual, bona fide romance.

Lauren couldn't let herself fall in love with someone who didn't love her. And since she was not, and never had been, the kind of woman who was made for sex as sport—never mind a relationship or a marriage run as the business Mitch wanted it to be—it was time she got their date back on the impersonal, unemotional track it was supposed to be on. Smiling at Mitch in a way meant to keep him safely at arm's length, at a way she sensed he hated, she said, "Anyway. Enough of that." Then turned and headed for the dining nook next to the kitchen.

His disappointment at the way she'd abruptly shut him out again evident, Mitch helped her take the cardboard containers out of the paper sacks. "Our dinner's probably cold," he said, frowning.

"There's no probably to it," Lauren agreed. The sides of the containers weren't even lukewarm. "But not to worry." She beamed a smile at him. "I'm an ace at heating kung pao chicken and moo shu pork in the microwave." Dining alone as much as she had the past two years, she'd had lots of practice.

"I TRIED CALLING YOU last night," Payton Heyward said the next morning over their weekly breakfast date, "and got Grace Deveraux instead. She said you had leased your home to her.''

Was it her imagination, Lauren wondered, or was her father looking a little hot and uncomfortable this morning? As he'd sat down, he'd been moving a little stiffly, too. But then, that could have been due to the mild arthritis that had been bothering him for the past few years. Trying her best not to show her concern—she knew he hated it when she fussed over him—she smiled and said, ''Yes. I did.''

''So where did you sleep last night?'' Payton continued, perplexed.

''At Mitch's,'' Lauren replied and watched the color drain from her father's face. ''It's not the way it sounds,'' she said hastily.

Unfortunately, her father wasn't buying it.

Payton clamped his lips together tightly. ''I want the two of you to marry, Lauren. Not shack up together.''

Lauren didn't want to just live with a man without benefit of marriage, either. She picked up her knife and began spreading strawberry preserves on her buttermilk biscuit. ''It was only a one-night thing, Dad.''

Payton looked at her as if that was even worse.

Too late, Lauren realized how that must have sounded and defended herself further, ''Nothing happened, Dad.'' That was, if you could discount the kisses Mitch had given her earlier, and she couldn't quite do that, either. Because those kisses had been wonderful. Warm, enticing, erotic.

Payton lifted a skeptical eyebrow, and Lauren blushed despite herself. Trying to make the evening sound as dull as possible, she continued truthfully, ''When we got to his place last night, we just talked and ate Chinese food and watched a movie, and then he slept on the sofa bed in his study and I slept in his bed.'' And it was odd how comforting and truly relaxing that had been. She'd felt truly at home in Mitch's place.

The only disconcerting moment had come when she'd been selecting a movie from his collection of videotapes and DVDs and she turned and saw him with her cell phone in his hand. He'd explained he was just looking over the features, comparing her brand of phone with his, but she'd felt a little funny about it just the same. Not that there was anything he could have learned about her from looking at her cell phone—except who had called her recently, or who she had called, and there was nothing secret about that. Nevertheless, it had felt funny to have Mitch encroaching on her territory without permission—maybe because it was the sort of thing her father would have done. Only her father probably would have been doing it deliberately to glean information on whom she had been in contact with.

Payton harrumphed. "I'd like to say the fact you had such a dull time when you spent the night with Mitch is reassuring to me, Lauren, but it's not."

The faintly disapproving expression on her dad's face reminded Lauren of other times, when Payton'd been trying to protect her from getting involved with the wrong man. And, as it turned out, much to her chagrin, rightly so. "I thought this was what you wanted, for the two of us to get close," Lauren persisted.

"It is." Payton rubbed the back of his wrist, as if it was bothering him. "But I also want you to have a wedding ring on your finger. Having the two of you act like platonic, rather than romantic, friends will not accomplish that."

Lauren admitted she wouldn't mind marrying Mitch if Mitch were wildly in love with her, but he wasn't. Hence, she couldn't even consider it, because no matter how physically and emotionally attracted she was to Mitch, she didn't want a relationship that was based on a mutually profitable business deal.

"But an arranged marriage is not what I want, Dad," she said quietly, hoping that when the week ended, and she and Mitch chose not to get married, that her father would accept their decision and let it go, and not dangle any more prizes in front of them.

"You've still got four more dates to go." Payton shrugged, a little stiffly, and sat back in his chair. Abruptly, he looked optimistic again. "Maybe you'll change your mind by the end of the week."

And maybe, Lauren thought, as charming and fun as Mitch could be when he wanted to be, she wouldn't. Because the last thing she wanted was to marry a man who—like her father—was so involved with his business dealings that he would actually marry a woman in order to cinch a deal.

Chapter Ten

Mitch spent the morning meeting with Internet consultants, and working on a proposal for an e-commerce site. At noon, another client not under written contract, bailed in favor of doing business with an Internet auction site. Mitch scrambled to fill the space on their container ship headed for Jacksonville, and eventually got some cargo on there, but it was at a lower rate than the initial client would have paid, and it narrowed their already slim profit margins for the month.

Frustrated, Mitch went down the hall to Jack Granger's office. "We can't keep doing this," Mitch told Jack.

"For what it's worth, I agree with you," Jack said as he hit the screen saver button on his computer and a picture of a snowy mountain peak popped up on the monitor. "The sooner Deveraux Shipping enters the e-commerce shipping market, the better." Jack closed the file on his desk, too, and rested his clasped hands on top of it. "The problem is, I'm not the one making the decision. Your father is, and he thinks we can't afford it."

"We could if we start small," Mitch said. And he'd put together a proposal demonstrating how to accomplish just that. Now all he had to do was get Tom to listen and agree to it. "Have you heard from my father yet?" Mitch asked. His own e-mail to Tom was still unanswered.

Jack shook his head, looking equally disturbed by Tom Deveraux's unusual disappearance. "I'm sure he'll check in soon, though," he said confidently.

Mitch hoped so. This was the third day in a row Tom had failed to show up for work at the Deveraux Shipping Company offices. "If you hear from him, please ask him to call me on my cell phone," Mitch told Jack. He wanted to set up a time to talk to Tom about his e-business proposal, and he wanted to tell him that Grace had moved out—two things that were best done in person, or at the very least, during a phone conversation.

"Will do," Jack promised easily, making a note on the pad in front of him.

Mitch checked his watch. It was nearly five-thirty. Traffic would be brutal this time of day. "I better get going if I want to make my date. I don't want to be late."

"Lauren Heyward again?"

Mitch nodded.

Jack shook his head wistfully. He looked at Mitch as if he had never seen such a romantic fool. "You must really like her to be going against your father's wishes this way."

That was the problem. Mitch did really like Lauren, business deal aside. As for whether she was somehow involved in any counteraction or deal stealing against their company, that Mitch couldn't say. He'd checked out the list of incoming calls on her cell phone last night, but the call from Lance had registered "private" on the caller ID history. Which meant he had no phone number to check out, and no last name. The "Lance" Lauren had been swearing to secrecy last night could have been anyone. Furthermore, Mitch ruminated, just because Lance was doing something to help Lauren and her father's business, it didn't necessarily mean he was also hurting Mitch or his firm. What Lance was doing could have had nothing to do with Mitch and the Deveraux Shipping Company whatsoever. Lauren could be completely innocent of any industrial espionage.

Jack regarded Mitch respectfully, his own reservations about the situation still evident. "But, on the other hand," Jack said, "if your relationship with her leads to a better working relationship between our two shipping companies, or even the merger you've been wanting, Deveraux and Heyward shipping companies would both benefit because they'd be better able to fend off the increasing competition from the Internet auction sites."

Mitch agreed. The only problem was that he'd begun to lose his enthusiasm for bringing about such a coup. It wasn't that they didn't need the merger. With competition stiffening daily, both companies needed to combine forces and take up a bigger share of the market, more than ever. Mitch's real regret centered around Lauren. He was pretty sure she would see the merger as proof positive that all he had ever really been interested in was the joining of the two companies. And while that had been true in the beginning, when her father had first pitched his proposal to them, it was no longer the case. Now Mitch was genuinely interested in Lauren. To the point he wished he had never allowed himself to be talked into the agreement with her father. Because now, even if everything else worked out, she was never going to believe he was interested in Lauren, for Lauren, and not for some business deal....

LAUREN MET MITCH at the door of 10 Gathering Street. Although they were supposed to go out to dinner shortly at Magnolia's restaurant downtown, she was still in rumpled khaki slacks, a much laundered denim work shirt and paint-splattered sneakers. She'd swept her golden-brown hair onto the back of her head and secured the tousled length of it in a tortoiseshell clip. Her cheeks were tinged with pink, her dark brown eyes shimmering with excitement. She looked so pretty and sexy, in fact, it was all

Mitch could do not to sweep her into his arms the moment he crossed the threshold and take her straight upstairs for the tenderest, most intimate lovemaking session of her life.

Oblivious to the lusty direction of his thoughts, Lauren grabbed his hand and tugged him along beside her as she hurried him through the downstairs hall. "Oh, Mitch!" she enthused breathlessly, looking every bit as glad to see him as he was to see her. "I can't wait to show you what I just found! You're never going to believe what I just discovered!"

Given how happy and excited she looked, Mitch could think of only one thing. "Buried treasure?" This was, after all, a very old house that had once been inhabited by some very wealthy Charlestonians.

"Even better." She tightened her grip on his palm, her hand feeling warm, soft and capable in his as she took him to the first-floor library, chattering excitedly all the while. "I was checking out some of the bookcases, you know, dusting them, and then suddenly, I felt something funny— a little piece of wood sticking out of one of them. I thought it was just a piece of scrap wood or something that had gotten stuck in there when they were constructing it, so I pulled on it a little and *voila!* The door started to open." Lauren flashed Mitch a dazzling smile and paused to demonstrate.

Right on cue, the bookcase swung open, revealing a twelve-foot-square room hidden behind the library. It had been decorated in a very feminine manner. There was a pale pink-colored Aubusson rug covering the floor, a burgundy-silk chaise and delicate rose-patterned wallpaper on the windowless walls. Books of love poems were scattered around the room. A big old-fashioned steamer trunk sat in one corner. Next to it was the outline of another door, and a lever next to it. It looked like a love nest or trysting place from another era.

"Where does that lead?" Mitch asked, inclining his head at the door.

"I don't know." Lauren bit her lip and looked perplexed. "I hadn't gotten that far— I just found this room a few minutes ago."

Intrigued, Mitch continued to look around. His gaze fell on an exquisite crystal vase filled with red, white and pink roses that were so fresh the petals were just beginning to open up. "Nice flowers," he murmured, taking in the subtle feminine fragrance.

"They aren't mine!" Lauren said. "And I didn't dust in here, either."

Mitch turned to Lauren in surprise. "You think the previous owners or Realtors who sold the place to your father put them in here?"

Lauren shrugged. "I think it's highly unlikely. I mean, they didn't bother to dust or clean up the rest of the house. Why would they clean up this little room? Besides, I'm not sure they knew about it. I called my father and asked him if they had any secret rooms here, and he said 'Not that he knew of.'"

Mitch mulled that over. It was possible this was just a fluke. It was also possible it was a device meant to distract him from company business. Mitch tested the chaise and found it very comfortable indeed. Folding his hands behind his head, Mitch looked up at Lauren and asked, "Did you tell your father what you'd found?"

"Not yet. I wanted to show you first."

Mitch tried not to attach any significance to her revelation. It wasn't easy. Since the romantic, hopeful part of him wanted to do just that.

"Mitch—" Lauren sat down next to Mitch on the chaise "—I think someone may have been using this room to, uh, well, rendezvous with someone else."

Mitch lifted his eyebrow in speculation. With Lauren

leaning over him like this, her thigh brushing his, that was certainly his inclination. "You mean an illicit affair?"

Lauren's smile widened merrily as she tried to figure it out. "Why else would you meet in a windowless room in the middle of a deserted mansion?"

Good point. Mitch decided he better get up if he didn't want to end up making love to Lauren here and now. He rose, electing to satisfy his curiosity instead. "Let's see where this other door leads."

"Okay." Lauren moved closer to him, inundating him with her signature fragrance. Mitch pulled the lever. The door swung open onto a narrow hall with no lighting. "I always wanted to be Nancy Drew," Lauren murmured.

Maybe it was because she was such a take-charge woman, but Mitch had no problem imagining Lauren hot on the trail of some mysterious happening. "And I had a thing for the Hardy boys. Do you have a flashlight?"

Lauren shook her head.

"I've got one in the glove compartment of my car. Wait here. I'll go get it." When he came back, Lauren was pacing the small room.

"Let's go," Lauren said impatiently. She latched on to his sleeve. "You lead the way."

"So much for playing a girl detective," Mitch said dryly as they entered the narrow brick passageway with the wooden floor. He would have expected it to smell dank and stale, but instead it smelled like fresh air and spring flowers.

"There are some jobs that are just meant for men. This is one of them. And as I recall—" Lauren paused to shoot him a teasing glance "—the Hardy boys were quite fearless."

"Sure, for characters in a book," Mitch said, liking the sensation of having her pressed so close to his side. "I doubt they would have gotten into some of those scrapes in real life. If they'd had a lick of sense they would have just called the cops first and solved the mystery later.''

''If they had,'' Lauren returned, studying the long and winding passageway in front of them, ''the books wouldn't have been nearly as exciting.''

''You read them?'' Mitch wrapped an arm around Lauren's shoulders as they rounded yet another corner.

''The complete sets of both,'' Lauren confirmed, pressing herself companionably against his side. ''I wanted a boyfriend just like Frank.''

Aware Lauren was trembling slightly, whether from the chill of the passageway or the uncertainty, he didn't know, Mitch slanted Lauren an amused glance. ''Why Frank and not Joe?'' he probed.

Lauren had to think about that for a second. ''Frank was older, more mature, less impetuous,'' she said finally, wrapping her arm around his waist. ''He was also tall and handsome, and he had dark hair.''

Simultaneously, Mitch realized Lauren could have been describing him. As he looked at her in a way that made Lauren acutely aware of what she had just said, she turned her glance back to the passageway ahead and steadfastly avoided Mitch's eyes. ''Did you read Nancy Drew?'' she asked cheerfully.

''No, but Amy did, so I heard all about her adventures. I've got to say, she sounded like quite a babe.''

Lauren smiled sweetly, but still didn't look at him. ''I identified with her a lot,'' she admitted candidly.

''Maybe because *you're* a babe,'' Mitch said. He grinned when he saw her look away. No doubt about it. She was as aware of him as he was of her.

''How much farther, do you think?'' Lauren asked in an oddly muffled voice.

''Not much farther,'' Mitch said confidently, figuring with the distance and direction they had gone, they had to be near the perimeter of the mansion. Six steps later, he reached another dead end. And another hidden door, with a hidden lever. Mitch pushed the door open. And the two of them found themselves standing in the neglected flower gardens just outside the ivy-covered back wall of the mansion.

"Wow," Lauren said, feeling more worked up about a property than she had in a long time. "In three and a half days and four more dates, I'm going to own a home with a hidden room and a secret passageway." *This was so great.*

"I wouldn't get too excited about that just yet," Mitch warned with a frown as she shut off his flashlight.

Lauren tensed in irritation. "Why not?" Lauren turned to him and noticed how handsome he looked in his charcoal-gray polo shirt and slacks. He had obviously shaved before coming over, too. The spicy, sandalwood fragrance of his after-shave clung to his skin.

Oblivious to the libidinous nature of her thoughts, Mitch tapped the flashlight against his side. "Because someone has obviously been using that room, and sneaking in and out of here at night."

"Who?" Lauren's glance trailed idly down his braced thigh before returning to his face.

"Beats me." Mitch shrugged his broad shoulders. "Maybe there's a clue in the room. In the meantime—" he stepped back inside the corridor and tapped the walls "—maybe you should consider having this passageway walled off."

After all the romance that had happened there? Lauren thought. He had to be kidding. Only he wasn't.

She looked at him firmly. "Not a chance! That would be like destroying history."

"Better safe than sorry," Mitch said as he closed the outside door and led the way back. "And until you know who is using that room and why—"

Okay, so maybe he had a point, Lauren conceded reluctantly. Maybe she did need to be a tiny bit sensible about this. Already thinking, Lauren dashed on ahead of Mitch. "Maybe there's a clue in the steamer trunk or some of those books." She rushed back into the room and opened the lid of the trunk. Inside it were several beautiful ball gowns from many years ago. Satin dancing shoes. Pressed flowers. And a packet of ribbon-wrapped letters, yellowed with age. Lauren paused. "I feel funny about reading this."

Mitch shot her an empathetic look that let her know he wasn't as unromantic as she'd first thought, then said quietly, "How else are you going to know who they belonged to or who should have them now?"

"You're right," Lauren agreed with relief. She carried the letters over to the chaise and sat down in the middle of it. "These letters obviously should be with someone. I've got to find out whom."

Gently, Lauren worked open the first envelope, and because she knew Mitch was every bit as curious as she, began to read the first aloud to him:

Dearest Eleanor,

I used to look forward to the days I spent at the helm of my ship, sailing from port to port. No more. Now all I want is to be back in Charleston with you. But even that is not as free of difficulty as I would wish for us. I had hoped by now that Dolly would have accepted that I do not love her, and therefore, cannot marry her. But she insists on holding me to my promise. And swears she will put a hex on us for all eternity if I continue with my plans to one day tell everyone of my love for you. I do not believe such nonsense. And you should not either, my love. For we will be together one day soon. That, I promise you. In the meantime, I will leave Boston in another few days. As soon as we get the ship loaded again and be home again before you know it.

All my love,
Douglas

Lauren looked up, shocked. "This letter is about the curse put on your family," Lauren said.

Mitch groaned as he sank down on the chaise beside her. "Not you, too. I am so tired of hearing about that."

Lauren swiveled toward Mitch. They were so close her bent knee brushed his thigh. She studied the skeptical expression on his face. "I take it that means you don't believe in the legend?" she guessed.

Mitch's dark eyebrows lowered like thunderclouds over his eyes. "The curse is a self-fulfilling prophecy. If you believe there is no way you can live happily ever after with the love of your life, then you won't be able to do it."

Deciding to play devil's advocate for the heck of it, Lauren cited a little history. "Well, so far, your aunt Winnifred was widowed shortly after she married her husband. Your parents divorced. So did you."

"True—" Mitch traced the thinning denim over her knee with his thumb "—but Chase is happily married now."

Lauren tried but couldn't quite keep herself from leaning into Mitch's mesmerizingly soft, seductive touch. In fact, she was so aroused, it was all she could do to ask as he continued to stroke her knee with the same slow, thoughtful strokes, "You think his relationship with Bridgett is going to last?"

"Oh, yeah." Mitch smiled his approval of his older brother's match. "Absolutely."

"I'm glad to hear it." Lauren smiled enthusiastically. "That means the curse is broken."

"Even if it wasn't," Mitch proclaimed determinedly, his

hand stilling abruptly on her knee, "I am going to be the exception to the rule. The one person in the family who *does* live happily ever after."

"Brave talk." Lauren returned his teasing look with a smile. "But don't you think it odd that I would discover this here, now, when I am dating you?" *What were the odds of that?*

Mitch shrugged, wrapped his arms around her waist and lifted her over onto his lap. "The only thing I consider odd is that I've been with you, like this, in such an intimate setting and I haven't kissed you once today," he whispered as he lifted her face to his and claimed her with a hot, passionate kiss that shook her to her very soul. It felt so good to be held against him that way, so good to be wanted, Lauren thought. Needing to be closer yet, she wreathed her arms around him and opened her mouth to the insistent pressure of his. And that was when they heard it. The sound of something—or someone—moving in the passageway behind the secret door.

Simultaneously realizing they were no longer alone, Mitch and Lauren broke apart. "Did you hear something?" Lauren demanded breathlessly as she jumped off Mitch's lap.

"Yes." Mitch also vaulted to his feet. "And it sounded like it was coming from over there." Mitch strode to the secret door. Lauren was right beside him as he pressed the lever and watched it open. Just outside the portal, on the floor of the passageway, was a bouquet of fresh spring flowers wrapped in satin ribbon.

MITCH TURNED BACK to her, a quizzical expression on his face. "Don't look at me," Lauren said, holding up her hands in a gesture of surrender. "I have no idea who put those there."

"Well, there's one way to find out." Mitch grabbed the flashlight and rushed into the passageway, a determined look on his face. Lauren followed all the way to the end. But there was no one there. Nor was there anyone in the garden. There was, however, a long chiffon scarf, scented with rose perfume, caught on one of the bushes.

"Well, this definitely wasn't here before," Lauren said grimly.

Mitch dashed around the house, to the street, while Lauren took a closer look at the garden. She had just searched every nook and cranny of the overgrown garden when Mitch returned. "Did you see anyone?" she asked.

He shook his head. "Although there are several dozen places, whoever left this could have disappeared. Other gardens, houses, back gates."

"I wonder whom the flowers are for," Lauren said as she picked up the bouquet of daisies, baby's breath, lilies, azaleas, lilacs and sweetpeas she had dropped.

"Probably whoever has been trysting in this room," Mitch said.

"I figured that, silly. I meant who are the lovers?" Lauren persisted.

Mitch's gaze turned speculative. "I can only think of one person in Charleston who might know," he said.

"And that would be…?"

"My aunt Winnifred. She's not just the social doyenne of Charleston, she's an expert in both the public and private history of the area, too."

Chapter Eleven

"I'd always heard there was a secret rendezvous place for Captain Douglas Nyquist and Eleanor Deveraux," the fifty-year-old Winnifred Deveraux told Mitch and Lauren soon after she and her butler, Harry Bowles, had arrived to see the hidden room. "But I don't think anyone knew where it was until now," Winnifred said, her patrician features tightening into a problematic frown as she and Harry sat down on opposite ends of the chaise, while Mitch and Lauren seated themselves side by side on the steamer trunk.

"It makes sense, though," Winnifred continued thoughtfully, smoothing the skirt of her elegant pale blue dress. She settled her trim, petite frame more comfortably on the chaise. "This mansion was owned by Douglas Nyquist's cousin, at the time Douglas and Eleanor fell in love. And she was reportedly very sympathetic to the young lovers and their predicament."

Mitch would have been, too. To be in love with someone and not be able to see and be with that person would be a lousy way to have to live. If he were in that situation—in love with someone his family did not sanction—he wouldn't care what anyone said. He would move heaven and earth to be with her.

"What do you know about what happened back then?"

Lauren asked, appearing as if her sympathies were squarely with the young lovers.

Seemingly in no hurry to get to the social occasion she had scheduled for that evening, Winnifred smiled and lifted a delicate hand. "It was arranged from the time he was a child that Captain Nyquist would marry Dolly Lancaster. The match made sense. The Lancasters were merchants and the Nyquists were seamen. Both families stood to profit. As the children were growing up, both families were very prosperous, but as Douglas and Dolly reached marrying age, the Nyquists invested a great deal of money on a sleek new ship design that didn't quite pan out, and the Nyquists fell on hard times financially."

Just like the Heywards now? Mitch wondered silently. "How did Dolly feel about marrying someone who was no longer as wealthy as she was?" Mitch asked curiously, wondering if there were even more parallels in these two situations than they knew.

Winnifred lifted her hands in a helpless gesture. "Dolly wasn't happy that Captain Nyquist's wealth was diminished, but she felt that over time, with help from her family, Douglas Nyquist would be able to recoup his family fortune."

"That was probably true, wasn't it?" Lauren interjected, looking as caught up in the story as Mitch. "I mean, all businesses have their ups and downs. But if you know how to make a business a success, you can overcome your mistakes and do it again. You just need the time and opportunity."

"And funds," Mitch added, wondering, even as he spoke, how Lauren would react to that. But instead of looking guilty or self-conscious over the subtle parallel he was trying to make, Lauren merely nodded earnestly, agreeing.

"Yes," Lauren said. "It always helps to have some capital to start with. I wouldn't have been able to build up my own real estate business if my father hadn't believed in me enough to underwrite my office costs the first couple of years.''

Was that why Lauren was working so hard behind the scenes to bail her father out now? Mitch wondered. Assuming, of course, her father was in some sort of financial trouble because he had fallen into one of the major pitfalls of business and expanded much too fast.

''Anyway, as I was saying,'' Winnifred continued informatively as she touched a hand to her beautifully coiffed hair, ''about the time Douglas and Dolly reached marrying age, Douglas met Eleanor, and fell head over heels in love with her. But Douglas knew he was promised to Dolly and that his father—Joseph Nyquist—was counting on him to marry Dolly and bail the rest of them out financially, so Douglas followed through with a ring and a proposal and tried very hard to live up to his obligations.''

''But in the end he couldn't,'' Mitch guessed, remembering all too clearly how miserable it had been to be married to a woman who didn't love him any more than he loved her, in the end.

''Right,'' Winnifred said. ''And although Dolly didn't actually love Captain Nyquist, Dolly was very upset when he broke it off with her. At first Dolly tried to get Douglas back with a charm offensive. When that didn't work, she tried pressure from their families and friends.''

''But that failed, too, didn't it?'' Lauren guessed.

Winnifred nodded. ''Yes. And that was when Dolly began to get obsessed with the hurt and humiliation she had suffered at Douglas's hands. Meanwhile, Eleanor—who wouldn't give Douglas the time of day until he had ended things with Dolly—realized that she loved Douglas as much as Douglas loved her, and Eleanor wanted to be with him more than anything. But Eleanor's heart went out to Dolly because she knew how angry Dolly was. So Eleanor told Captain Nyquist that until Dolly found another beau, or her family could make another match for her, Eleanor wouldn't see Douglas publicly or let him court her. But as months went by, and Dolly showed no signs of even thinking about marrying anyone else, Eleanor and Douglas became very impatient. And they started seeing each other on the sly, in their secret place. Dolly heard rumors of their trysting and she swore the two of them would never find any happiness. And to make sure of that, she went to a gypsy and put a curse on Eleanor and Douglas's love for each other.''

"They didn't believe the hex had any power, did they?" Mitch interrupted.

"No, they didn't, until Captain Nyquist's ship went down just off the coast of Charleston in a tropical storm.''

"Eleanor must have been devastated," Lauren said, shifting slightly closer to Mitch.

Winnifred nodded as she settled more comfortably on the chaise. "And worse, Eleanor blamed herself for Captain Nyquist's death. She felt that if she had put her own desires aside and made him marry Dolly, he would still be alive. She was inconsolable. And she caught pneumonia that very winter, and later died of what some say was a broken heart.''

Mitch turned to Lauren, wanting to finish this part of the story himself. "Since then, as legend goes, every Deveraux has been doomed—at least where love is concerned.''

"Although Mitch doesn't believe that," Winnifred added for Lauren's sake.

Mitch shrugged. "There's no disputing that the family doesn't have the best track record when it comes to romance, but I think we Deveraux have made our own mistakes, independent of any curse.''

Lauren didn't act as if she disagreed with Mitch's thinking. "What happened to the Nyquist family?"

"The Nyquists sold their mansion at 10 Gathering Street and moved to Virginia for a fresh start," Harry added.

Winnifred smiled at her devoted butler with long-standing affection. "Harry's quite the history buff."

"As well as timekeeper," Harry said, consulting his pocket watch. He looked at his employer fondly. "If you don't want to be late for your soiree, we'd best be on our way."

"Well, we can't have that, can we?" Winnifred quipped when Harry helped her to her feet.

"Thanks for stopping by," Lauren murmured. She and Mitch walked Winnifred and Harry to the front door.

"My pleasure!" Winnifred beamed.

"What should I do with the letters?" Lauren asked, concerned.

"Why not keep everything as is for right now?" Winnifred suggested. "Until I talk to my brother, Tom, and see what he wants to do."

"That sounds fine," Lauren said.

As soon as the door closed, Mitch turned back to Lauren. Her dark brown eyes had a distant, bemused expression. "Why so pensive?"

Lauren shrugged and she led the way up to the second floor, down the hall to the east wing. "I was just thinking about Eleanor and Captain Nyquist," she said as she beckoned Mitch into a suite of rooms that she had cordoned off as her private living quarters during the upcoming renovations.

As they walked in, Mitch checked out the changes she had made. The card table and folding chairs she'd brought in the night before were resting against a wall. She'd had a big four-poster bed delivered that was so high off the floor a stepstool was required to get into it; a nightstand, complete with clock, light and telephone, beside it. A brocade sofa still encased in plastic sat before the window, overlooking Gathering Street. There were shopping bags of brand-new stuff bearing a popular department store logo stacked willy-nilly, and several rugs of different sizes that needed to be unrolled and placed. Mitch noted she had her work cut out for her just trying to bring some order to the space.

Frowning sympathetically, Lauren continued, "Douglas and Eleanor never really got to be together. Publicly, anyway. Douglas's father must have felt so bad after his son died. I mean, the curse aside, Joseph Nyquist was responsible for keeping his son from the love of his life. That would be hard to live with."

"I don't feel sorry for Joseph Nyquist," Mitch said, admiring the antique mahogany table and four chairs Lauren had set up before the fireplace. He turned back to Lauren, ready to lend a hand in any way she needed. "What kind of father asks his son to bed a woman to bail him out?"

Lauren took a mattress pad out of the plastic cover and carried it over to the bed. Once there, she opened it and shook the wrinkles out of the quilted fabric. "Maybe Joseph didn't want to do it but the family didn't have any other options. You heard Winnifred. Times were tough and then there were forces they couldn't control—like the failure of that new ship design."

Or, in our case, Mitch thought, *increased competition from the little guys and e-commerce.* Mitch walked over to help Lauren make up her bed. "Would you do it?" he asked casually as they struggled to tuck the springy elastic edges around all four mattress corners.

"What?" Finished, Lauren reached for the contoured sheet.

"Bail your father out that way," Mitch supplied as they quickly made up the bed with soft taupe sheets and covered it all with a silky damask bedspread in the same hue as the linen.

Lauren walked over to get four down pillows. She

brought them back to the bed and shot him a haughty look. "He'd never ask me."

"He asked you to date me," Mitch pointed out as they slipped the cases on the pillows.

With a beleaguered sigh and a very pointed look at him, Lauren qualified, "My father did that because he wants to see me married. And, for some reason I can't begin to fathom, has decided you are the man of my dreams."

Mitch liked the sound of that—he wanted to be the man of Lauren's dreams—even if she wasn't yet convinced that was the situation at all. But he couldn't let himself be distracted from his mission here, which was to find out what was really going on behind the scenes. "Suppose your dad did ask you to marry for purely monetary reasons." Mitch walked around to her side of the bed. "Would you volunteer to help him?"

Lauren kicked off her shoes and climbed up the step-stool. Kneeling on the bed, she arranged the pillows the way she wanted them against the headboard. "One hundred years ago I wouldn't have had much choice—I would have had to do what my father asked."

She was ducking the question, Mitch thought. Subtly changing it to something easier to answer.

Mitch turned his glance from the snug fit of the khaki slacks across her hips and waist, and walked over to get several bolster pillows, in the same damask silk as the taupe spread. "I'm talking about now," he said. " He kicked off his shoes and climbed up onto her massive four-poster bed, too.

Lauren sighed. "Today is different." Lauren took the bolster pillows from him and sitting cross-legged on the bed, began arranging them.

"How so?" he asked. Deciding to test out the bed, Mitch stretched out lengthwise on the king-size mattress. To his pleasure it was just as comfortable as it looked.

Lauren shrugged and sat back, with her hands braced

behind her. She was sitting on the hem of her shirt, and the fabric of her much-laundered denim work shirt pulled across her full, round breasts.

Looking intrigued by the intensity of his questioning, she tilted her head consideringly at Mitch. "Women have choices. We don't automatically have to do what our fathers ask of us," she said softly after a moment.

"Suppose your father asked you to marry someone for the sake of the family business and you had to make a choice and this was the only way to save Heyward Shipping." Mitch rolled onto his side and propped his head on his hand. He was more aware than ever of the clean, sexy fragrance of her hair and skin—of the mounting desire he felt for her, the desire that could send his judgment to Hades. "What would you do?" he pressed on relentlessly, doing his best to keep his suspicions hidden about what Lauren and her father might or might not be up to, under wraps. "Would you marry the man?" He searched Lauren's dark brown eyes for the truth concealed deep within her. "Or say no to the betrothal and the deal that would save your family business."

LAUREN STARED AT MITCH. *What had gotten into him?* She didn't like his questions. And didn't see any need for them, either. "No," she said firmly. "I would not." Instead, she would urge her father to find another way to rescue Heyward Shipping. Deciding to push back on him with a series of very revealing questions of her own, she asked, "What about you, Mitch? If you had lived fifty to one hundred years ago, would you have married to save the family business?"

To Lauren's dismay, Mitch didn't even hesitate. "Of course," he told her matter-of-factly. "That's the way things were done."

Lauren hitched in a deep, bolstering breath, and tried not to think about how being this close to him made her feel—which was hot, restless and full of desire. "What about now?" Lauren pushed on boldly, trying hard not to notice how the soft, knit fabric of his charcoal-gray polo shirt defined his broad shoulders and nicely muscled chest. "Would you marry to save your family's business today?"

This time Mitch did hesitate. "I suppose," Mitch said reluctantly at last, half his mouth curling down into a frown, "if there were no other way, I would marry rather than see the Deveraux Shipping Company bite the dust. But if that were my agenda," he said, an unexpected edge creeping into his low tone as he looked her straight in the eye, "I'd at least be honest about it."

Was there an accusation there? Lauren wondered uneasily. Or was it just her imagination that Mitch was taking this all a little too personally? Aware her heartbeat was picking up, and that she was a little too fond of the intoxicating sandalwood and spice fragrance of his after-shave, Lauren studied him. "You'd really hurt someone that way," she noted pragmatically, doing her best to keep the depth of disappointment to herself. She'd thought Mitch was so much more romantic and passionate than that!

"You think in a situation like that, a woman should be romanced?" he asked in a low, astonished voice.

"Well, if you at least tried to find the basis for some attraction between you, the whole situation would be a lot easier." Otherwise, she couldn't imagine sharing a marriage bed, as couples had been forced to do in years past.

Mitch scoffed, as if he couldn't have disagreed more. "Tell that to Dolly Lancaster," he said.

A little shiver went down Lauren's spine as she eased away from Mitch. "What do you mean?" she demanded warily.

"Captain Nyquist gave it his best shot when he was romancing Dolly, only to renege on it later, when he decided he couldn't go through with the marriage after all because he was in love with someone else."

"So?" Lauren asked.

"So Dolly wasn't the least bit grateful for his efforts to find a way to conjure up some chemistry between them," Mitch said impatiently. "Instead, she felt led on and deceived when it all fell apart."

"Look, I'm sympathetic to what Dolly went through, too," Lauren said, leaning toward Mitch earnestly. "I understand that her pride and her feelings were hurt, especially if by then she did love Captain Nyquist. But as for what she did in return... She put a curse on the entire Deveraux family, Mitch." Which was something that didn't seem to shock or surprise Mitch at all, Lauren noted unhappily. Lauren flattened both her hands on the bedspread. "Surely you can't condone what Dolly did—even if it was in revenge."

"I can't sanction her actions, but I do understand her resentment of Eleanor Deveraux." Mitch sat up abruptly so they were both sitting cross-legged on the center of Lauren's big comfortable bed, knee to knee. "Dolly probably thought if Eleanor hadn't been around, Douglas Nyquist would have gone through with their marriage."

"And maybe he wouldn't have gone through it in any case," Lauren persisted just as determinedly. "Eleanor or no Eleanor."

"Why would he have done that?" Mitch asked, taking one of her hands in his.

"I don't know." Lauren's irritation with Mitch grew. She didn't know why he was on the wrong side of this issue! Lauren withdrew her hand from his and blurted out the first excuse that came to her mind. "Maybe Captain Nyquist just didn't think he could fake it in the bedroom!"

Mitch grinned, amused. His look grew even more challenging. "Could you?"

"What?" Lauren froze, her heart pounding in her chest.

"Fake it," Mitch said.

Her breath coming quick and fast, Lauren regarded

Mitch warily. She wasn't sure why, exactly—maybe it was the dusky light coming in through the windows in her room, but his eyes had never seemed such a deep, vivid blue. "I don't know where you are going with all these questions," she said, swallowing hard.

Mitch steadfastly ignored her effort to steer the conversation to another, less intimate track. He took her wrist, turned it over and stroked the tender inside of it. "Could you kiss a man like you meant it if you didn't?"

Lauren flushed guiltily. Aside from the very real, very passionate kisses with Mitch, all she had really done up to now with the other men she had dated and even the two men she had been engaged to—was try to conjure up passion where there ultimately was none. *But how had Mitch known that?*

Determined to keep what surely had to be one of the most embarrassing and humiliating secrets of her life, Lauren tipped up her chin and pretended a sexual sophistication she did not—maybe never would—possess. "I suppose," she said slowly, watching with satisfaction as an answering fire ignited in Mitch's eyes, "that it would all depend on what was riding on it. If the stakes were high enough, sure," she fibbed audaciously, daring to meet him on a level playing field. "I know I could."

"Really," Mitch said as he sized her up with a humor-filled glance.

"Really," Lauren declared mulishly, aware Mitch hadn't even tried to put the moves on her and she was already tingling from head to toe.

"Then let's just put that boast to the test," Mitch drawled, moving swiftly toward her.

The next thing Lauren knew, she was lying flat on her back and Mitch was stretched out beside her on the bed, one of his knees wedged intimately between hers.

Lauren tensed, aware everything was about to change.

"You wouldn't dare kiss me just to prove a point," she said. "Not after the very businesslike deal we made!"

But Mitch merely grinned, not about to be put off now that he had her in his arms again. "I wouldn't bet on that," he said in a low sexy voice that stirred her senses. His lips moved down her neck, eliciting tingles wherever they touched.

Before she could do more than rake in one quick breath, he had framed her face with his hands and pressed his lips to hers firmly, possessively. Heart pounding, she kissed him back just as hungrily, knowing what Mitch didn't. That despite what her father wanted—and she swore to herself she didn't—despite the repeated warnings she had given herself, she was falling dangerously, wonderfully, head over heels for Mitch Deveraux. To the point she no longer cared what happened at week's end. She only cared about the here and now, and the fire of desire raging in her soul. For the first time, the only time, in her life, she truly wanted to be with a man. Knowing these overwhelming feelings might never happen again, knowing she might never feel so consumed by a man, so possessed, she wasn't about to walk away.

So for the first time in her life she forgot about protecting her heart and put everything she had into the reckless kiss—fitting her lips to his, slanting her head at just the right angle, finding just the right way to caress his teeth and tongue. She expected fireworks in return, and she got plenty. Mitch's lips were firm but yielding, his tongue plundering deep as their kiss took on an even more urgent turn. It felt so good to be wanted and held this way, Lauren thought as Mitch clamped an arm protectively about her waist, rolled onto his side and dragged her even closer, so near their bodies were almost one. Her breasts pressed against the solid wall of his chest as he murmured his pleasure, then drew back a little, altering the angle, increasing the depth and torridness of their kiss. She felt his erection pressing against her, hot and urgent, and her excitement mounted, fueled by the rasp of their breathing and the feel of his hot, hard body so close to hers. She caught her breath, as lost in the miracle of longing as he. She had waited a lifetime to be kissed and wanted and possessed like this.

Mitch hadn't meant for the situation to get out of hand. But it had. Instead of the kiss testing Lauren's loyalty, or determining just how far she would go to help her father— and maybe, by association, herself—it was revealing far more telling things. Like how much he wanted her. And needed her. Needed this. In ways that had nothing to do with the way the situation would benefit him, financially or professionally.

She made him feel like taking risks. Not just in business, which was easy, but in his personal life, which was not. She made him feel as if all things were possible, including an intimate liaison between the two that went far beyond the seven dates for which they had reluctantly signed on. The two of them had discovered something special here. The question was, did she realize it, too?

He let the fiery kiss come to a halt and drew back. As their gazes locked he saw a new and ardent excitement shimmering in her dark brown eyes. "So," Mitch drawled, still wondering what was in her heart. "Did you mean it?" 'Cause the kiss had sure felt as though she did, he thought. "Or were you faking it?"

"What do you think?" She let out a soft, ragged sigh.

"I think," Mitch said, already unbuttoning her blouse, "we need to try that again." And try it they did as she clasped his head, lowered it to hers and kissed him with a fervor that surprised them both. In no particular hurry, he opened her blouse the rest of the way, pushed it off her shoulders, down her arms. He sighed his pleasure as his glance roved her breasts. They were full and round and soft—rosy nipples budding against the transparent light blue lace. He smoothed the creamy flesh with the pads of his thumbs. "Just as I thought," he murmured, fastening his lips on her breasts, suckling her gently through the cloth. "Beautiful."

Lauren let out a soft moan. Her back arched. Her thighs fell even farther apart. Knowing he had to undress her and see the rest of her, Mitch removed her bra, slacks, socks.

"Just so you know," Lauren gasped as he worked off her panties, too, "making love doesn't mean we're getting married."

Passion flowed through him, fierce and hot, as Mitch shrugged out of his clothes, as well. Naked, he stretched out beside her. Chuckling softly, he caught her around the waist. "Never figured, even for one second, it did." Getting Lauren to marry him would take a lot more than just this.

"Glad we got that straight," Lauren murmured, tugging him back into her arms.

"Me, too," Mitch murmured as he stroked the silken insides of her legs, from knee to thigh. Feeling her begin to slide inexorably toward the edge, he caressed the satiny petals until the dampness flowed. His fingertips made lazy circles. Moved up, in, out, and then back again. Over and over he loved her, kissing her hotly, rapaciously, all the while. Lauren gasped, arched, bucked, until at last she was there, right where he wanted her, shuddering with release. And it was then, when she looked at him, her eyes full of wonder, that he knew. This was a first. Not just for them, but for her.

"You never...?"

"No." Lauren gulped, her slender body still quivering in his arms. "I didn't think I could."

Eager to please her even more, he slid his hands beneath her, he guided her thighs apart. Then driven by the same urgent need as she, he lifted her against him and surged into her, slowly, deliberately. Still kissing, caressing, he took everything she offered and gave her everything in return. Moving together, toward a single goal, until she gasped with arousal and wrapped her arms and legs around him needing to make her his and only his. And he continued with deep, then shallow strokes. Until both of them were breathing frantically, trembling. And then suddenly they were there, as one, catapulting over the edge before coming slowly, reluctantly, back to earth again.

Mitch collapsed against her, loving her softness, her warmth, the uninhibited way she had just made love with him. Worried, however, that he might be too heavy for her, he rolled, so they were lying on their sides.

Mitch looked at Lauren's rosy face and kiss-swollen lips and smiled. He didn't know how it was possible, but he wanted her again. Lauren might not know it yet, might not want to accept it, but this was not, he decided firmly, going to be a one-time-only love affair. This was real. It was passionate. It was lasting. He didn't give a damn how or why it had begun. And in time, he promised himself, she wouldn't, either.

Lauren swallowed as she moved even farther away from him and regarded him in silence. Clearly, Mitch thought, she wanted to trust him, but she was not quite able to, probably because of how and why their relationship had begun.

She wet her lips. "Mitch, I'm not sure this is the right time, but there's something I need to say."

Uh-oh. Here it comes.

"I'm not doing this for my father or the deal we made with him."

Mitch had already guessed as much, given the depth and genuineness of her response to him, but he was glad she'd felt the need to clarify it. Honesty was always helpful. Especially in situations like this. It was lying and withholding information that got people into trouble.

"I made love with you for me," Lauren continued softly.

Which was, Mitch thought, just the way it should be. Because the only reason to ever make love with someone was because you wanted to be with that person. "The same is true for me," Mitch stated seriously, even as her expression relaxed in relief.

But that didn't explain everything, however. There was one more thing he wanted to inquire about.

MITCH RESTED his elbow on the bed, and propped his head on his upraised palm. "You've never had an orgasm before."

Because I wasn't in love, Lauren thought, then immediately banished the notion. She wasn't, was she? In love with Mitch? This was just lust, wasn't it? Wonderful, life-altering, mind-blowing, passionate lust?

"I don't know," Lauren fibbed just as her phone began to ring. Mitch scowled at the interruption as Lauren turned to get it. "I hope that's not your father."

"Me, too," Lauren murmured, dragging the phone into bed with them. The last thing Lauren wanted was her father guessing what had just happened, or was happening, between her and Mitch and saying, "I meant for you to be together as in married." It was bad enough that Payton had paired the two of them together *romantically* for *business* gain. "Hello."

"Lauren, darling, it's Winnifred! Is Mitch still there?"

Lauren breathed a sigh of relief that it was only Mitch's aunt. "Yes, actually, he is," she said, deciding this was exactly the kind of distraction they needed.

"Could you put him on the line, too, so I can speak to you both at once?" Winnifred asked over the din of the party around her.

"Of course," Lauren said. She told Mitch what was going on and held the receiver so they both could hear.

"We're both here now, Aunt Winnie." Mitch smiled as he put his face close to Lauren's. "What is it?"

"The two of you have got to watch out for Eleanor Deveraux's ghost!" Winnifred warned with utmost seriousness on the other end of the telephone connection.

Mitch rolled his eyes. "Not that again, Aunt Winnifred!"

"I'm serious, Mitch!" Winnifred retorted.

"Why would she appear to either of us, when you're the only member of the family who has actually seen our heartbroken ancestor?" Mitch asked with a beleaguered frown.

"Chase and Bridgett think they may have had a visit from Eleanor on their wedding night," Eleanor continued.

Mitch scoffed and shot Lauren a can-you-believe-this glance. "Sounds more like too much champagne to me."

"Listen to me, you two!" Winnifred scolded emphatically. "If Eleanor's belongings are in the secret room at 10 Gathering Street, then she will obviously be there soon, too. So be on the lookout and let me know if you do spot her, because I would love to talk to her."

Mitch wrapped an arm around Lauren's shoulders in a gesture that seemed to state they were in this—whatever it was—together. "I promise we'll call you if and when we see Eleanor's ghost," Mitch told his aunt sincerely.

Winnifred thanked them and ended the call so she could go back to her party.

Lauren put the phone back on the nightstand beside her bed. Acutely aware of her nakedness—and his—she held the sheet against her breasts and turned to look at Mitch. He was so warm and strong and tall, and he made love to her better than she had ever dreamed, but she couldn't let herself depend on him to rescue her from this situation or any other. Not when she knew she was perfectly capable of handling it herself.

She looked Mitch straight in the eye. "A ghost did not leave those flowers," she stated firmly.

MITCH WAS GLAD this subject had come up again. He had known he was going to have to deal with the fact that Lauren had obviously had a love-struck intruder in her new home, before the evening ended. "Which means," Mitch speculated, "that someone else has been using that secret room without permission."

"Well, they can't keep doing that," Lauren said heatedly. "I live here now."

Mitch lifted his eyebrow in surprise. He had just assumed Lauren would not want to live there until the locks had been changed, the house secured from any further trespassers.

"You can't stay here alone tonight," Mitch said, shocked she would even consider it.

"Careful," Lauren warned as she bounded out of bed and began to dress. "You're sounding like my very overprotective father."

"And in this case, he'd be right." Mitch reluctantly left the bed and reached for his boxers. He looked at Lauren sternly. "You need a man to protect you." And now that they'd made love, Mitch knew exactly who that man was. He didn't care how their relationship had started, or even why, he just knew where he wanted it to go. Which was to a more permanent, traditional arrangement.

Lauren rolled her eyes as she ran a brush through the mussed length of her golden-brown hair. Abruptly, she looked more like the determinedly single woman her father had described. "Look, Mitch, it's very sweet. But you don't have to come to my rescue just because we made love once. I've lived on my own for nearly seven years now," she told him in a low, exasperated tone. "I know how to protect myself."

"I still want to be here," Mitch stated just as stubbornly,

studying the new color that swept into her fair cheeks. "Unless you'd rather I call your father and ask him," Mitch amended when Lauren continued to look unreceptive to his suggestion.

Lauren's lower lip shot out petulantly. "Don't you dare," she warned bluntly.

Mitch lifted an eyebrow, wondering why she was so opposed.

"I don't want my dad thinking he has to come to my rescue," Lauren said fiercely as she hunted around for her socks, and then sat down on the bed to put them on. "I am a grown woman. I can handle this."

Regardless of what Lauren might or might not be trying to put over on him in a business sense, there was no way he was leaving her alone. Not after the way they had just made love. Mitch shrugged. "Then *I'll* stay with you tonight." He didn't mind. It might even give them a chance to make love again.

Lauren sized Mitch up with a provoking glance as she vaulted back to her feet and brushed the bangs out of her face with the heel of her hand. "You know my father wouldn't approve."

For that reason alone, Mitch could see Lauren expected him to back out. But it wasn't her father Mitch was trying to please—it was Lauren. He closed the distance between them in two quick strides. He cupped his hands around her shoulders and looked deep into her eyes. "Your father isn't involved in what goes on between you and me behind closed doors. Is he?"

"Well, no," Lauren allowed as she raked her teeth across her delectably soft and full lower lip.

Then that settled it as far as Mitch was concerned. Mitch shrugged, aware he had never wanted to spend time with a woman as much as he wanted to spend time with Lauren. "Then for tonight anyway it's just the two of us," he said.

"I DON'T KNOW about this," Lauren said as soon as they got back from their errands an hour and a half later and made a beeline for the hidden room, which appeared—to their mutual relief—to have been undisturbed in their absence.

Mitch switched on the baby monitor and then knelt to place it beneath the chaise lounge, well out of sight. "How else are we going to know who's coming in here, and when? We already established if the intruders hear our voices inside the hidden room, they won't come on in."

Lauren shrugged again. "We could set up a hidden video camera."

"Good idea. If we don't catch anyone trespassing tonight, we'll get one first thing tomorrow. Until then, a baby monitor it is." He took her by the hand and led her from the room.

By mutual agreement, they collected their packages and went quietly up to the second floor, to the spacious bedroom Lauren had claimed as hers. Lauren set the other half of the baby monitor, the listening component, on the fireplace mantle, and turned it on also.

"Sitting, dining and bedroom in one," Mitch said as he carried the sacks of food to the table and four chairs that were set up in front of the fireplace. With effort, he kept his eyes away from the bed where they had made love earlier. "I hate to say it, but it almost looks like you could be comfortable here while the renovations are under way."

Lauren had her back to the rumpled covers on the bed, too, even though that meant sitting right next to, instead of opposite, Mitch at the table. "Believe me, there's no place I'd rather be than right here while the renovations are going on," she said determinedly, looking happy to talk—and think—about anything but the intimate turn their relationship had taken. Lauren opened a bottle of springwater and poured some into paper cups, while Mitch ladled Charleston crab cakes and coleslaw onto paper plates. She smiled warmly as she related in a low, honest tone, "There's nothing more exciting than seeing a wreck of a house transformed into a showplace before your very eyes."

Mitch could see how that would be very satisfying. He regarded Lauren curiously, admiring her ability to "rough it" every bit as much as her ability to visualize—and then bring about—success, in both her business and personal life. "Have you renovated every home you've purchased?"

"Yes." Color swept Lauren's cheeks, making her look even prettier. She handed Mitch a buttermilk biscuit and tore open a packet of strawberry jam. "At first I did it because it was economically feasible. I wanted a home of my own in the historic district and all I could afford was a fixer-upper. But once I realized how much fun it was to buy something in need of tender loving care and bring it back to life, that's the only kind of property I have purchased."

"How many have you bought and lived in so far?"

"This is my fifth place. And hopefully my last, at least as far as my own residences are concerned. I think I'll still fix up properties, but just for resale."

"It's an awfully big place." Mitch broke open a biscuit. "Twenty-four rooms."

Lauren shrugged her slender shoulders. "I'll put my realty office downstairs. That'll take up a couple of rooms at the very front of the house."

It was going to take more than Lauren's business to fill up the mansion with the kind of joie de vivre it deserved. "And the rest?" Mitch asked curiously.

She grinned as she cut into a moist and fluffy crab cake laced with spices. "I'll probably fill them with children."

Mitch noted she hadn't said anything about a husband. Or getting married. He figured he could change her mind about that, because if there was any woman who should be married to a man who really loved and cared for her, it was Lauren. "How many children?"

"I don't know." Lauren's dark brown eyes sparkled charmingly. "Maybe three or four or five."

Mitch thought about his own family life, growing up. Boisterous hadn't begun to describe it. "Four is a good number," he said.

"Any number is fine, just so long as it's more than one." Lauren's eyes darkened unhappily as she related, "It's lonely growing up without any brothers or sisters."

Mitch nodded, understanding her regret about that. "I imagine that's so," he lamented quietly. He didn't know what he would have done after his parents' divorce if he hadn't had his siblings.

Lauren studied him over the rim of her paper cup, her eyes darkening with compassion. "You count on your siblings, don't you?"

Mitch nodded. "I don't know how we would have made it through the hard times without each other."

She sighed wistfully as she forked up the last of her fries. "You're very lucky."

"You could be lucky, too." Mitch opened the box containing their lemon meringue pie.

"It's a little too late for siblings, Mitch."

"Maybe by birth," Mitch allowed as he served them both a generous piece, "but you could always get them by marriage."

Lauren caught her breath at the determined look he gave her. She paused, put her fork down and sat back in her chair. "What are you saying, Mitch?" she asked cautiously.

Mitch reached across the table and took her hand. "That maybe your father's idea of hooking us up together wasn't so far-fetched after all." He could see them dating long after the week ended. He could even see them getting serious about each other. Serious enough to marry. Serious enough for Lauren to become a real part of the Deveraux family.

Unfortunately, Mitch noted, his feelings weren't shared by Lauren.

A panicked look on her face, Lauren withdrew her hand and stood. "I thought I made it clear that I wasn't interested in an arranged relationship with anyone."

"That was four dates ago," Mitch reminded her as he too pushed back his chair and got to his feet.

"Three and three-quarters," Lauren corrected, swallowing hard, "and the decision still stands."

Mitch surveyed her, head to toe, victoriously taking in her flushed face, trembling body and quickened breathing. "Tell me that after you make love with me again," he said softly, "and I'll believe you."

Until then he was determined to show her how wonderful their lives could be, if she proved as trustworthy as he hoped. His pulse racing, Mitch took Lauren into his arms and threaded his hand through her hair. Before he could so much as kiss her again, however, they heard a sound, like a door opening and closing, coming from the speaker on the baby monitor.

It was followed by a woman's voice.

Chapter Twelve

•

"Oh, Douglas," the soft cultured voice murmured over the one-way transmitter as Lauren and Mitch stared at the baby monitor on the fireplace mantel. "I knew we'd be found out eventually, but...I so did not want this to happen," the woman finished wistfully.

There was a rustling sound, the sound of something opening and closing. The door again. And then only silence.

Mitch muttered an oath as he released Lauren and dashed toward the door to her bedroom. Lauren had a few choice words to say as she, too, made a run for the staircase. Together, they barreled through the hall to the library, hitting light switches as they went. Mitch reached the bookcase first, and pushed the hidden lever. The door swung open. To Lauren's acute disappointment, the lovers' hideaway was as empty as it had been earlier in the day. Mitch dashed across the room, hit the second lever and rushed out into the tunnel, Lauren hard on his heels. To no avail. There was no one in the overgrown formal garden, no one in the alley, no one walking or running or hiding along Gathering Street that they could see.

Lauren swore again and paused, still breathing hard, her hands on her hips, as they looked up and down the moonlit street. "Maybe they left a clue," she said, sprinting back around the house, toward the secret room.

"We can only hope," Mitch said as he jogged alongside her.

But to their dismay, there were no clues as to who had been there, or why.

"The intruder took the flowers she left earlier," Lauren noted.

"And something else, too," Mitch said grimly as he methodically searched through the heavy steamer trunk. "The packet of love letters between Eleanor Deveraux and Captain Nyquist are gone."

Lauren sat down on the chaise, still struggling to catch her breath. "What are your aunt Winnifred and your father going to say when they found out we lost them?" she asked, already regretting their carelessness. They knew they'd had an intruder. They should have anticipated something like this would happen and taken care to safeguard the letters!

"Truthfully…" Mitch shrugged, and paused. "They probably won't be nearly as interested in what happened to the old letters as they will be in the turn our relationship has taken."

Lauren flushed at the unexpected temerity of Mitch's remark. She knew she and Mitch had behaved impetuously. There had been no helping it. She had never felt as spellbound by a man or as caught up in the moment as she had when they had ardently made love earlier that evening. And though she knew they shouldn't have crossed that barrier when they knew this was just an arranged courtship that was bound to end, and end soon, due to their very different feelings on love and marriage, she couldn't quite make herself regret the intimacy. Mitch might think a relationship between a man and a woman should be run as efficiently and cerebrally as a business, but for a time anyway, he had been as caught up in the passion as she.

"They're not going to know about that," Lauren told Mitch determinedly. Because if their families found out, they would read all sorts of things in the liaison that just weren't there. Like love. And the possibility of a real and enduring marriage.

Mitch's sexy smile broadened even more. A knowing gleam appeared in his ocean-blue eyes. Looking impossibly handsome he leaned forward, his hands clasped between his spread knees. "You don't think they'll guess when they see the two of us together?"

That was the problem. Lauren knew they would. "Our making love was a mistake, Mitch."

It had made her think that a relationship between the two of them was not just possible but probable. And thinking that way was delusional.

Mitch grasped her hand and tugged her onto his lap. "Do you really believe that?" he asked gently, lacing both hands around her waist. "Or are you just upset because your father knew what was going to happen between us before you did?"

Lauren sighed. "He didn't predict what happened earlier, Mitch." If her father knew how impetuously she had behaved, Lauren was certain he would disapprove.

"Sure he did." Mitch tightened his arms around her and held her in place when she attempted to vault off his lap. Looking deep into her eyes, Mitch continued, "Your dad knew there would be sparks. And he knew if we spent any amount of time together that those sparks would ignite into a full-blown flame. You just don't like the fact that he was right and we weren't."

Lauren's shoulders stiffened in indignation. "What are you saying?" she demanded hotly. "That you didn't expect us to make love, either?"

Mitch shrugged his broad shoulders. "I'm a planner,

Lauren. I don't do anything without considering the pros and cons very carefully. And yet tonight…when I held you in my arms…I stopped thinking, planning, weighing what would or would not work to best advantage, and just went with what I was feeling at that moment. I wanted you, Lauren," he murmured, looking deep into her eyes. "More than I've ever wanted any woman."

That was true for her, too, Lauren conceded reluctantly to herself. For a few brief minutes, they had both been swept away—Mitch by physical need, she by her feelings for him. But prior to that, Mitch had courted her every night, at her father's explicit instructions, merely as a means to an end. A business end! She couldn't forget that, Lauren reminded herself sternly, any more than she could forget what Mitch Deveraux had told her at the outset. Mitch believed, as her father did, that a marriage could and should be run like a business arrangement in order to be successful. Whereas, all she wanted was passion and romance and love, the feeling that she, and their marriage, mattered above all else. That was not likely to happen with a businessman like Mitch, no matter how gentle and considerate a lover he was. Lauren flattened her hands against the solid wall of his chest and pushed herself off his lap. "Wanting someone and belonging with them are two very different things," Lauren announced icily as she turned on her heel and exited the secret room.

Mitch caught up with her in the adjacent library and moved to block her way. "You're telling me what just happened meant nothing at all to you?" he demanded, standing with his legs braced apart, his arms folded in front of him.

That was the problem, Lauren thought. It meant everything to her. But she knew he did not feel the same, even if he wanted the physical passion between them to continue.

She wished she could lock him out as easily as she could

lock her doors. But it wasn't happening. He was getting into her heart despite her best efforts to keep him at arm's length emotionally. Lauren swallowed hard. "I'm telling you it's past midnight, Mitch. And our date is over," she said in a voice that was not to be denied. She looked him straight in the eye. "The danger is gone. And I want you out."

"YOU'RE BACK," Mitch said to his father late the following afternoon.

Tom Deveraux walked into Mitch's office at Deveraux Shipping Company. He was impeccably groomed as always and dressed in his customary business attire of a light blue cotton shirt, dark suit and tie. But there were circles under his eyes and a new haggardness in his face that made Mitch realize his father was—for whatever reason—under tremendous strain again.

"I'm still not caught up on all my e-mail yet, but I heard you wanted to see me," Tom said.

Wondering again just what it was that would keep his very business-oriented father from even looking at his own e-mail for the past couple of days, Mitch picked up a folder from his desk and handed it over. "I have some preliminary facts and figures on what it would take to put up a minimum e-commerce site for the company. I'd like you to at least look at the proposal and think about it. And I've prepared a second proposal, for a merger of Deveraux-Heyward. I'd like you to look at it also, and really think how our two firms could benefit if we joined forces."

Tom frowned, looking even less receptive to the idea than before. He sat down on the edge of Mitch's desk, still cradling the folder in his hands. "You know how I feel. Doing business over the Internet robs you of the personal relationships with your customers. It all becomes very impersonal, and then there's no loyalty to any one shipper.

In the short run, it may not be a problem, but in the long run," Tom predicted sternly, "it will be."

Mitch stood and moved restlessly to the window overlooking Charleston harbor. "Look, Dad, I know you grew up doing business that way."

"And so did my father and his father," Tom said as he too looked at the container ships being unloaded as they spoke. "It's a proven, time-honored way of providing services, Mitch. Not to mention that if we switched a big portion of our business to e-commerce, we'd have to let a lot of our sales force go."

That problem, Mitch realized in frustration, was one he had no answer for. A lot of the sales force had worked for the company for years.

"I don't want to pink-slip those people, Mitch," Tom continued.

"Neither do I," Mitch agreed sincerely.

Tom shrugged. "Then…?"

"I'll work on that aspect of it," Mitch promised.

Tom joined Mitch at the window and looked at him, man to man. "I appreciate the work you're doing here, son. And I've read some of the articles in the trades lately that portend e-commerce as the real future of the shipping industry, but I think they're missing the point on one thing. The primary component of e-commerce is price not quality of service. I think customers will continue to pay more for quality of service if they know that when they ship with Deveraux their goods get there on time, in prime condition. That's not the case with a lot of these cut-rate firms."

Mitch nodded and went back to his desk. He sat down behind his computer and printed a few more pages for his father to look at. "I agree. However, our latest marketing research shows that although only five percent of business is done through e-commerce today, in three years fifty percent of business will be done over the Web. The same data shows that if the Deveraux and Heyward shipping companies don't shift to e-business in that time span, that at least one, or maybe both of them, will be out of business.''

Tom continued to pace Mitch's office. "You're sure about this?"

Mitch grabbed the papers out of the laser printer and handed them to his father. "Dad, I've run the figures every way I can think of—the result is the same."

"Which is why you're pushing so hard for a merger," Tom concluded.

Mitch nodded, glad his father was finally willing to hear him out instead of dismissing the idea outright. Mitch leaned back in his swivel chair. "There's a new generation of container ships coming out that are bigger, faster, more fuel efficient. They're more automated and they require smaller crews. Payton Heyward added two of them to his fleet last spring."

"And in the process may have overextended his company," Tom pointed out.

Even if he had, Mitch knew that Payton was at least headed in the right direction. Deveraux Shipping was still lagging behind.

Mitch went on to the next component of his business case. "If our two firms joined forces, we could cut back where we both compete. Divide our resources so we're no longer vying with each other, and that would start bringing costs down for both of us." And hence make those ships Payton had bought suddenly a lot more affordable.

Tom regarded Mitch with respect. "You've given this quite a bit of thought," he noted quietly.

"Yes. It's all in there." Mitch inclined his head at the folder his father was holding. "Why don't you read it, and then we'll talk some more."

Mitch could see his father was taking his proposal seriously for the first time. "All right," Tom said thoughtfully. "I'll let you know what I think as soon as I've had a chance to give your plan the kind of thoughtful consideration it deserves.''

Mitch knew there was one more thing he had to talk to his dad about before Tom holed up in his office. ''Have you been home yet?'' Mitch asked reluctantly, still hoping he wouldn't have to be the one to break the news.

''No,'' Tom replied, obviously perplexed. ''I came straight from the airport. Why? Everything's all right with your mother, isn't it?''

That, Mitch really didn't know. ''She moved out while you were gone, Dad.''

Tom blinked, stunned. ''Back to New York?'' he asked hoarsely.

Mitch shook his head. ''No. She's leasing Lauren Heyward's home from her.''

Mitch noted that once his father had absorbed the information he didn't look as surprised as Mitch would've expected him to look. ''I thought this might happen,'' Tom said eventually.

''Why did you leave like that?'' Mitch decided to confront his father point-blank. ''I've never known you to just walk out on everything for three days before.''

''I had some—'' Tom stopped, looked as if he was mentally kicking himself for nearly having said too much, and then tried again. ''There were just some things I needed to do,'' he said finally.

Mitch had only to look at the inflexible expression on his father's face to know it would do no good to press for further information. Tom had said all he was going to say on the subject.

''How are things going with you and Lauren Heyward?'' Tom asked, changing the subject smoothly.

That was something Mitch would like to know. He'd thought they were going great—until they'd made love for the first time, anyway. Since then, Lauren had kept him at arm's length, both emotionally and physically. "We have our fifth date this evening," Mitch said.

"And then, two more, and you'll get what you want out of this arrangement," Tom surmised.

Not exactly, Mitch thought, because what he wanted was Lauren. And given the way she had shut him out of her home, her heart and her thoughts last night, that was not likely to happen. The way things stood at the moment, Mitch wouldn't even be able to claim the prize he was to be awarded for dating Lauren for one week. Which meant, of course, that after all this effort, not to mention the way he had begun to open himself up to Lauren, heart and soul, it was all going to be for naught.

Mitch sighed. "Just because Payton Heyward will be willing to merge shipping companies at that point doesn't mean it will happen, Dad. You are going to have to want it, too." So far, Mitch knew, his father wasn't convinced a merger was either necessary or desirable. But maybe Tom's feelings would change once he read Mitch's detailed pitch of the potential benefits of the merged businesses. And maybe if Tom could be convinced to change his mind, Lauren could be persuaded to change her mind, too.

"If I agreed to this—and I am speaking strictly in the hypothetical," Tom stipulated bluntly, tapping the file folder in his hands, "I'd want to keep up a firewall between the organizations, at least for a while. And I'd want one of our executives on his executive team, and I'm sure Payton would want one of theirs on ours, as well."

Realizing that was the least of their worries, Mitch broke in, "He's already thought about that, Dad."

Tom lifted a speculative eyebrow. "And…?"

"He wants it to be me." *But only,* Mitch thought, suddenly feeling as if he had the weight of the world on his shoulders, *if I follow up this week of courtship by marrying his daughter.*

"THOSE TWO SECURITY GUARDS you brought in last night were completely unnecessary," Lauren said the moment she and Mitch met to collect books for the literary drive.

Maybe for her, Mitch thought as he helped her carry some empty boxes to his car. He had needed to know Lauren was safe, and since she wouldn't let him stay…

Trying not to notice how pretty she looked in a lavender boat-necked sweater and matching linen jeans, Mitch turned his eyes to hers. "Did they bother you?"

"No." Lauren scowled at him as she tucked her shimmering golden-brown hair behind her ear and waited for him to unlock the trunk. "I didn't even know they were there until this morning, when I walked outside and saw the locksmith."

Mitch lifted the trunk lid, placed his own boxes inside, then turned to help her with hers. "Did you get all the locks changed and a dead bolt installed on the secret passageway?"

Their hands brushed as Lauren handed over her boxes to him. "Only because the locksmith refused to leave until he'd done the work," Lauren bit out.

Mitch shrugged, not about to apologize for his efforts to keep her safe. She was beginning to mean a lot to him and he wanted her to know it. "I told him if you protested, to give me a call and I'd come over."

"So he said," Lauren retorted dryly as she reached into her pocket and produced a check. "Here is what I owe you."

"You don't have to do that." Mitch pushed her check back at her. "It was a gift."

Lauren's eyes gleamed with resentment as she stuffed the check into his sport-shirt pocket anyway. "One my father would approve of, no doubt," she said sarcastically.

"You're angry," Mitch noted calmly as the two of them went toe to toe and nose to nose.

"Oh yes."

He continued to study the flushed contours of her face.

"How come?" he asked curiously. Most of the women he knew would be flattered a man cared about their safety.

Lauren squared her shoulders defiantly and took a small, self-conscious step away from him. "For starters, because it was so presumptuous of you," she stated furiously. "Deciding, *not asking,* what I wanted to do about my safety."

Mitch shrugged again and leaned against his car, crossing his legs at the ankles and folding his arms in front of him. "I would have been happy to ask you if you had still been speaking to me, but you weren't."

Lauren slanted a glance at the couple strolling along the sidewalk a few houses down, on the other side of the street. "I said good-night!" she reminded him.

Mitch retorted, "Right before you escorted me out the door."

"With good reason," Lauren insisted stubbornly. "Our date was over."

Mitch shook his head at her. "That's not why you threw me out and you know it."

The flush in Lauren's cheeks deepened attractively. "Then what was the real reason?"

Mitch grinned triumphantly. "Because you knew if I stayed any longer we would end up making love again."

Lauren took another step back. "Don't be ridiculous."

Mitch straightened, and not caring who might happen along and see them, closed the distance between them and took Lauren in his arms. "You're the one who is being ridiculous if you think it's not going to happen again."

"It's not." Lauren splayed both her arms against his chest.

"Maybe not tonight," Mitch allowed, knowing—given Lauren's current mood—that he had some cozying up to do.

"Maybe not ever," Lauren scoffed.

"But it will happen," Mitch promised, tightening his arms around Lauren protectively.

Lauren tilted her face up to his, but made no further effort to move away. "Dream on."

"I intend to," Mitch said. He would also work to make those dreams a reality—soon. Because right now, Lauren—not work—was his top priority.

Lauren's soft lips curved resentfully as she stepped out of the circle of his arms. "Much as you might want to, Mitch," she told him ruefully, "you can't control what happens between the two of us."

"I don't want to control it," Mitch said, ignoring the truculent set of her chin and the turbulent emotion churning in her dark brown eyes. "I want whatever happens to just happen." He leveled a lecturing finger at her. "You're the one who wants to control events. Make rules. Decide with some random or obligatory standards what is going to be allowed and what is not allowed between us."

Lauren's shoulders stiffened as she brushed his hand away. "Someone has to exercise a little judgment," she said defensively.

Mitch found it odd to be making the exact opposite of the argument he would usually make. But then, being around Lauren…falling hard for her…was changing him. Maybe more than he'd realized up until now.

"Is that what this is?" he demanded hotly, wishing he didn't recall how soft and luscious her lips were or how well she kissed. He stepped even closer. "Because I'd say what you are doing is refusing to listen to that little voice that tells you what you should really be doing. And that's another thing we executives learn to do—follow our instincts." And right now his instinct was telling him that Lauren was having to work overtime to keep him at bay.

Lauren swallowed. "Listen to me, Mitch. We have three dates left, if you include tonight. When that ends, I'll have my house. You'll have your merger—"

Knowing what she was about to say, knowing he didn't want to hear it or even consider it, Mitch cut her off. "If I can get my father to agree to it," he delineated just as stubbornly. "So far that isn't a done deal."

Acting as if he hadn't spoken, Lauren continued firmly, deliberately, as she got out the list of places they were supposed to go to collect books for the literacy drive. "And then, that will be the end of us."

No, Mitch thought, it wouldn't, not if he had anything to do about it.

To MITCH'S DISAPPOINTMENT, picking up the donated books and taking them to the community center took up the first two-thirds of their date, and Lauren had plans for the other half that didn't include anything the least bit romantic or intimate in nature.

"You want to go and buy a refrigerator now?" Mitch asked in disbelief as soon as they had returned to her house.

"A mini-fridge," Lauren specified cheerfully. "The kind college students have in dorm rooms. I'm going to put it upstairs, in my suite."

Mitch watched Lauren get out of his car and rifle through her purse. "I thought you were going to have a refrigerator delivered to the house today."

"I meant to." Lauren plucked her keys from her shoulder bag, then zipped it shut. "But between dealing with the locksmith first thing this morning, and showing property to a prospective buyer all afternoon, I never got around to it."

Mitch consulted his watch. "It's almost ten-thirty." They'd had a dinner of hamburgers and fries, between stops, but he had hoped to make that up to her by taking her somewhere really romantic for dessert and a glass of wine as an end to their fifth date.

Unfortunately, Lauren was thinking along completely different lines.

"The electronic-superstore is open until midnight." Lauren gave him a cheerful, efficient glance as she headed for her own car, which was parked in the driveway. She unlocked all four doors with a click of her remote keypad. Then tossed her purse, the award certificate and the travel book-light they had given her for volunteering in the back. "So, if you want to follow me over there…"

She wasn't getting rid of him that easily. Mitch followed her. "Nah," he said, already opening the passenger door and getting in. "I think I'll ride with you."

Her expression composed, Lauren slid into the driver's seat. "You're going to leave your car here?"

Mitch pushed the seat back as far as it would go, to make room for his long legs. "I'll get it when we come back." He reached for his seat belt and fastened it around his middle.

"But that'll be inconvenient," Lauren protested.

"I don't mind." Mitch smiled, noting how fresh and pretty Lauren looked, even after all the running around and hard work they had done. "Besides—" he inclined his head at her seriously "—you're going to need someone to carry that refrigerator up the stairs."

"I'll have it delivered."

Mitch stretched and rested his left arm along the back of the front seat. "Why, when I can easily do it for you?"

Abruptly, Lauren seemed to realize this was not an argument she would win with him. "Fine. Whatever," Lauren said, looking openly annoyed as she put the key in the ignition and started her car.

"Aggravated again?" Mitch observed as he settled more comfortably in his seat.

"Exasperated," Lauren corrected through mutinous lips. "And yes, I am."

"Why?" Mitch asked, wondering just what it would take to make her weaken.

Lauren kept her eyes trained away from him. "Because you make everything so difficult."

Difficult to be together and ignore each other, you mean. "I'm just trying to follow the spirit of the agreement we made with your father in regard to our dates." He narrowed his glance at her teasingly. "And that probably means riding in the same vehicle for the duration of the social engagement."

"Probably," Lauren agreed dryly.

Although, Lauren thought grumpily, the enforced intimacy wasn't doing much for her attempts to put up an emotional wall between her and Mitch that could not be crossed. Whenever he talked to her, or engaged her in even the most trivial of conversations, she found her resistance to him fading just a little bit. She knew if she allowed the seductive mood to continue, she'd be back in his arms and in bed with him again in no time.

To prevent that from happening, she punched the stereo button. "Would you mind if we listened to this?" she said, and then the book on tape began playing. And Mitch was finally quiet.

Not that this was necessarily a good thing, Lauren reflected as she turned her car into the superstore parking lot some fifteen minutes later. Mitch wasn't interested in the mystery novel she was listening to. Instead, he focused all his attention on watching her drive. The lack of conversation had only served to heighten the physical awareness and resulting tension between them.

"Well, here we are!" Lauren said brightly, parking in the spot closest to the door.

"Awfully busy for this time of night," Mitch said.

Lauren shot Mitch a curious glance. This time of night and on weekends was when they were busiest. "You must not do a lot of shopping at night."

"I don't do a lot of shopping, period," Mitch said.

Lauren could believe that. Just as she believed Mitch ought to make a lot more time in his schedule for leisure activities.

Together, they walked past the cash registers. They were making their way to the appliance section in the back of the store, when they saw Grace Deveraux. She was wearing a nylon jogging suit and sneakers. Beside her was a very handsome twenty-something man with shoulder-length, sun-bleached hair. He was dressed in a white tank top and navy-blue athletic pants that revealed his fantastic body and tan.

Mitch did a double take, as did Lauren. "Who the heck's that?" Mitch asked, gaping at the Fabio look-alike who was standing very close to his mother.

"His name's Paulo. He's the hottest yoga instructor in Charleston," Lauren said in a low voice only Mitch could hear. "I think your mom is taking private lessons from him."

"He looks like a guy on the cover of a romance novel," Mitch said.

He was also standing close enough to Grace to hint at some sort of intimacy between them that went beyond whatever lessons Paulo was giving Mitch's mother. And that surprised Lauren. Grace Deveraux had never had a reputation for chasing after younger men. Nor had Paulo ever been known to date his clients.

Abruptly aware she was being watched, Grace turned and caught Lauren and Mitch gawking at her. For a second, she looked guilty—as if she'd been caught doing something she would rather her children not know about—then her pretty face regained the pleasant composed look she always wore on morning TV. "Hello, Mitch, Lauren." Grace strode forward and introduced everyone politely.

"What are you doing here?" Mitch asked his mother as he shook Paulo's hand.

"We're buying some music for my yoga sessions," Grace explained.

Lauren noticed, as did Mitch, that Grace had quite a selection in her handheld basket.

"If you want, Lauren and I can run you home when you're done," Mitch offered helpfully.

"Thank you, darling, but that won't be necessary," Grace said just as politely. She looked Mitch in the eye. "Paulo and I are having a late dinner together when we're finished here."

Lauren felt Mitch tense. Sensing a storm coming on if she didn't get him out of there before he said something he would regret, Lauren took Mitch's hand in hers. She smiled at Grace Deveraux and Paulo. "Speaking of late, we really need to go pick out a mini-fridge for me. So, later, everyone..."

"That was a little abrupt," Mitch complained as Lauren tugged him out of the music section, toward the vacuum cleaners.

"You were about to put your foot in it." Lauren led the way past the washers and dryers.

Mitch's lips set unhappily. "My mother's got no business gallivanting around with someone that young."

Lauren took a deep breath, figuring now was probably not the time to tell Mitch she had once taken lessons from Paulo, too. "Paulo's a nice man," she said.

Mitch smirked, and still holding on to Lauren's hand, doubled back around to the front of the store. "He's half her age. And I doubt she would be doing this if Dad hadn't left town without telling anyone where he was going or when he'd be back."

"It may be a lot more complicated than you think." They could be friends. And even if Grace was interested in Paulo, well—she was a grown woman. She had a right to pursue whatever sexual pleasure or emotional connection she wanted, without comment from anyone else, including her grown children.

"That still doesn't mean what she is doing with Paulo is right," Mitch retorted gruffly. "Damn it, I never would have figured my mother would be easy prey for a fortune hunter like that!"

Lauren did not like the presumption in his low voice. Nor did she believe, as Mitch apparently now did, that his mother would let herself be made a fool. She gave Mitch a warning glance, which he promptly ignored. "Mitch…"

"I want to catch her before they leave." Mitch released his hold on Lauren and strode over to the checkout line. "Mom, before I forget, Dad and I wanted to ask you if you would consider doing the voice-over for the new Deveraux Shipping Company promotional video we send out to prospective clients."

Grace sized her son up for just long enough to let everyone know Mitch wasn't fooling anyone with his impetuous request. Finally, she gave him a cordial smile that did not reach her eyes. "Just let me know when and where you need me to show up." She looked back at the dwindling line ahead of her, then dismissed Lauren and Mitch with a tight smile. "We're up next. I'll see you later."

Lauren took Mitch's arm, and once again led him away. She waited until they got almost back to the appliance section again before she spoke. "Smooth, bud. Real smooth."

"What do you mean?"

Not about to let him off the hook after the way he had just behaved, Lauren returned his long-suffering glance with a cynical smile all her own. "You just made that up, didn't you?"

Mitch shrugged, looking guilty but not apologetic. "We do use promotional videos. And we will be making a new one if the merger between Deveraux-Heyward goes through."

Lauren shook her head. "Doing that won't stop your mother from hanging out with Paulo, if that's really what she wants."

The corners of Mitch's mouth turned down in dismay. "Whose side are you on?"

"Your mother's," Lauren told Mitch grudgingly. "You have no right to try and manipulate her. It's as bad as the way my father is trying to control who I see or don't see by stipulating that I date you every night for seven days."

"But you're doing what your father wants you to do anyway," Mitch retorted.

"With my eyes wide open," Lauren conceded, wishing she weren't so aware of the heat and strength emanating from Mitch's tall, strong body. Wishing she didn't want so very much to make hot, wonderful love with him again. "Because I really want to own the house at 10 Gathering Street. And I'm angry enough about that." She was angry at herself and Mitch for agreeing to the deal and her father at concocting it. Because that "arrangement" had spoiled whatever romance and love she and Mitch might have one day found all on their own, had her father simply introduced the two of them in a much less pressured way, or better yet, let them discover each other on their own.

Mitch refused to look away. "What I am doing for my mother is for her own good," he said just as hotly. "And as for you, your father is just trying to ensure your happiness."

"I don't care," Lauren insisted stubbornly, aware that the differences between them had never seemed more pronounced. She angled her head up to better see his face, looked him straight in the eye and made her feelings on the subject perfectly clear. "I would never forgive anyone in my family who made secret deals or plans behind my back, no matter how noble or protective the gesture." It was bad enough, she thought, what had already been done with her knowledge.

MITCH THOUGHT ABOUT what Lauren had said while Lauren selected a mini-fridge, paid for it and arranged for it to be taken out to her car. She was dead wrong about what he was trying to do for his mother, of course. Grace needed to be busy right now, so she wouldn't make a foolish mistake by getting romantically involved with Paulo. If helping out Deveraux Shipping was key to that, then so be it. He knew they would all benefit in the long run. His parents, because they would be forced to spend at least some time together on such a project. And himself, because he would know he had at least tried to keep Grace from embarrassing herself, and the family, with a yoga instructor half her age.

As for Lauren, well, that situation was going to be a lot trickier to manage. He knew for certain now that if Lauren found out about the secret dowry her father had offered Mitch to marry Lauren, and Mitch had not told her about, Lauren would never forgive him. She would feel too betrayed.

Hopefully, she would never have to know—even if the two of them did end up together, as he was beginning to hope. Because if he did marry Lauren, Mitch admitted, it would not be because of anything her father had offered him. It would be because the two of them had fallen recklessly, head over heels, in love.

Chapter Thirteen

"Interesting. Going for the rainbow effect?" Mitch remarked Saturday evening when he arrived to pick Lauren
up for her father's black-tie birthday party. She had been
incredibly put together on all five of their previous dates,
but tonight she looked breathtakingly beautiful in a shimmering floor-length gown of beaded taupe silk chiffon. The
strapless bodice hugged her midriff, emphasizing the slenderness of her waist and the fullness of her breasts, and
leaving her graceful neck and soft, silky shoulders bare.
At her waist, the fabric became wispier, the beading more
sparce, and the gown flared out so it moved when she
walked, adding to the overall sexiness. Her high silver evening sandals had spiked heels that made her look several
inches taller and she had put her hair up in a simple, elegant style. Mitch wanted nothing more than to sweep her
away to some romantic hideaway and make mad passionate love to her all night long. But he knew it wasn't possible—not yet—not until after they had attended the cel-
ebration for her father. Once their sixth date ended,
however, all bets were off, as far as he was concerned. For
then they were going to be on their time. Subject only to
their own whims and desires; no one else's....

"The only way to tell if you can live with a color of
paint on the wall is to put a little bit of the paint on the

wall and live with it for at least a week," Lauren said. She smiled at Mitch as she fastened simple but elegant diamond studs in her ears. "You try and look at it in all different types of light, at all different times of a day."

"What's the verdict so far?" With effort, Mitch tore his eyes from Lauren and studied the slashes of peach, gold, green and marine blue on her foyer walls.

Lauren pursed her lips into a sexy moue as she followed Mitch's glance. "I can't decide."

"Somehow, I knew that," Mitch drawled, pivoting back to face her. If he hadn't known it before, he knew it now— Lauren Heyward was the only woman on earth for him.

"I want something dramatic enough to really make a statement, and yet sort of soothing and tranquil, too," Lauren continued thoughtfully.

Mitch grinned as he pushed back the edge of his tuxedo jacket. "Or in other words, no gray."

"Not a lick of it." Lauren picked up her evening bag.

"Why don't you hire an interior designer to decide for you?" Mitch asked, drinking in the intoxicating fragrance of her perfume.

She shot him an amused glance as he held the door for her. "That would take all the fun out of it."

"Somehow, I knew that, too," Mitch said wryly.

Lauren went into the front parlor, closing the drapes and turning on the overhead light. "I think this is the place where you give me a lecture on how I need to delegate more," Lauren said.

"No way." Mitch followed her around the downstairs as she checked the doors to make sure they were locked and turned on lights here and there so they wouldn't have to come home to a totally dark house.

"How come?" She slanted him an inquiring glance as they completed their check of the first floor.

And suddenly Mitch couldn't contain his need for her anymore. "Because I like you just the way you are,"

Mitch said, drawing her close enough for a sweet, lingering kiss. Knowing they'd never make it to the party at all if they continued kissing, and surprised by the tenderness that swept through him whenever he was with her like this, Mitch let the embrace end as sweetly and softly as it had begun.

Lauren looked up at him mistily as they moved apart.

"You about ready to go?" Mitch asked, wondering if she felt about him as he did about her.

THE HOTEL BALLROOM where the party was being held was still being prepped when Mitch and Lauren arrived some fifteen minutes later. "I hope this doesn't prove awkward for us," Mitch said as he nodded at his ex-wife. Jeannette Wycliffe was standing in a corner of the ballroom, clipboard in hand, firing off instructions to the catering staff.

"I'm sure it will be fine," Lauren told him confidently. "We all want this party to be a success. Jeannette isn't going to do anything to wreck her rep as the most innovative events planner in the city."

Mitch hoped not. Recalling the bitterness of his divorce, however, he did not have the same faith. "All the same, I'm going to steer clear of her," he said as Jeannette disappeared through a pair of double doors.

Lauren headed for the gift table being set up, then turned to Mitch, a concerned look on her face. "I left my father's birthday present in the back of your car. And I want to give it to him as soon as he gets here, before all the other guests arrive."

"Not to worry. I'll go get it," Mitch said, glad to help make this evening a success in any way he could.

"All right." Lauren beamed her relief. "I'll stay here and see if there's anything else I can do."

Mitch headed out and returned five minutes later. Lauren was nowhere in sight. Jeannette, however, spotted him immediately. She walked over to him, clipboard still in hand. "Looking for your heiress?" his ex asked sarcastically.

Mitch sighed, the gift box still in his hands. This was the kind of witchy trouble he'd been expecting. "If you've seen her—"

"She just slipped into the coatroom with Ron Ingalls," Jeannette informed Mitch. "I don't know what they were whispering about, but whatever it was, it looked pretty intense to me. I hope you don't interrupt anything if you go in there."

So did Mitch.

Then again, he conceded, still reluctant to let anything spoil the evening ahead, maybe this was his chance to find out a little more about what was going on between Lauren and Ron Ingalls. And if whatever it was had anything to do with either the Heyward or Deveraux shipping companies. Ignoring the uneasy feeling in the pit of his stomach, Mitch thanked Jeannette and headed for the coatroom. He was about to go in when he heard Ron say soothingly, "There's no reason for you to be disappointed."

"Yes, there is," Lauren countered, upset. "I'd hoped to have everything worked out by tonight."

Tensing, Mitch ducked out of sight so he could continue to listen, unobserved.

"It practically is," Ron stated happily. "I mean—he's obviously interested. He said as much to me on Wednesday, when the two of us talked about it."

Mitch had lunched with Ron on Wednesday, and they had talked about the ship Ron wanted to unload for a bargain price. Was that what Ron was referring to? Or was it something—someone—else?

"And you know by everything he has said and done so far that he gets on well with your father and would like to make the necessary commitment—as soon as he can set everything up anyway," Ron continued persuasively. "So

I don't understand why you can't tell your dad what you've got up your sleeve.''

"Because as far as my dad's concerned, it's not a deal until it's signed, sealed and delivered,'' Lauren whispered emotionally, as if much was riding on whatever it was she and Ron were conspiring about. "And we're just not there yet. Something could still go wrong, and I couldn't bear it if I disappointed him again, especially after what happened last year.''

What had happened last year? Mitch wondered. Was Lauren somehow responsible for the ship order her father had had to cancel, and the inevitable financial loss that had followed in terms of the lost deposit?

Without warning, Jeannette came up behind Mitch and pinched him on the arm, startling him so much he almost dropped the gift box. "You ought to be ashamed of yourself,'' Jeannette whispered in Mitch's ear. "Eavesdropping like this.''

Mitch lowered his face to Jeannette's, intending to tell her to lay off, just as Lauren and Ron rounded the corner.

Mitch wasn't sure what Lauren thought was going on between him and his ex-wife. But he knew, by the way the color first drained from and then flooded Lauren's face, that whatever Lauren was thinking was going on there was not liable to make her think more kindly of him.

"Get everything taken care of?'' Jeannette asked Lauren and Ron brightly, stepping away from Mitch. Once again, to Mitch's relief, Jeannette was all business.

"Sure did.'' Ron smiled at Mitch and extended his hand. "Say,'' he continued gregariously, "have you had any more time to think about that ship…?''

"NOTHING WAS GOING ON,'' Mitch reassured Lauren the very first moment he had her alone again after dinner had been served, the gifts presented to Payton and unwrapped.

But Mitch and Jeannette had shared a secret—Lauren

had noticed that the moment she rounded the corner and saw Mitch and his ex-wife standing with their faces so close together just outside the coatroom. Lauren didn't like feeling like the odd woman out, when *she* was the woman on the date with Mitch. "Then what were you talking about?" Lauren asked, point-blank.

To Lauren's disappointment, instead of answering her outright, Mitch hesitated. And it was in that second of hesitation that Lauren saw the second flare of guilt and evasiveness in his eyes. And she knew, whether Mitch meant to do it or not, he was holding her at arm's length, just the way her father always had. Only telling her what he felt she ought to know, nothing more, nothing less. "Never mind," Lauren said as her temper inched ever higher. "I'm sorry I asked that. It really isn't any of my business," she concluded flatly.

But suddenly Mitch seemed to think it was. He clasped her arm just above the elbow. "Look. Jeannette was just goading me—"

"About…?" Lauren prodded when Mitch showed no inclination of continuing.

Mitch shrugged. "My interest in you, among other things. I was about to tell her to back off, when you came out of the coatroom. That's what you interrupted. If I seemed on edge, then or now, it's because I know I shouldn't let her get to me, but when it comes to you, she does."

What Mitch was saying made sense. And yet, deep in her heart, Lauren had the feeling Mitch still wasn't telling her everything. And she didn't like that one bit. She wanted to feel she could trust him.

Looking determined to resurrect their earlier carefree mood, Mitch changed the subject smoothly. "Your father really seemed to like his new putter," Mitch said.

"Of course I do. It was wonderful," Payton Heyward said, coming up behind them and joining in on the conversation. "But as nice a gift as that was, Lauren, you still haven't given me what I really want." Payton continued to look at Lauren with obvious disappointment. "I arranged this week of dating to give you two a chance to get to know each other under after-hours circumstances. And what do I see when I look across the room tonight but the two of you behaving about as intimately as a lamp and a rug."

Lauren stiffened under the onslaught of her father's unexpected—and undeserved—criticism. So what if she was suddenly rethinking her closeness to Mitch? Was she supposed to just forget about the tête-à-tête with his ex-wife that she had just witnessed, or the sly, knowing looks Jeannette was still sending Mitch every chance she got? Looks that seemed to make Mitch increasingly tense and on edge?

"And that in turn makes me wonder," Payton Heyward continued, oblivious to the real reason for the tension between Mitch and Lauren, "if maybe you aren't behaving this way because you're afraid to let your guard down with Mitch for fear of what would happen if you did."

"And what would you have me do?" Lauren retorted, frustrated that she hadn't been able to give her father the big surprise she had been planning and working on for weeks now. The gift that would have shifted his focus from her to him and kept conversations like this one from happening!

Payton sipped his sparkling water and lime as he looked at Lauren gently, and said, "I want you to open yourself up to the possibilities, Lauren, and give Mitch—give this arranged courtship—a chance to work out, instead of spending all your energy trying to resist him, as well as any other romantic feelings such closeness might engender."

"And how should I do that?" Lauren demanded emotionally, feeling more boxed in than ever by her father's expectations and demands. Did he want them holding hands during his birthday party? Kissing? Looking deep into each other's eyes? What?

"I think you know the answer to that," Payton said, giving Lauren a level look. He paused, choosing his words carefully. "I made this bargain with you, and I'll own up to my part of it two days from now, no matter what the outcome of the prescribed courtship. But in the meantime, I expect you two to honor not just the letter of the agreement but the spirit of the deal. And that is all I have to say on the matter." Payton turned on his heel and walked away.

Lauren stared after her father, fuming, as the music started up and couples moved onto the dance floor that had been cleared in the center of the hotel ballroom. She crossed her arms in front of her and regarded Mitch belligerently. "He probably wouldn't be happy unless I was sitting in your lap," she told him sarcastically.

"I don't think you have to go that far," Mitch said dryly.

"Then what do you think he'd have me do?" Lauren demanded, her temper inching ever higher. First Mitch had shut her out. Then her father had scolded her for not behaving amorously enough. A first, if there ever was one! And now Mitch was taking her father's side in criticizing her! If all that wasn't grounds for fury, she didn't know what was.

Mitch shrugged. "I don't know precisely what your father wants, but I imagine he wants you to look as if you want to be here with me instead of edging away from me like I have the plague."

Lauren was now keeping her physical and emotional distance from Mitch again for her own protection. Because she knew how weak-willed she was when it came to Mitch Deveraux. A touch, an intimate look, a kiss, all were things that would lead them straight back into bed. She knew it, and she was betting, so did Mitch.

"Your father probably thinks," Mitch continued, "that you're afraid to smile at me or dance with me or in any other small way allow yourself to enjoy being with me because you're afraid if you do that, something just might happen."

"Please. You're not that irresistible," Lauren fibbed, reminding herself that their relationship, such as it was, was a business deal, nothing more, nothing less. She'd been foolish to think—hope—the two of them were in love. Because people in love didn't shut each other out the way Mitch had shut her out earlier. That, she knew for certain.

"You're telling me there's no lingering combustion between us?" Mitch said warily, suddenly looking just as unhappy—and full of temper—as she felt.

"Not a drop," Lauren said determinedly as she clasped Mitch's hand in hers. "And to make sure you and my father both understand that, I'll prove it."

LAUREN DANCED with Mitch for the rest of the evening. She touched his hand, his face, looked deep into his eyes and smiled. And she did it all and still kept her heart under lock and key. By the time her father's birthday party drew to an end, she was pretty proud of herself for showing up both Mitch and her father. They'd said that she couldn't resist Mitch if she allowed herself to be physically close to him—well, she had!

Mitch, however, wasn't nearly as happy. The minute the clock struck midnight, he let go of her, stepped back. "It's official," he said crisply. "Our date's over." Then he turned on his heel and walked away.

Lauren stared after him, watching as he left the ballroom and headed out into the lobby. Unsure whether he was coming back or not—surely he wouldn't just leave her here without a car or a ride home—Lauren made a pass by the punch bowl, said good-night to her father, who was still surrounded by a few well-wishers, including Ron Ingalls, then wandered out into the lobby herself. As soon as she crossed the marble floor, a bellman tapped her on the shoulder. "Miss Heyward?"

"Yes."

"This is for you." The bellman slipped an envelope bearing the hotel insignia into her hand.

"Thank you," Lauren said. Heart pounding, she made her way across the lobby, found a deserted corner, as far away from the ballroom as possible, and sat down on one of the plump garnet-red sofas. She opened the envelope and found two things inside. An electronic key and a room number. There was no name. No note. Nothing.

She didn't need it.

She knew darn well whom it was from.

LAUREN THOUGHT ABOUT not going up there. About leaving Mitch Deveraux high and dry. Two things stopped her. One, she didn't want her father to see her get a cab home—that would lead to questions she did not want to answer, and probably another lecture on not living up to her end of the bargain as well. And two, she didn't want to forfeit her chance to tell Mitch exactly what she thought of him, and what he had just done. She headed for the elevators and made her way to the fifth floor. She marched down the hall to the room, put the electronic key card into the door, waited for the light to turn green and then opened the door.

Mitch Deveraux was reclining on the king-size bed. He had taken off his tuxedo jacket and tie, and loosened the first few buttons on his shirt. "I didn't think it would take you long to get up here," he said.

Trying not to notice how darkly handsome and dangerous he looked, Lauren marched even closer. "You have a lot of nerve."

"No, lady, you have a lot of nerve." Mitch pushed away from the bed in one smooth motion and squared off with her. "Where did you get off coming on to me that way!"

Lauren swallowed hard around the sudden dryness in her throat and tried to look as if she had zero interest in the confrontation that had been brewing between them for hours now. So what if she had touched his face, his hand, looked deep into his eyes and smiled? He knew she'd been putting on a romantic show just to prove her point—that she *could* resist Mitch, even when they were physically and or intimately close. "You're the one who dared me to do it!" she accused in a low silken tone.

And in her estimation, she had passed the test with flying colors.

"Okay, then." Mitch gave her lips a long, thorough once-over that swiftly had her knees weakening and her body tingling, then dropped his gaze to her breasts, hips and thighs for a leisurely survey before returning ever so slowly and deliberately to her face. "I dare you to make love with me here and now."

Lauren ignored his baiting as her heart began to race. "That's not a dare I want to take," she informed him coolly.

One corner of Mitch's mouth lifted in a taunting smile. "So you're afraid," he presumed wickedly.

She drew herself up to her full height, propped her hands on her hips and glared at him willfully. "I am not!"

Mitch inclined his head slightly to one side. "You weren't afraid the other night," he recalled.

Refusing to encourage him in the slightest, Lauren frowned. "I was a fool the other night."

"You were a passionate, daring woman the other night."

Lauren swallowed, wishing she had something a little more substantial and a lot less sexy than the glittering silk-chiffon ball gown and evening sandals. "We went over why what happened then should not happen again," she explained with a great deal more patience than she felt.

Mitch nodded, not buying it for a minute. "So what was that downstairs in the ballroom just now?" he asked mildly.

Lauren folded her arms in front of her and gave him a feisty smile. "We were dancing."

"That's one word for it," Mitch agreed.

Lauren knew she shouldn't take the bait—she couldn't help it. "What's another?"

"Teasing."

Lauren's jaw dropped at the sexual implication in his low tone.

"And to make things worse, you were only coming on to me like that to prove a point," Mitch continued.

Lauren's cheeks flushed self-consciously. "Well, it looks like I demonstrated it aptly!"

"The only thing you showed me down there," Mitch countered indolently, "was that you can be every bit as much of a control freak as your father."

Lauren drew a shocked breath. "That's not true," she protested heatedly. She and her father were nothing alike!

"Then prove it to me," Mitch said. "And really let loose tonight."

Lauren had known it was risky coming up to his hotel room, when their emotions were running so high. She had counted on her fury keeping them apart. Instead, it was driving her right into his arms.

"Mitch," she murmured helplessly as he closed the distance between them and wrapped his arms around her.

"Kiss me, Lauren," Mitch whispered, looking impossibly handsome and incredibly determined in the soft light.

Lauren's heart pounded all the harder as she delivered the obligatory protest. "I—"

Mitch's eyes darkened ardently. "You know you want

me." He rubbed his thumb sensually across her lips. "As much as I want you."

Lauren splayed her arms across his chest, wedging as much distance as she could between them. But already her lips were parting, her body melting into his. "We're headed down a dangerous road," she whispered, her breath coming as raggedly and erratically as his.

"I don't care," Mitch whispered back just as passionately. "I've got to have you."

And, as it turned out, Lauren had to have Mitch, too. The minute he took her lips in a fierce burning kiss, she knew there was no turning back, no turning away. Like it or not, want it or not, the two of them were meant to be together. Tonight. And maybe for all time....

Desire thundering through him in waves, Mitch flattened the hard length of his body against the softness of Lauren's. He swept the insides of her mouth, languidly at first, then with growing passion, until she was lost in the touch, taste and feel of him. Her soft, delicate hands stroked his chest and shoulder with slow, seductive strokes. Rising on tiptoe, she met him, kiss for reckless kiss. Reveling in the soft surrender of her body pressed against the rock-hard demand of his, Mitch backed Lauren toward the bed. Unhooking and unzipping, he kissed her long and hard and deep. Kissed her until she moaned, deep and low, in the back of her throat, and his own blood began to boil.

Whisking off her lovely gown, he knelt before her, positioning himself between her thighs. Her taupe lace bustier gripped her waist, ribs and breasts. The top of her transparent lace garter belt covered her delectably from her hipbone to just below her navel. Beneath that were several inches of the silky-smooth flatness of her abdomen, and the equally sexy flare of her hips. Thong panties covered a nest of enticing golden-brown curls. Garters stretched down her bare, lusciously silky thighs, and sheer taupe stockings covered her very sexy legs before disappearing into her stiletto-heeled evening sandals.

Mitch removed her shoes one at a time, kissing the insides of her knees as he did so.

Lauren shuddered and placed the heels of her hands on either side of her on the bed.

"I meant what I said about really letting go tonight," Mitch murmured, looking up at her.

"I think I'm ready to try," Lauren whispered back, scooting to the edge of the bed and wrapping her arms around his neck. And that was all the encouragement Mitch needed. If this wasn't heaven, he didn't know what was, he thought as his tongue teased her lips apart and then plunged into her mouth again and again, tantalizing and compelling, while one of his hands caressed the most feminine part of her and his other flattened against her spine before moving deftly to her breasts. Dispensing with the bustier, he caressed her breasts with his palms, rubbing his thumbs over the tender crests. "You are so beautiful, Lauren," he murmured, touching his lips to the sweetness of her skin, even as he divested her of the rest of her impossibly sexy lingerie. "So hot, so wet." He kissed her everywhere, tantalizing and exploring, until she moaned and surged against him helplessly. And then she was taking him by the arm, pulling him up onto the bed beside her. Dark brown eyes luminous and filled with desire, she undressed him, too. Stroking and exploring, caressing and kissing every inch she uncovered. Until he was naked, too. Shuddering, unable to hold back the feelings he had for her any longer.

Shifting, so she was beneath him on the bed, he covered her with his body. Lauren wrapped her arms and legs around him and lifted her hips to his. He penetrated her slowly, cupping her bottom with both hands, lifting her and filling her with the hot, hard length of him. And then they were one. Kissing, sweetly and lingeringly, deeply and passionately. Joining forces. Moving toward a single goal, climbing ever higher.

Mitch felt Lauren shudder as she arched and plunged, the insides of her thighs rubbing the outsides of his. Until at last he relinquished control and gave himself to the passion, to her, and they were plummeting together, blissfully over the edge.

Chapter Fourteen

Lauren woke with the most wonderful sense of well-being. She was burrowed deep in the covers, a man's strong, warm arms wrapped around her, his body pressed close to hers. Remembering how and why she'd gotten there, Lauren struggled to wake up all the way and found herself being turned gently from her side to her back.

Looking as happy and satisfied as she felt, Mitch smoothed the tangle of hair from her face and kissed her temple. "Morning," he said softly. And she had only to look into his eyes to recall all the erotic, sensual things they had done. And wanted to do again.

Blushing shyly, Lauren looked up at Mitch.

"I'm never going to forget last night," he told her, his gaze lovingly roving her face. And then, to Lauren's delight, Mitch made it a morning neither of them was ever going to forget.

Several hours later, showered, wrapped in white hotel robes and sharing a room-service breakfast, they faced a dilemma of a different sort. "We need to talk about this," he said quietly.

Sensing the seriousness of his mood, Lauren curled even deeper into her chair. "I think this is one of those cases where actions speak louder than words," she said.

Mitch studied her over the rim of his coffee cup. "I'd

like to believe that, if I thought you weren't going to run away from me—from what we've found—again.''

Lauren reminded herself they only had one date left before Mitch and she both got what she wanted from her father. As much as she would like to forget how and why her relationship with Mitch had started, she couldn't do so. And that being the case, she knew there was only one path to take. She drew a breath, looked Mitch straight in the eye and said solemnly, ''I admit I'd like some breathing space—''

Mitch frowned. ''So you can pretend we didn't start a love affair?''

Lauren's heart pounded as she studied his reaction gravely. ''Is that what we've done?''

''It sure feels like it to me.''

Lauren drew a shaky breath. She toyed with the belt on her robe. ''This isn't like me, Mitch.'' She forced herself to meet his eyes and be totally honest about this much. ''I'm not the kind of woman who can enjoy a strictly physical affair.''

Mitch's blue eyes darkened and his lips compressed. ''This isn't strictly physical.''

And yet, she thought, her worry deepening, Mitch hadn't once mentioned love. And passion without emotional commitment wasn't enough—not for the long run. And what she wanted, Lauren admitted to herself silently, was someone who was in it for the long haul, just as she was. Not someone who was just in it for what he could get from her father. Knowing he was the kind of man who needed a concrete reason for beginning and ending anything, Lauren fished around for an excuse. ''You're not even my type,'' she said finally.

''What is your type?'' He indulged her.

The exact opposite of men like you and my father, Lauren thought wryly. Out loud she said, ''The sensitive, non-business-oriented man.''

Mitch sat back in his chair. He picked up the last strip of bacon and broke it in half. "Has that worked out for you?"

"No." Lauren accepted the portion he gave her and munched on it quietly.

"Why not?" Mitch asked as he poured them both some more coffee from the carafe.

Lauren stirred cream into her coffee. "You really want to hear this?" She didn't want to tell it; it was embarrassing.

Mitch flexed his shoulders. "How else am I going to understand where you're coming from—and I do want to understand you, Lauren."

Lauren looked in his ocean-blue eyes and saw that was true.

"Your father told me you've been engaged twice," Mitch prodded.

Lauren sighed. She should have figured she would have no secrets. "That's right. And both relationships ended up being unmitigated disasters." To the point she had sworn off all men for a while.

Mitch's eyes softened sympathetically. "What happened?" he asked gently.

Lauren traced the rim of her cup with her finger. "My first fiancé was an artist I met in college. He was terribly gifted but he couldn't hold down a regular job to save his life. As a consequence he was always short on cash, and he was always borrowing money from me."

Mitch rolled his eyes. "I bet that went over well with your father."

"You have no idea," Lauren said just as dryly. "Anyway, it ended when I realized I was really just a way to pay his rent."

Mitch made a commiserating face. "Ouch."

"No kidding." Lauren sighed, remembering how much

that had hurt, and how she had sworn it would never happen again.

"What about fiancé number two?" Mitch asked curiously as he polished off the rest of his mushroom and cheese omelette. "What was he like?"

Finding her appetite had evaporated, Lauren toyed with the fruit on her plate. "He was a college history professor. We met at an exhibit at the Charleston Museum. He was very much a stand-on-his-own-two-feet sort of guy, and very protective of me."

Mitch looked intrigued. "Sounds good so far."

"It was," Lauren admitted. "Until I realized that he wanted me to stay at home while he worked, wore the pants in the family and made all the decisions."

"He just came right out and said that?" Mitch looked amazed.

"I wish," Lauren lamented candidly. "It would have saved me a lot of grief. But, no, he was much more subtle than that."

"Then how did you find out?" Mitch asked.

Lauren grimaced. "We were looking for someplace to live after we got married. And he sent me over to look at this beachfront cottage that had just gone on the market and wasn't too far from the university where he taught. I was supposed to tell him if I liked it."

"And...?"

"It was wonderful. Adorable. And, I found out accidentally when the Realtor showing it to me spilled the beans, it had already been spoken for, because my fiancé had already put a contract on it while pretending to want my input on whether to buy the property or not. Of course, I knew I couldn't be with someone who could go behind my back and subtly manipulate me into doing what he wanted me to do, so I ended it. My father keeps saying the third time around is bound to be the charm for me. But I don't know." Lauren shook her head sadly as she got up and restlessly roamed the room. "My gut feeling keeps telling me it's just not that easy."

No KIDDING, Mitch thought as he walked over to the window and looked out on the traffic in the city streets below. *Because if Lauren ever found out about the deal he'd been offered by her father, the deal he had yet to tell her about, even after they made love, she would never forgive him.*

Lauren came over to stand beside him. She had a concerned look on her face. "You look...upset."

Thinking how very beautiful she looked, even with damp hair and no makeup, Mitch traced the curve of her face with the back of his hand, said gently, "I was wishing your father hadn't made that deal with us."

"I know." Lauren tucked her hands in the lapels of his robe and smiled up at him wistfully. "I've thought that, too. But he did. And I want 10 Gathering Street." She shrugged her slender shoulders and continued earnestly, "I'm aware we have one more date to go, but I really feel, in my heart, that the property is already mine. And I know you need and want the Deveraux-Heyward companies merger just as much, so...since we're both benefiting, and since we both went into this with our eyes wide open, all our cards on the table, it really isn't the same thing as what happened to me with fiancé number two, because it's all aboveboard and out in the open."

Except it wasn't, Mitch thought uncomfortably. *Not on his side, and maybe not even on hers.*

"It's not as if you have anything to gain from continuing to see me after tonight's date," Lauren continued logically.

"But I do want to see you after tonight," Mitch said, meaning it with all his heart. He didn't care what she had done up to this point—that was water under the bridge as far as he was concerned.

"I know," Lauren said sincerely. "And I want to see

you, too. But as for the rest of it, I could use the funds my father promised me if I married you, because fixing up the mansion and restoring it to its former glory is going to cost a lot of money. But I don't need them," she told him stubbornly, "and more to the point, I don't *want* them, so first chance I get, I'm going to tell my father to forget about the marriage bonus."

"No," Mitch said, determined to protect Lauren in every way he could now that she was his woman in every way but name. "I don't want you to do that." He regarded her seriously. "It's something your father wants to do for you, and I don't think you should refuse such a generous gift from him because it would hurt his feelings. Besides, I know if we eventually do decide to marry that we'll marry not due to any business deal or potential profit to the two of us, but because of the way we feel about each other."

Lauren wrapped her arms around his waist and cuddled against him playfully. She gave him a teasing wink. "I thought you were all for the marriage-run-as-a-business-instead-of-a-relationship theory."

"I was." Mitch grinned back, enjoying her company more than he had ever enjoyed any woman's. "But being with you has made me see things differently, Lauren," Mitch said honestly, bringing her closer yet and looking deep into her eyes. "There's only one reason two people should ever get married," he murmured, kissing first her temple, then her cheek, then her lips. "And that's because they're in love, and they want to spend the rest of their lives together."

And, one day soon, if things worked out the way he wanted, the two of them would be doing just that.

MINUTES LATER, Mitch was in the bathroom shaving when he heard a cell phone go off. Wondering if it was hers or his, he turned off the water, wiped his face and eased the door open. Mitch tensed when he saw Lauren perched on a chair next to the window, her back to him, talking in a low excited voice. "I understand…you have other people you work with. No, no, he's going to be so happy when I tell him, believe me. Monday and Tuesday would be great. I am sure he can rearrange his schedule. Well, I'll make him. Oh, thanks again, Lance, you are a lifesaver. I mean it. Bye." A blissful expression on her face, she hung up.

Mitch walked into the room still blotting his face. Maybe it was time for some of that pillow talk he had been so wary about. Working hard to keep his suspicions to himself, Mitch nodded toward the phone. "Was that anything important?"

Lauren hesitated, then shook her head. "Just something for my dad I've been working on for quite a while," she said vaguely, refusing to elaborate. "Kind of a present, although it's sort of for business, too." She gathered up the glittering silk-chiffon ball gown she'd had on the night before. Her emotions suddenly in check, she looked past him at the lavishly appointed bathroom. "My turn?"

Mitch nodded, and started doing up the fasteners of his white tuxedo shirt. Oblivious to his doubts about her trustworthiness, Lauren swept past him into the bathroom. "I'll just be a minute."

If she wouldn't tell him, there were other ways to find out what Lauren was up to. Mitch pushed aside his guilt, waited until the door shut, then headed for her cell phone. He punched a button and the list of incoming calls popped up, starting in order of last received. Again, to his frustration, it said merely Private. Swiftly, he scrolled through the numbers for the past couple of days. Ron Ingalls came up several times, so did her father, even Mitch, and his mother, who no doubt was calling Lauren about the house-hunting they were engaged in. But nothing that would tell him who Lance was.

More baffled than ever, Mitch put the phone back down

just as Lauren came out of the bathroom. Not sure whether she had seen him with her phone or not, he turned his attention away. *I'm not cut out for this,* he thought culpably. He'd never make a good industrial spy. It required too much subterfuge. And yet, like it or not, he had to protect the family company. Especially since he was the one talking merger with Lauren's father.

A cordial but distant expression on her face, Lauren turned her back to him and asked, "Can you help me with my zipper?"

"Sure." Wondering all over again if he could really trust Lauren as much as his emotions were telling him he could, Mitch obliged, his fingers brushing the silky bare skin of her back.

"Mitch?" Lauren murmured as he struggled with the hook-and-eye fastener at the top of the zipper.

"Hmm?"

"How well do you know Ron Ingalls?"

Mitch tensed. If he didn't know better, he would think Lauren was now checking out *him.* Fortunately, she had no reason to mistrust him. "We're business acquaintances," Mitch said, keeping his tone noncommittal. Finished, he put his hands on her shoulders and turned her to face him. He looked down into her face. "Why?"

Lauren smiled, and looked, if possible, even more emotionally distant as she tucked her gleaming golden-brown hair back into the style she had worn the night before and secured it there with two long pins. "He really went out of his way to do a favor for me. I need to get him a gift and I'm not really sure what I should buy." Lauren was still fussing with her hair as she moved to the bureau. "I thought maybe you might have some idea what would be appropriate."

"A fruit basket?"

Lauren frowned as she checked her hairdo in the mirror. "Something a little more personal than that. Besides—"

she shrugged as Mitch came to stand beside her and she searched Mitch's face for clues "—I'm not sure if Ron is a fruit aficionado or not. I can't recall ever seeing him eat any, even when it was on a buffet."

"You've got a point there." Mitch paused, glad Lauren apparently hadn't seen him messing with her cell phone again. He would not have wanted to try to explain that. "Ron plays a lot of golf," Mitch continued informatively. "Maybe you should give him a pass at a course he's been wanting to try."

"That's a good idea. Thanks." Lauren stood on tiptoe and kissed him on the lips. "We've only got one problem," Lauren said as she turned back to face him. "We can't leave the hotel at eleven in the morning dressed like this." She swept a hand toward her evening gown and his tuxedo.

Mitch shrugged, and did his best to put his doubts aside. Whatever Lauren was doing was probably all a lot more innocent than it seemed, including the phone calls. "If you'd prefer to wear the hotel bathrobes…" he teased.

"I'm serious." Lauren's lower lip jutted out. "Some of the guests at my father's party were staying over last night. Plus, a lot of very prominent people lunch here. There's no telling who we might run into in the lobby." She might not have been all that cautious in the heat of passion last night, but she wanted to be cautious this morning.

"So we won't go through the lobby." Happy to protect her from gossip, Mitch picked up the phone.

Minutes later, they were being escorted ever so discreetly out the service entrance to their car by the hotel manager. Mitch paid him handsomely for his effort and then drove her to 10 Gathering Street.

Lauren groaned again as she saw the contractor trucks sitting at the curb. "You're having work done on the weekend?" Mitch asked, surprised.

"I forgot. I told the electricians to go ahead and get

started with the rewiring this morning. And yes, I know it will cost a lot more to have them working today instead of during the week, but I want to go ahead and get the house as safe as possible as soon as possible, and getting the rewiring done will greatly reduce the risk of fire.''

''Can't argue with you there. If it keeps you safe, it's well worth the extra cost.'' Mitch leaned across her to study the front of the house. They both frowned as they considered a tactical approach to the problem. ''Looks like they're working on the downstairs,'' he said.

''Front and back,'' Lauren noted. Which vetoed a back-entry. Wishing she had worn something a little less sparkly the evening before, Lauren slunk a little farther down in her seat. She put her hand over her face. ''I really don't want to run into those guys dressed like this.'' They were the most skilled craftsmen in all of Charleston, but were prone to teasing. Usually, she didn't mind their wisecracks, and gave back as good as she got. But this morning she wasn't up to any joshing—however genial—about the sudden, sexual turn of her relationship with Mitch. It was too new, too precious, too private. Plus, they all knew and did work for her father. She didn't want to chance anyone deciding to act paternally and share information with her father. It was bad enough the prediction he had made the evening before—that she was afraid to let her guard down for fear of what would happen—had been oh so correct!

''We could go to my place in Mount Pleasant,'' Mitch suggested lazily.

Lauren didn't have to think very hard to know what would happen if they did—they'd be back in bed in no time. ''I don't have any clothes there, either.''

Mitch merely grinned, letting her know her hypotheses had been right on the money. ''Yet,'' Mitch corrected with a smoldering look that set Lauren's pulse racing. ''If I have my way, that'll soon change.

Lauren flushed. She had the feeling, by impetuously

continuing her affair with Mitch, she had gotten in way over her head. "Back to the problem at hand," she said crisply, waving Mitch on.

Obediently, Mitch turned the Lexus away from the curb and continued driving down the shady, tree-lined street. "What about at your dad's apartment in the city?" he asked almost too casually. He braked at a stop sign and searched her eyes. "Do you keep anything there—for emergencies?"

Funny, Lauren mused, perplexed, that Mitch would think to suggest that. "Actually, I do," she said, a little embarrassed she hadn't thought of that idea herself. "It's easier than having to go home and change if I drop by and Dad asks me to play a quick round of golf or go out sailing or something. And there's not going to be anyone there this morning. Since it's the weekend, he should be at the house in Summerville or playing golf at the country club there." This late on a Sunday morning, her father would not even be in the city.

Noting the way was clear, Mitch stepped on the accelerator again. "You want me to drive you over there?" he asked, looking eager to help.

"Would you mind?" Lauren asked as a horse-drawn carriage full of tourists turned into the street in front of them. "I need to drop off another key to 10 Gathering Place anyway now that I've had the locks changed."

"Not at all," he said, seeming pleased by the solution they'd found.

Her father's apartment building—which catered to executives who actually lived elsewhere but wanted a place to stay when they were in the city during the week—was as quiet as always over the weekend. Lauren used her "emergency" key to let them inside the penthouse. "Feel free to look around and make yourself at home," she said. "I'm going to go change."

HERE IT WAS, Mitch thought as Lauren disappeared into the guest bedroom to change her clothes. The perfect opportunity to explore and see what he could find out about Lauren and her father and what they might or might not be planning behind the scenes. And it hadn't taken much effort on his part to get here, either, he thought guiltily, moving about the spacious penthouse apartment, feeling more like a spy than Lauren ever would.

Bypassing the master bedroom and bath, Mitch checked out the living room and the small galley kitchen and, finding nothing suspect, moved to the study beyond. Like the rest of the apartment, it was neat as a pin and showed no clue that Payton Heyward had fallen on hard times. The bookshelves were filled with books on the shipping industry, business management, tour books about the many ports his company served and several golf books and videos.

In one corner there was a computerized putting cup and an automatic putt return, as well as several custom-made golf clubs. Frustrated, Mitch turned his attention to Payton's desk. There was nothing on it except a Palm Pilot and a humidor. Which was odd, Mitch thought, since he had never known Payton to smoke, or even offer anyone a cigar. His mood tense, Mitch opened the lid of the humidor and his jaw dropped at what he saw.

Chapter Fifteen

It had to be her imagination, Lauren reassured herself
firmly as she stripped off her evening gown from the night
before and slipped into a white short-sleeved golf shirt and
buttercup-yellow shorts. Mitch had not been eager to come
over here and have the chance to look around. Just because
Mitch and his father were her father's fiercest competitors,
just because the two men were about to engage in complicated merger discussions, was no reason for Mitch to
try to spy on her father through her.

And yet, Lauren couldn't deny the fact that, for the second time in a week, Mitch had been messing around with
her cell phone back at the hotel. The first time, he had said
he was just comparing her model phone with the type he
already had. But today, she was sure he had been handling
it again when she had walked out of the bathroom and
surprised him.

She didn't want to think he was using her, especially
after the wonderful way he'd made love to her, and the
way she was falling head over heels in love with him. And
yet... Lauren sighed.

It had to be her imagination, Lauren told herself firmly
as she knelt to put on her shoes, then, on a whim, elected
against it. Either that, or a misconception on her part. Deciding there was one way to find out what Mitch was really

up to—if anything—she eased the door open ever so gently. And slipped back out into the hall, padding silently through the empty living room, past the equally empty kitchen to her father's study.

Her heart sank at what she saw.

Mitch was standing at her father's desk, her father's Palm Pilot in his hand. "What are you doing?" she demanded, upset.

Mitch looked up at her, his expression grim. "I'm checking you and your father out. And I have to tell you," he continued angrily, "after what I just found, I'm very glad I did."

Lauren blinked in confusion. She was the one who should feel betrayed here! Not him! "What are you talking about?" she asked hoarsely.

Mitch's lips thinned into an unhappy line. "Why didn't you tell me your father was ill?"

LAUREN BLINKED, stunned by the unexpected accusation. "He's not!"

Mitch regarded Lauren with a skepticism that stung. "You don't know?"

"No. And I don't believe you, either," Lauren said emotionally.

"Then believe this," Mitch directed flatly as he flipped open the lid of the expensive humidor. The electronic controls showed it had not been turned on or used to store cigars. Instead, it had been filled with a half-dozen medicine bottles, the dates on some of them going back months. "And this." Mitch opened a desk drawer and revealed several medical books, a thermometer, a notebook and pen. "The calendar on your father's Palm Pilot reveals he's been having medical tests and doctor's appointments for the past six months."

Lauren scanned the notebook Mitch had given her, her pique with him momentarily forgotten. "According to these notes, my father's been having fevers and a lot of pain for months now," Lauren said. Finding that her legs would no longer support her, she sank into a chair and, trembling, looked over at Mitch. "No wonder he's suddenly in such a hurry for me to find a reliable man and get married. He's dying!"

"Hey," Mitch corrected quickly as he crossed to her side, his pique with her apparently forgotten. "We don't know that."

"Then why hasn't my father told me about any of this?" Lauren demanded, tears running down her face, aware she had never felt so concerned and upset as she did at that moment.

Mitch touched her shoulder gently. "He probably just didn't want you to worry."

Lauren wiped her tears away, then stood and studied Mitch intently. "And you didn't know about it, either," she surmised tightly.

"Not until just now," Mitch admitted reluctantly. "Although my father and I both suspected that your father had to have some ulterior motive for wanting the merger. His complete change of heart was too sudden to be taken strictly at face value."

"Which is why you've been investigating him," Lauren guessed.

Mitch replied matter-of-factly. "I had to scout out the truth, Lauren. For both our sakes. I walked into a relationship and marriage blindly once before, without knowing what Jeannette really wanted from me. I couldn't allow the same thing to happen again. And I certainly couldn't allow it to happen to my family's company." He paused, then continued more gently, "I'm not proud of what I've had to do to discover the truth. But I'm not going to apologize for it, either."

Lauren sighed, too shaken at the news to dwell on her anger with Mitch for not coming to her with his suspicions.

She plucked a tissue from the holder and blew her nose. "I knew my father had arthritis, that a few times when I've seen him lately he looked a little flushed. But...if there's something more wrong than that—and it looks like there is—he should have told me, Mitch."

Mitch leaned against her father's desk. He folded his arms in front of him, and continued to study her contentiously. "There's one thing I want to know, Lauren. What does all this have to do with Lance?"

Wishing she could ignore the accusing note in Mitch's low tone, Lauren dropped her crumpled tissue into the waste can. She frowned at him, noting unhappily, "You really do suspect me of something nefarious, don't you?"

"Look—" Mitch spread his hands in front of him, struggling to be fair "—I know Ron Ingalls is somehow involved in whatever is going on with Lance."

"Yes, he is," Lauren was only too happy to point out. "In fact, Ron was instrumental in trying to arrange my deal with Lance."

Mitch studied her in frustration. "You're not going to tell me what it is, are you?"

"Believe me, I plan to discuss it with you," Lauren retorted heatedly, deciding it would serve Mitch right if she kept him in suspense a little longer. "But not until after I have spoken to my father and found out exactly what he's been keeping from me."

Mitch followed her as Lauren went back to the bedroom, grabbed her shoes and evening clothes. "What are you going to do?" he demanded impatiently, still looking darkly handsome and dangerous in the tuxedo he'd worn the night before.

"I'm going to go with you while you change clothes at your place," Lauren told him flatly, already heading for the door. "And then I want to see your brother Gabe."

"THESE REALLY AREN'T the kinds of questions you should be asking me," Gabe said when Mitch and Lauren had caught up with him at the hospital several hours later. "You should be talking to your father."

"I want to know what I'm likely dealing with before I confront him," Lauren said. She knew she needed to be prepared. And she needed enough information to keep her father from giving her a snow job again, to protect her feelings. "You're a doctor. You must know what kinds of illnesses these medications are used to treat." Lauren handed over the list of names she had copied down from the pharmacy bottles.

Gabe studied the list reluctantly. "This first medication is used to lower cholesterol, the second two work together to control blood pressure, these three here all relieve joint or skin symptoms, this one is a stomach acid-reduction drug."

"Which means what?" Lauren asked, still as baffled as ever.

"That your father's health obviously is not as good as he or you would like. But as for what specifically is wrong with him, again, I think you should ask him," Gabe said kindly but firmly.

Realizing they had gotten all the information they were going to get from Gabe, Lauren and Mitch thanked him and left the hospital in silence. They paused by Mitch's car. Lauren turned to him, knowing she had no right to ask but realizing she was going to anyway. "Would you go with me to see my father?" she asked quietly. She needed someone with her when she confronted him. She needed Mitch.

"Sure." Mitch squeezed her hand reassuringly.

They drove to Summerville in record time. Payton was upstairs when the butler let them in, so they waited for him in his study downstairs. Too nervous to sit still, Lauren paced. Mitch tried to engage her in conversation, but she couldn't concentrate on a thing he was saying. Finally,

Mitch took her in his arms and held her close. "It's going to be okay," he said, smoothing her hair with his hand.

"What if it's not?" she whispered, trembling, knowing that she had already lost her mother and she couldn't bear to lose her father, too.

Mitch tilted her face up to his. "It will," he whispered comfortingly once again, and bent his head to kiss her. And that was when Payton Heyward walked in.

"WELL, WELL, WELL," Payton said as Mitch and Lauren broke apart. "If this is what you came to tell me, I approve."

Blushing hotly, Lauren disengaged herself from Mitch and walked toward her father. Abruptly, she was as filled with resentment as before. "It's not," she said quietly.

Payton's expression abruptly became as serious as Lauren's. "What is it?" he said, realizing there was something very wrong.

Lauren crossed her arms in front of her. "Mitch and I dropped by your apartment this morning."

"We saw all the medicine in the humidor on your desk," Mitch explained.

"I can't believe you're sick and you didn't tell me!" Lauren accused emotionally.

Payton frowned. "I'm fine."

Lauren threw up her hands in exasperation. "Dad, please. Come on. I've already talked to a doctor. I know what some of those medicines are used for. Now, are you going to give me the straight story or what?"

Payton released a beleaguered sigh and gestured for them to have a seat.

Lauren was still trembling as she and Mitch took the chairs in front of Payton's desk.

Looking more relaxed than Lauren could ever hope to feel under the same circumstances, Payton leaned against the front of his desk, and continued matter-of-factly, "I have lupus."

"What?" Lauren asked, panicked. Mitch shot Lauren a reassuring glance, reached over and took her hand, and held it tightly.

"It's an autoimmune disease that causes inflammation in the body," Payton explained.

"Like arthritis," Lauren guessed.

"Except this is a little more serious," Payton allowed reluctantly.

Lauren swallowed hard around the growing lump in her throat. "Could you die?"

Payton hesitated. "In certain cases it can be fatal, but it can also be quite mild."

Lauren held on to Mitch's hand, drawing strength from his steady presence. "What kind do you have?" she asked her father.

"Mild."

Lauren gave a big sigh of relief, then studied her father suspiciously. "You're not lying to me about that, are you, Dad?" She would hate it if he was.

"No, honey, I'm not," Payton told her gently. "And if you'll think about it, you'll realize it's true. I haven't missed more than a day or so of work, here and there. I sometimes get a little fever or some joint pain, but that's been controlled pretty well by medication. And my doctor says that once I get through this particular episode I may not have another relapse for years to come."

"And if and when you do…?" Lauren asked anxiously.

"Then they'll treat it again," Payton replied firmly. "And I'll be fine."

"If this is the case, why didn't you just tell me?" Lauren asked in frustration. She hated being shut out that way by those close to her.

"Because I didn't want you to worry," Payton explained kindly. "And—" Payton paused to look at Mitch

"—I didn't want any rumors about my health floating around when I was trying to stay competitive and arrange a merger between our two companies. I figured people would be suspicious enough just by the fact that I was willing to forfeit complete control of Heyward Shipping Company."

"I understand," Mitch said.

"Well, I don't!" Lauren cut in. She shot her father an angry glance. "You had me scared to death."

"I'm sorry." Payton grimaced in regret. "I had planned to tell you one day if it became necessary—"

"It was always necessary!" Lauren chided, upset. She vaulted out of her chair and squared off with her father. "I want us to be honest with each other. I want to know if there is something wrong you'll come to me, and that I can come to you, too."

Payton opened his arms to her. "I want that, too, honey." He took her in his arms and Lauren and her dad embraced for a long heartfelt moment.

As they drew apart, Lauren looked up at him, realizing that no matter how uncomfortable the answer, she needed to ask this too. "Is your illness why you were in a hurry to get me hooked up with Mitch?"

For a moment Payton looked taken aback by the question. As was Mitch, Lauren noted with relief. "I confess," Payton responded quietly, "it was sobering, learning I had an illness that could potentially be fatal in some cases. It made me realize that I wasn't as immortal as I'd like to think. And it also made me want to see you were taken care of, should anything happen to me," he finished gently.

Lauren squared her shoulders. "I can take care of myself, Dad."

"I know you can," Payton said with an affectionate smile. "But that doesn't mean you should live the rest of your life alone. Or refuse to meet a man I think would be the perfect husband for you.''

Lauren's feelings for Mitch were deep and abiding, but she wasn't ready to share them with anyone. Not until she and Mitch had discovered if they were really as in love as Lauren suspected they were, anyway. "We're not getting married just because you think we should," Lauren told her father calmly.

Payton regarded her with a knowing glance. "I never thought you would," he said just as quietly. "I thought you'd do it because it felt right."

Which was the irony of it, Lauren thought. Her relationship with Mitch did feel right—so right it scared her. "Well," Lauren took a deep breath, said finally, "if you really are doing okay, Dad—"

"I am," Payton reassured her firmly.

Lauren smiled, aware this wasn't how she had planned to announce her father's belated birthday present, but it would do, anyway. She searched her dad's face. "Are you feeling well enough to play some golf?"

Payton looked surprised. "Today?"

Lauren's grin widened. "I've arranged for you to have two days of private lessons at Pinehurst with Lance Murtaugh starting tomorrow morning."

Payton did a double take, as Mitch put it all together, finally understanding what all Lauren's mysterious phone calls of the last week had been about. "*The* Lance Murtaugh?" Payton said. "North Carolina's top golf pro?"

"The one and only." Lauren beamed.

Payton picked up the putter Lauren had given him for his birthday and cradled it between his hands. "I thought Lance Murtaugh didn't work with anyone but the very top professionals."

"Usually, he doesn't," Lauren said, downplaying how very difficult it had been for her to arrange the lessons. "But when I explained to him how much it would mean to you, he promised to look for a hole in his schedule and get back to me. If you want to do it, you've got to call him right away, Dad.''

"THAT WAS SOME birthday present you just gave your father," Mitch said as they waved goodbye and Payton headed for the prestigious North Carolina golf course where his lessons would begin the very next morning. The drive would take several hours but Payton had assured them both he was up to both the trip and the lessons.

"Yeah, well, he deserves it." Lauren stood watching until Payton's limousine disappeared down the driveway. She headed for Mitch's car, then turned to him, an impish grin on her lovely face. "Not that I didn't have some ulterior motive. I was hoping if Dad got into golf again, big time, he'd have a lot less time to be thinking about and meddling in my love life."

Mitch caressed her cheek with the pad of his thumb. "I'm sorry I suspected you."

"I'm not." Lauren smiled, her relief palpable. "Your sleuthing uncovered something I very much needed to know about my dad."

"I won't do it again," Mitch promised her softly, seriously, as he stroked a hand through the silk of her hair.

"That's good," Lauren returned just as solemnly. "Because trust is important. I couldn't bear it if I thought you were going behind my back or manipulating me the way my last fiancé did."

The last thing Mitch wanted to do was hurt Lauren. Or cause a rift between her and her father.

"And if this merger goes through," Lauren continued, oblivious to the disturbing nature of Mitch's thoughts, "it should actually help my dad, physically. You heard what he said his doctor told him." She inclined her head to the side. "Eliminating stress from his life will help him more than anything. If he knows the company is secure, our financial futures protected, I think he'll rest a lot easier.''

Mitch wrapped his arms around her, loving the way she felt against him, so soft and feminine and warm. Pushing aside his guilt for the moment, he studied her intently. ''Does this mean you approve of the merger?'' He wanted her approval, and that was something new, too. He had never much cared what anyone thought of him—he had just gone out and done what needed to be done. Period. Now to his surprise he was concerned about her reaction to his actions, too.

''Very much so.'' Lauren smoothed her hands across his chest, her touch as loving and wonderful as the look in her dark brown eyes. ''I want you and my father getting along. Having the two of you work together, at something you both obviously love, is even better.'' Wreathing her arms about his neck, Lauren stood on tiptoe to kiss him. Her lips were sweet and seductive beneath his. Making Mitch realize all over again how hard he had fallen for her and how much he had grown to love her in just one week.

When at last the gentle kiss came to an end and they drew apart, Mitch gave her the heartfelt apology he knew she deserved. ''I am sorry for deceiving you,'' he told her sincerely. He was even sorrier for not telling her at the start about the dowry her father had offered..

Lauren looked deep into his eyes, her forgiveness as evident as her previous hurt. ''Just don't do it again,'' she warned softly, her faith in him obvious.

Mitch wouldn't.

The question was, should he tell her now and risk her being so hurt she couldn't forgive him, or her father? Mitch wondered, his conscience prickling mightily. Or just talk to her father alone, the first chance he got, and tell him man to man he didn't want or need anything from Payton. That loving Lauren, being with her, was pleasure and privilege enough.

Chapter Sixteen

"I can't believe this is our last date," Lauren mused as the two of them took the Deveraux family yacht, the *Endeavor,* out for a moonlit cruise Sunday evening.

"Our last date under the terms of our agreement with your father," Mitch qualified readily as he selected a place several miles offshore and dropped anchor. He turned to her with a sexy smile. "It's also where our real relationship begins. I don't want us to stop seeing each other, Lauren."

Aware her heart was suddenly beating triple time, Lauren got out the picnic basket Mitch had packed, while he opened a bottle of wine. "I don't want that, either," Lauren acknowledged slowly as she paused to meet Mitch's eyes. Warily, she continued, "But I don't want us to be together just because it's what my father wanted, either." Because doing that would hurt both of them more than she could say.

"Then how about because it's what we both want?" Mitch asked her huskily as he stopped what he was doing, took her into his arms and held her close. His eyes filled with tenderness, he smoothed the hair from her face and continued with a soberness that warmed her heart and gladdened her soul. "Your father's illness have worked to drive home to me how precious time is. I don't want to waste a second of it.'' Tightening his grip on her, he brought her closer yet and kissed her cheek, her lips, her hair. ''I know I want to spend the rest of my life with you, Lauren,'' Mitch told her quietly. ''And I think you feel the same way about me.''

Lauren tilted her head up. Her heart pounded at all the love she saw in his eyes. It matched the feelings in her heart. She wreathed her arms around his neck and touched her lips lightly, persuasively, to his in a show of devotion. ''I do.''

Mitch ran a hand through the silk of her hair and looked deep into her dark brown eyes. ''Then show me,'' he whispered with a measure of satisfaction that had her pulse points pounding.

Lauren's knees weakened at the heat in his low voice, the desire in his deep blue eyes as his hands already began slipping under the soft cotton fabric of her T-shirt to the bare skin beneath. She had promised herself she wouldn't fall prey to her father's plan for her. That she would marry a man of her own choosing, not his. And yet, here she was, falling in love with Mitch, to the point where she could no longer imagine a life without him.

''Show me how you really feel,'' Mitch continued persuasively as he lowered his lips to hers. He ran his tongue along the seam of her lips until her lips parted helplessly in surrender, and her heart was thumping so hard she could feel it in her ears. Lauren moaned, soft and low, as she fused her mouth to his. She trembled against him, aware of the need that seemed to grow even as it was met. Her abdomen felt liquid and weightless, and there was an answering moisture between her thighs that heralded her readiness for him.

Making the most of the moment given to them, they indulged in slow, kisses until their was no turning back, no question of their need or want for each other, no way they weren't going to be together from now on....

Taking their time, they continued undressing until they were naked beneath the stars overhead. His arousal pressed against her, creating an ocean of warmth inside her. Lauren stirred languorously as they reclined on the makeshift bed of their discarded clothing and Mitch taught her pleasure in ways she had never imagined. Needing to give as well as receive, she let out a soft groan and rolled so he was beneath her. Her hands and lips moved over him, delighting in the masculine feel and taste of his skin. She couldn't get enough of loving him and that filled her with a kind of wonder, even as she settled over him, caressing the velvety length of him, first with her hands, then with her lips and tongue. Whatever reticence she'd had, whatever reluctance to get involved, was gone now. She wanted to feel him deep inside her. She wanted him in her life.

"My turn," Mitch whispered.

Lauren sighed contentedly and moved onto her back, expecting him to take her then and there. She placed both her hands around his neck and brought his head down to hers. He kissed her until she was shuddering and so was she, and all coherent thought spun away.

"Now," she murmured.

But Mitch only grinned, and kissed his way down her neck, sensually exploring the delicate U of her collarbone, her shoulders and arms, the insides of her elbows and wrists, and finally the uppermost curves of her breasts. They had all the time in the world, and he was going to take it. Because tonight was a night she would remember the rest of her life.

He bent his head and traced the rosy areola with his tongue, brushed it dry with his lips and then suckled her tenderly. Eager to know all of her, he continued his slow, sensual exploration, until her head fell back and her body arched against him. Moving lower still, he stroked her with light butterfly kisses until she shook with her need for him and made a low, whimpering plea. "Mitch…Mitch…"

Needing to possess Lauren the way he had never wanted to possess any woman, Mitch moved back up her body. Sliding his hands beneath her, he brought her up to meet him. She opened up for him, surging against him, drawing him deeper, giving him what he needed, what they both needed. Until they were both perspiring, surging toward the outer limits of their control. Soaring into soft, sizzling love and shuddering pleasure.

Afterward, Mitch held Lauren close. The pinnacle of pleasure had passed, leaving them exhausted, replete and more than a little awed. So much had happened in just a week. And suddenly Mitch needed—wanted—to put it into words. He shifted so she was beneath him once again, and framed her face with his hands. "I love you, Lauren. With all my heart."

Lauren smiled up at him, her pretty eyes filled with tenderness. "And I love you," she murmured, the silence of the night around them broken only by the ocean water lapping timelessly against the hull of the boat.

"Then marry me, Lauren," Mitch murmured, stroking a hand through the tousled silk of her golden-brown hair. "And build a life and a family with me."

"Oh, Mitch," Lauren said softly, looking up at him in a way that was conflicted and yet still filled with all the joy they had found. He knew what she was thinking. It was all happening so fast. But it also felt more right than anything ever had, for both of them. "Tell me that's a yes," he said, knowing he would do and say whatever necessary to get her to say yes, she would marry him.

Abruptly, Lauren's features were flooded with relief. "It is," Lauren whispered ecstatically as she wrapped her arms around him once again. "It absolutely is!" She and Mitch kissed again. Gently. Rapaciously. And every way in between. Mitch chuckled as he swept her into his arms. "I don't know about you, but I think it's time we tried out that bed down below."

They made love throughout the night, each time better than the last, and Lauren woke the next morning wrapped in Mitch's arms. They made love one last time, slowly and tenderly, and then had a leisurely breakfast of coffee, juice and blueberry crumb cake in bed, before showering and dressing and heading back to shore.

"You want to buy a ring today and make it official?" Mitch said as he steered the yacht back into its slip and dropped anchor once again. He turned to regard her seriously, all the love he felt for her in his eyes.

"Actually," Lauren said, taking a deep breath and drawing on every bit of courage she possessed, "I'd rather the two of us just get married."

MITCH LOOKED at Lauren in a way that told her he wasn't sure what Lauren meant. He leaned against the steering wheel and folded his arms in front of him. "Without an engagement ring?"

"Or a big wedding," Lauren rushed to elaborate, before she could lose her nerve. "Or any of the hoopla." Nervously, she ran her fingers across the glass housing covering the navigation instruments. "Couldn't we just hop on a plane and go somewhere and elope?" She loved him so much she didn't want to risk anything, be it family or business or even random incidents in life, preventing them from spending the rest of their lives together.

To her delight, Mitch looked extremely amenable to her heartfelt suggestion. He dropped his arms and moved close enough to take her in his warm embrace. "Like Vegas?"

Lauren wrapped her arms around his neck and lifted her face to his. She had never in her life been this reckless or impulsive, but she couldn't say she wasn't enjoying it. "Or the Bahamas. Or Mexico," she suggested practically as she studied his expression, thrilled at the devotion she found. "I haven't done any research, but I am sure there are places where it's quick and easy and—"

A knowing look appeared on Mitch's face as he guessed dryly, "Painless?"

Lauren knew how this sounded—as though she was rushing into this for fear if she delayed something, one of them would change their mind, but that wasn't it at all. Wanting Mitch to understand that, she said, "It's just— I've been engaged twice, Mitch, and started the whole planning-a-wedding process and then ended up having to call it off. So I almost feel like if I were to do that again, I would either jinx it, or maybe it's just, given enough time, something is bound to go wrong with the whole big-wedding thing, and this feels so right to me, I don't want to even contemplate that happening." She wanted them to continue being together the way they had the night before.

Mitch paused, his expression conflicted. "Your father would be hurt," he worried out loud eventually.

Lauren disagreed. "He'd be happy. He wants us to get married, remember? He went to great pains and expense to arrange it. And besides, given his health right now... Well, the stress of trying to put on a wedding, while at the same time arranging a merger of our two family companies, could not possibly be good for him."

Mitch began to relax. "You're right about that," he said, smiling once again.

"Please," Lauren said, taking his hand in hers, "let's just do it."

MITCH DIDN'T NEED much more convincing. He didn't want anything messing up the love they had found, either. The fact that she was willing to be so practical and businesslike about the exchanging of their vows boded well for the marriage ahead. So, that evening, they were in the Caribbean. They said their vows on a beautiful beach at sunset, and then made love all night and all the following day. Only the fact that they had to tell their families, and wanted to do so in person, had them back on the plane to Charleston Wednesday morning.

"We'll take a longer honeymoon as soon as we can," Mitch promised Lauren as they settled into their roomy first-class seats.

Lauren tucked her hand in his and sat as close to him as she possibly could. "You're assuming the honeymoon is going to end the moment we get back to Charleston," she teased, gently tracing the sensually chiseled outline of his lips with her fingertip. "It's not. Our honeymoon will continue wherever we are, regardless of what we're doing, the rest of our lives."

Mitch put his arm around her shoulders and drew her farther into the curve of his warm, strong body. "Lady, I like the way you think," he murmured, pressing tender kisses in her hair.

"And I like the way you make me feel," Lauren whispered, leaning over to kiss the strong, suntanned column of his neck.

"Which is...?" Mitch took her face in his hand and pressed his lips to hers.

"Loved. Cherished. Admired."

"That's good," Mitch whispered, pausing just long enough to kiss her once again. He drew back, looked deep into her eyes. "Because I feel all of those things for you, too, you know."

Lauren smiled as contentment flooded her heart. "I know."

"And I love you, too," Mitch continued, kissing her passionately once again. "With all my heart."

Too soon, their plane landed at the Charleston airport. They got Mitch's car out of the parking lot and began driving into the heart of the city. "What should we do first?" Lauren asked.

Mitch knew he had to talk to Payton Heyward before they told him of the marriage. He didn't want Lauren privy to that conversation. He frowned, hoping like heck she would understand as he told her, "I hate to do this. But I've got some crucial business to take care of. So how about we go our separate ways and each do what we need to do. And then meet up again this evening and go see our parents together and tell them the happy news."

To Mitch's relief, Lauren grinned. "That sounds good to me."

"Six o'clock tonight at 10 Gathering Street okay with you?" Mitch asked as he turned his car into the historic district, and then waited for a horse-drawn carriage full of tourists to make it across the next intersection.

"Seems like old times. And that's great. I'll see you then."

Mitch dropped Lauren at her place, and saw her safely inside, then went straight to Heyward Shipping. Payton Heyward saw him immediately in the executive office. He looked tanned and rested from his days of playing golf at Pinehurst. "I was wondering when I would hear from you," he said.

LAUREN KNEW she'd promised Mitch that she would wait and see their parents together, to tell them about the marriage, but she also wanted to talk to her father alone first. She wanted to tell him, before he found out about the marriage, that while she was accepting the property at 10 Gathering Street, she would not be accepting any funds from him to renovate and furnish it. Those, she could manage on her own. She also wanted to thank her father for matching her up with Mitch. It galled her to have to do it, but she knew she owed Payton a debt of gratitude since he had fixed her up with the man who had indeed turned out to be the love of her life.

She entered the executive suite at Heyward Shipping and noted that his secretary was away from her desk. Figuring her father wouldn't mind if she barged in, she swept toward the door then stopped dead at the sound of the familiar voices inside the suite.

"I told you before. There is no reason Lauren has to know about any of this," Payton was saying in an irritated voice.

"Look," Mitch returned, his voice just as short, "I know what the original deal was, but I'm telling you it's no longer viable."

"You want more money and influence—is that it?" Payton demanded, sounding just as incensed, betrayed and disbelieving as Lauren felt.

"I'd like to know that myself," Lauren said bitterly, opening the door the rest of the way and walking in unannounced. Unable to believe how gullible and foolish she had been, to follow her heart instead of her head, Lauren clamped her arms in front of her and glared at her "new husband." Calmly, quietly, she asked, "Exactly how much is marrying me worth to you, Mitch?"

MITCH SWORE INWARDLY at his bad luck and her timing as he swung around to face his wife of just thirty-six hours. "Lauren," he acknowledged her reluctantly.

Looking as if she was ready to burst into tears at any second, Lauren stepped forward and snatched the legal documents from his hand. It took only a minute or so for her to read through the legalese and understand what had been going on behind her back all along. Mitch didn't have to be a mind reader to know that the knowledge hit her like a bullet to the heart. She stared at Mitch as if seeing a stranger she didn't particularly like or want to get to know. "My father offered you controlling interest in the family company to marry me?" she asked incredulously.

Guilt and regret swept through Mitch in equal portions. Too late, he realized he should have told Lauren everything before they married rather than chance she would never have to know, or find out about it on her own. Mitch looked her straight in the eye. "Just because he offered it doesn't mean I was going to accept it," he stated bluntly, hoping she would give him credit for at least that much.

"No, you wanted more," Lauren said bitterly, citing the gist of what she had apparently just overheard.

"If you'll let me explain—" Mitch said.

"What's to explain?" Lauren waved the papers with her hands like a call to arms. "It says it all right here in the contract you were about to sign. All you had to do was marry me and you got fifty-one percent of the Heyward Shipping Company, as well as chief executive officer position during the transition period. That's a pretty tidy chunk of change and power for a quick 'I do' with me in the Bahamas, isn't it?" she asked sarcastically, moisture shimmering in her dark brown eyes. "No wonder you wanted to cut our honeymoon short so you could get back to work. And you—" Lauren turned to her father, clearly so outraged and hurt she could barely speak. "How could you make a deal like this behind my back?" she demanded hoarsely.

Payton regarded her in exasperation. "I was trying to protect you!"

"Too bad I don't see it that way," Lauren said bitterly. She ripped the papers in her hand in two and dropped them into the trash. She removed her wedding ring and threw it at Mitch's feet. Her lips pressed together furiously, Lauren glared at Mitch, then her father, then back at Mitch again. "Just so you know, gentlemen. The deal is off because my marriage is being annulled!"

Mitch started toward her. "You're making a mistake."

"I think so, too," Payton agreed.

"Yes, well, you both would," Lauren snapped, determined, it seemed, to think the worst of both of them. "But for once I am going to do what you both want me to do, and view this situation in a strictly businesslike way. I'm going to forget about what's in my heart and go by the hard facts in front of me. I'm going to treat my romantic relationships with the unemotional attitude and efficiency used in business. And this contract tells me that as much as I'd like to believe otherwise that the reason Mitch followed your very explicit directions and married me was because of all he had to gain. And because of that, Mitch Deveraux—'' she paused to give him a withering glance ''—I don't ever—ever—want to see you again!'' She turned on her heel and fled.

LAUREN WAS NEARLY to her car when Mitch caught up with her. Aware she had never looked as beautiful to him as she did at that moment, in a sleeveless white dress, with her cheeks full of color and her golden-brown hair blowing in the spring breeze, he asked angrily, ''Don't you think you should give me a chance to explain?''

Lauren's shoulders stiffened. ''After what you did to me I don't believe I owe you anything.''

Knowing the love they shared was too precious to write off, Mitch explained patiently, ''I came here to tell your father the deal was off.''

''Right,'' Lauren echoed sarcastically, throwing her arms up. ''I heard. You wanted more than what he had initially offered, and I can't say I blame you. You got me into the sack and wed to you!'' She shook her head, re-calling. ''Nice work, too. Romantic idiot that I am, I didn't suspect a thing.'' Her eyes narrowed. ''Even after I caught you spying on me and my father!''

Mitch shoved his fingers through his dark hair. ''I never wanted you to find out about this.'' He regretted like hell not being able to protect her.

Believing none of that, however, Lauren sized him up deliberately. ''Obviously,'' she agreed sweetly. ''You knew I'd be ticked off. And that I'd call the marriage off. And I am.''

His own temper beginning to flare out of control, Mitch

regarded Lauren stormily. "Doesn't the time we spent together mean anything to you?" he asked, aghast she could be so willing to simply call a halt to everything.

That, Lauren thought sadly, was the problem. It meant more than she could possibly say. Determined not to let Mitch know that, she said, "You have a lot of gall asking me that."

His eyes narrowed even more. "Damn it, Lauren," he said hoarsely, "I love you."

If only she could believe that, Lauren thought with more sadness than she ever thought she could possibly endure. "No," she corrected dispiritedly, "what you love, Mitch Deveraux, is the whole concept of an arranged marriage and the opportunity my father offered you." She didn't know who she resented more—her father for making her love for Mitch all about money and power in the end, or Mitch for taking advantage of her behind the scenes that way. All she knew for certain was that she had never wanted to feel the way she did right now—so hurt and disillusioned she could barely breathe, never mind think coherently.

Mitch grasped her arms gently and pulled her into the warm, comforting circle of his arms. "You mean more to me than that. You have to know that," he told her desperately.

Refusing to let the seductive power of his touch distract her from what was really going on there, Lauren flattened her hands against his chest and pushed away from him. "It's still not enough, Mitch." Her heart breaking, she regarded him haughtily. "And it never will be."

Mitch knew he had made some mistakes, for which he had apologized. But he had also told Lauren and showed her that he loved her in every way he could. And she still didn't believe him. Feeling more hurt and frustrated than he ever had in his life, he compressed his lips into a disapproving line and warned, "If you walk out on me now,

Lauren, it really will be over.'' Because it meant she had deceived him—when she'd promised to love and cherish him, through good times and bad, for the rest of their lives. It meant their marriage, brief as it was, had never been a real one after all. It meant their relationship was as flimsy and unsubstantial as the legal papers that had signified its end, able to be easily torn apart, destroyed.

''Good,'' Lauren retorted, looking every bit as hurt and angry as he felt. Her eyes glimmered wetly as she spun on her heel and stalked away. ''Because that is exactly what I want. For my relationship to you to be over once and for all.''

Chapter Seventeen

"I've finally had time to read and study your proposals for a Deveraux-Heyward merger," Tom Deveraux told Mitch several days later. "They're good. Providing Payton Heyward is still interested—"

Relief flowing through him, Mitch ushered his father into his office and shut the door behind him. "He is. I talked to him this morning."

Tom sat down in a chair in front of Mitch's desk and steepled his hands in front of him. He looked at Mitch with the unmitigated respect Mitch had always wanted as Mitch poured them both a cup of coffee. "You want to set up a meeting then?"

Mitch sat down in the leather swivel chair and checked the calendar on his desk. He was glad he had found out what was behind Payton's desire to merge companies and marry off his only daughter. Payton's illness had explained his actions, and that, plus a thorough accounting of the Heyward Shipping Company books, had provided the reassurance Tom and Mitch both needed to be able to trust Payton Heyward and his motives.

"How about later this afternoon?" Mitch suggested. "Payton and I were planning to meet around four, anyway, to discuss ways to better compete with the e-commerce companies that have been stealing our business—without cutting any of our existing sales forces.''

Tom sipped his coffee. ''I agree, we all need to continue to find cheaper ways to do things, while at the same time protecting the jobs of our current employees. It's the only way to stay competitive in today's market. And I had an idea about the sales force. I think we should bring in some instructors and start giving classes on the Web. We're going to need designers and programmers to maintain the Web site anyway, so why not train anyone who's interested—and I imagine a lot of the younger workers would be—to do business that way. We'd be giving them an added skill. And since they already know the shipping business, and the way things are done, it would be better for us, too, than hiring people with only a computer science background, for instance.''

Glad he finally had his father onboard, Mitch grinned. ''Sounds good, Dad.''

''Thanks for taking me into the future,'' Tom said.

Mitch looked at his dad. It had taken him nearly eight years to prove himself to his father, but for the first time, he felt they were working side by side, as equals. It was a good feeling. ''Anytime,'' he said thickly.

Tom grinned, stood and reached across the desk to shake Mitch's hand. ''So count me in on that meeting with Payton, and we'll start talking merger.''

''Will do.'' Mitch picked up his phone—he wanted to tell Payton that Tom would be joining them at the club.

Tom started to head out the door, then stopped and came back to Mitch's desk before Mitch could complete his call. Tom gave him a searching look. ''You know I never interfere in the personal lives of you and your siblings—''

Mitch gave his father a forbidding glance and slowly put the receiver back in its cradle. ''Then don't start now,'' he warned.

''Can't help it.'' Tom's eyes narrowed in concern. ''I

saw you the other night with Lauren Heyward—before the
two of you took the yacht out. The two of you appeared
to have something special.''

"Arranged by her father," Mitch qualified.

Tom shrugged, clearly not understanding what difference that made. "So?"

"So," Mitch said with mounting bitterness, "therefore
it doesn't count, according to Lauren."

Tom frowned, disagreeing. "She can't mean that."

"She does. Besides," Mitch sighed, admitting his own
culpability about this much, "she has every right to be
angry with me. I wasn't honest with her." Briefly, Mitch
explained the deal Payton Heyward had offered him—controlling interest of the company stock—if he married Lauren. Mitch shook his head, recounting with sincere regret,
"I should have told Lauren about it from the beginning
instead of keeping it a secret. If I had, well, we might still
be married today. Regardless, *that* wasn't a motivating fac-
tor for me."

Tom took another sip of his coffee and regarded his
second-eldest son thoughtfully. "Has your marriage been
annulled?"

Mitch shook his head and suddenly unbearably restless,
began to pace the confines of his office. "Only because
Lauren hasn't gotten around to giving me the papers," he
told his father as he poured himself a cup of coffee, too.
"As soon as she does…well, then it really will be over."

"Not necessarily," Tom said.

Mitch shoved a hand through his hair. "I hurt her,
Dad."

"Does that mean she can't forgive you?" Tom countered in a calm, compassionate way. Silence fell between
the two men. Tom set his coffee down and approached
Mitch. "Look, son, I know how you feel," he commiserated, clamping a warm, paternal hand on Mitch's shoulder. "Your pride is hurt. You know you did wrong and

you're sorry you hurt Lauren, but at the same time you also feel like she should be more understanding of what you're going through, and more able to forgive you.''

Mitch released a long, frustrated breath and closed his hand tightly around his coffee mug. ''That pretty much sums it up.'' He looked at his dad, man to man, son to father. ''How'd you know that anyway?''

''Because,'' Tom explained gently, his eyes glimmering with the depth of his own regret, ''that's how I felt with your mother when we started having difficulties years ago. I was at fault, so was she. But instead of continuing to go after her with the same unflagging determination that I approached my work here at the company—or the same relentlessness you pursued the merger with Heyward and our foray into the e-commerce world—I gave up and walked away. Figuring if she ever came to her senses, she would come back to me. That was a huge mistake on my part. I should never have walked away from Grace, no matter how hurt and angry we were over the breakdown of our marriage.''

''From what I can recall of that time,'' Mitch said quietly, ''Mom didn't want you anywhere near her.'' And in some respects, he amended sadly to himself, she still didn't.

''You're right—she didn't,'' Tom said, for once making no effort to hide his own misery and regret as he looked straight into Mitch's eyes. ''And I let her go because I was so hurt and angry. The point is, if we hadn't let all that time elapse, if we hadn't let our wounds fester to the point they became unmanageable, if we had just stuck together and kept trying to work things out, your mother and I might still be together to this day.''

CONCLUDING IT WOULD benefit her to be as busy as possible, Lauren spent the three days following her split with Mitch showing houses nonstop to Grace Deveraux. Unable to find an existing property suitable for her needs, and unwilling to go through the laborious renovation process, Grace finally decided she wanted to build something brand new and had purchased a piece of property on the beach at Sullivan's Island. Lauren paired her up with an architect renowned for turning his clients' dreams into reality, and then turned her attention back to 10 Gathering Street.

Saturday afternoon she was on a ladder listening to "I Will Survive" on her compact disk player and using a steamer to get the layers of old wallpaper off the dining-room walls when the doorbell rang. Deciding she didn't want to talk to anyone about anything, Lauren ignored the insistent ring and kept right on working.

Eventually it stopped, as she knew it would.

And then her father walked in, the key she'd given him for emergencies in hand. The first thing she noted was that he was in a rather formal-looking business suit and tie— as if he'd just come from an important business meeting. The second was that he looked better, stronger than he had in a while. "I'm here to apologize," Payton said. "I hope you accept it."

Lauren regarded her father warily, knowing if he hadn't interfered in her life she wouldn't have fallen in love with Mitch and then had her heart broken all to pieces when she discovered Mitch and Payton had both deceived her and manipulated her for business gain.

Lauren compressed her lips tightly. "That all depends on whether or not you ever plan to do anything like this again."

Payton quirked his eyebrow and countered dryly, "Arrange a marriage for you? I hardly think so. Particularly when you're still married to the love of your life."

Lauren blew out an exasperated breath. "Not for long if I have my way about it, and I will."

Payton's gaze narrowed all the more. "Oh, Lauren. Don't make my mistakes," he pleaded softly.

"What do you mean?" Lauren turned off the steamer and climbed down the ladder. She set the rented tool on a blanket on the floor. "You never tried to get your marriage to Mom overturned."

"But I did live in denial." Looking as full of regret as she felt, Payton sat down on the front staircase. "The whole time she was sick, I thought—hoped—it wasn't as serious as the doctors kept telling us it was."

Her father's confession stopped her cold. More willing to listen now, Lauren joined him on the third step up. "Is that why you spent more time at the office than at home, even at the end?" Lauren asked softly, remembering how hurt she had been about that.

Payton nodded, the sadness in his eyes mirroring the feelings deep inside her. "I pretended it wasn't happening, the same way you're pretending you aren't in love with Mitch Deveraux."

Lauren blinked back the tears gathering in her eyes. "It doesn't matter whether I love Mitch or not," she said thickly, struggling to rein in her emotions. "He lied to me."

"So did I," Payton admitted with heartfelt regret as he searched her eyes. "And I dare say you still love me."

"That's different," Lauren said stiffly, getting back to her feet once again.

"How?" Payton watched her pace the grand foyer restlessly.

"Because—" Lauren stammered.

Her father waited.

"You were trying to do what was best for me," Lauren said finally.

"So was he," Payton countered gently.

Lauren whirled to face him. "But he was my husband!" she protested.

"And I'm your father!" Payton stood, too. He gave her a paternal pat on the shoulder and continued soberly,

"We're not perfect, honey. No one is. Sometimes people make mistakes. Part of loving them is forgiving them."

LAUREN'S FATHER'S WORDS were still ringing in Lauren's ears when he let himself out and she went back to steaming off the wallpaper.

Somehow, though, now the woman-wronged spirit of the music didn't quite fit her mood. Again, the doorbell rang. Again, Lauren decided to ignore it. She had too much to think about. Too much to try to figure out. And that was when the front door opened, bathing her in a square of yellow sunshine, and Mitch walked in, a stack of official-looking legal documents in hand. Lauren didn't even have to ask where he'd gotten the key. She knew her father had given it to him. Nor did she have to ask what he had been doing, as he was dressed in the same formal-looking business clothes her father had been dressed in.

"If I didn't know better, I'd think you and my father were double-teaming me," she quipped lightly. "To try and get me to see things your way."

"I admit your father and I see eye to eye on the subject of my marriage to you," Mitch said.

Abruptly, Lauren felt herself getting angry. "You two have got to stop getting together and deciding my life for me," she said, trying not to notice how wonderfully handsome and determined he looked.

"Your father wants us to stay married."

"Only because he doesn't understand how complicated the situation between us is," Lauren countered. *Only because he doesn't understand how unwilling I am to let you, Mitch Deveraux, break my heart all to pieces.*

Smiling coolly, Mitch went on as if she hadn't spoken. "He also didn't want me to go ahead with these papers until after I had talked to you first. But I told him I had to do it. It was the only way you would know we were free and clear of the situation that has brought us so much unhappiness in the end.''

Lauren took another look at the papers in Mitch's hands. And suddenly she had an idea what they were. No doubt Mitch had tired of waiting for the annulment papers she had promised she would get, and had arranged for the end of their foolhardy marriage himself, so they could both be "free and clear of the situation that had brought them so much unhappiness."

Feeling as if both her heart and her spirit were broken, Lauren stayed right where she was. "Leave them by the door. I'll read and sign them later," she commanded just as tranquilly. And turned back to the wall before he could see the anguish in her eyes.

Ignoring her orders, Mitch walked over to stand next to the ladder. "Thanks," he said mildly, appearing prepared to wait her out indefinitely as he tilted his face up to hers. "But just for the record, these papers don't require your signature."

She should have known he would try and one-up her in this matter, too. "Gee." Lauren scowled and pretended an insouciance she couldn't begin to feel as she tilted her face down to his. "You can get an annulment without my knowledge? Who would have guessed?"

Mitch sighed, abruptly looking not so patient after all. "Just come down here and read the papers, Lauren. Then we'll talk."

Able to see she wasn't going to get him to leave until she complied with what he wanted, Lauren switched off the steamer and stepped carefully down the ladder. A mistake, for as soon as her feet hit the floor, she was aware all over again how tall and strong he was. And how much she wanted to be wrapped in his arms, feeling safe and protected and desired again. Doing her level best to ignore the way her knees were trembling and her heart was thudding against her ribs, Lauren wiped her hands on the hips of her khaki work pants and then took the papers.

"It's a little late for a prenuptial agreement, but it's not too late for a postnuptial agreement," Mitch explained matter-of-factly. "So I talked to your father, and the two of us had one drawn up."

"There you go again," Lauren said, piqued. She braced herself for the fireworks to come. "Joining forces and doing things together without my knowledge or permission." Would the two men she loved most in the entire world *never* learn?

"Hey! I tried to get you involved," Mitch said in his own defense. "You refused to return my calls, and instead insisted on an annulment."

Lauren swallowed, turned her eyes from his and continued to read. "It says here you refuse to accept any dowry for either dating or marrying me, that you will not now or ever hold any part of Heyward Shipping Company stock, even if a merger does occur. And that should said merger occur, it will be negotiated and handled by Payton Heyward and Tom Deveraux—you are excusing yourself from any involvement in said merger."

"Right."

Lauren let the papers drop to midthigh. She stared at him making no effort to hide her puzzlement. "Why would you do that?" she asked, aghast. She knew how long and hard Mitch had worked trying to make the merger happen. He'd said himself it was the one way—maybe even the only way—to prove to himself and his father how much he could do for the family company, given half a chance. It was also the only way he could finance their two companies' entry into the e-commerce shipping world, and still keeping expanding and adding state-of-the-art ships to their fleets.

"Because my marriage to you means more than any job," Mitch explained patiently, looking as if he meant to make her his again, this time with no holds barred. "To the point, I've told my father to find a replacement for me because I'm getting out of the shipping business entirely."

Lauren handed the papers back to him. "You can't do that!" she said as a little gasp was wrung from her. "You love the shipping business."

Mitch tossed the papers aside, turned back to her and took her all the way in his arms. "Not as much as I love you," he said, continuing to look down at her in that all-consuming way that made her feel for the first time—the only time—in her life, as really and truly loved as she was meant to be.

Lauren's heart did a flip-flop in her chest as she thought about what all this meant. The ache in her throat intensified as she tilted her face up to his. "Did you tell my father that, too?"

Mitch nodded, his expression solemn and direct. "He said I was a fool. And I told him I'd been a fool to let you get away, but no longer. I'm here to stay, Lauren," Mitch promised her resolutely, before continuing in a rusty-sounding voice, "I'm telling you here and now I'll do whatever I have to do to work this out because you mean more than anything in the world to me."

The tears Lauren had been holding back slipped down her face.

Using his fingertips, Mitch gently wiped the moistness from her face. "I'm sorry, Lauren," Mitch whispered rue-fully, wrapping his arms around her and bringing her as close as she had always wanted to be. He stroked a hand lovingly through her hair. "I should have told you from the get-go what your father had up his sleeve."

Relief flowing through her in waves, Lauren met his eyes. "Why didn't you?" she asked thickly.

"I thought you'd probably refuse to date me at all if you knew just how far your father was willing to go to bring the two of us together,'' he admitted quietly, his regret evident.

''You're right about that. I would have,'' Lauren confessed slowly.

''And,'' Mitch continued, ''I didn't think it mattered since I had no intention of ever taking him up on the secret part of his offer, the dowry.''

Lauren hesitated. As much as she loved Mitch—and she did, with all her heart—she still needed to know that their love had nothing to do with business. ''What about all the stuff you said about an arranged marriage being the way to go?'' she asked warily after a moment, thinking that he had never looked more caring or more devoted to her than he did at that very moment.

Mitch regarded her with quiet confidence. ''I still believe a husband and wife need to talk things out and negotiate the things that are important to them, just the way you do in business. But the rest of it was just a way of getting under your skin.''

Lauren grinned and ran her fingers through the neatly combed layers of his thick dark hair. ''You did that all right,'' she teased back.

''Does this mean you're willing to give us another chance?'' Mitch asked gruffly.

Lauren nodded and tugged him closer. She brought his head down to hers and they indulged in a kiss that left her feeling glowing and alive. When at last they drew apart, she whispered tearfully, ''Oh, Mitch, I'm sorry, too. I should have listened to you when you tried to explain.''

He held her tenderly, his arms warm and strong around her, and looked deep into her eyes. ''We're together now, that's all that's important.''

''You're right about that,'' Lauren agreed as he lowered his lips to hers and delivered a masterfully possessive kiss that left her spirits soaring.

''So what do you say I give you a hand with this wallpaper,'' he suggested cheerfully, already unbuttoning his suit jacket.

"Later," Lauren said, taking him by the hand and leading him toward the stairs. Knowing she had never felt happier or more content, she turned to him and smiled. "First, we have a honeymoon to continue."

"MITCH?" LAUREN SAID an ecstatic time later.

"Hm?"

"I want you to tear up that post-nuptial agreement you signed because our fathers were right. Our families need someone of the next generation to run the Deveraux-Heyward company. They need you. And I want you to realize all your dreams, just the way I have mine."

Mitch studied her, all the love he felt for her shining in his eyes. "You're sure about this?" he asked softly, still willing to give it all up.

"Very." Lauren cuddled even closer, knowing she had never been more certain of anything in her life. "I think that's what married love is all about, making sure your mate is fulfilled on all levels. And I know the shipping business makes you very happy, so I say go for it and make us all proud."

"You are one very smart and very generous lady." Mitch kissed her slowly, tenderly. "I just wish all my siblings could be as content as we are."

"Maybe they will be," Lauren supposed joyously. "After all, you and Chase have found your mates. Maybe Amy and Gabe will, too."

"Hm." Chase smiled. "I wonder who will be next."

* * *

Look out for My Secret Wife *in November 2003*

SILHOUETTE®
SPECIAL EDITION™

AVAILABLE FROM 17TH OCTOBER 2003

GOOD HUSBAND MATERIAL Susan Mallery

Hometown Heartbreakers

When Kari Asbury revisited her home town she never expected to bump into ex-fiancé Sheriff Gage Reynolds. But could Kari find the courage to overcome their past and stand by the man she'd always loved?

TALL, DARK AND IRRESISTIBLE Joan Elliott Pickart

The Baby Bet: MacAllister's Gifts

Ryan Sharpe was blatantly masculine, sexy and…irresistible. He could be with anyone, but his passionate pursuit told Carolyn he wanted *only* her. Dare Carolyn believe he'd still want her when he learned her secret?

MY SECRET WIFE Cathy Gillen Thacker

The Deveraux Legacy

A secret sex-only marriage was the only way Dr Gabe Deveraux knew to help best friend Maggie Calloway have a baby. But soon Gabe was forced to admit the truth—he'd secretly loved Maggie for years.

AN AMERICAN PRINCESS Tracy Sinclair

When Shannon Blanchard won TV's hottest game show, she never dreamed that her prize of two weeks at a royal castle would change her life. Until she set eyes on tall, dark and dangerously attractive Prince Michel de Mornay…

LT KENT: LONE WOLF Judith Lyons

Journalist Angie Rose wanted to unveil the hero…the mysterious millionaire that was Lt Jason Kent. But how could she expose Jason's secrets when their passion—*her heart*—revealed they were meant to be together?

THE STRANGER SHE MARRIED Crystal Green

Kane's Crossing

Two years ago Rachel Shane's husband vanished. Then, without warning, a rugged stranger with familiar eyes sauntered into her life professing amnesia. He was *all*-male and every inch a dangerous temptation…

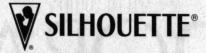

THE
COLTONS
A Colton Family Christmas

JUDY
CHRISTENBERRY

LINDA
TURNER

CAROLYN
ZANE

4 FREE

books and a surprise gift!

We would like to take this opportunity to thank you for reading this Silhouette® book by offering you the chance to take FOUR more specially selected titles from the Special Edition™ series absolutely FREE! We're also making this offer to introduce you to the benefits of the Reader Service™—

- ★ FREE home delivery
- ★ FREE gifts and competitions
- ★ FREE monthly Newsletter
- ★ Exclusive Reader Service discount
- ★ Books available before they're in the shops

Accepting these FREE books and gift places you under no obligation to buy, you may cancel at any time, even after receiving your free shipment. Simply complete your details below and return the entire page to the address below. *You don't even need a stamp!*

YES! Please send me 4 free Special Edition books and a surprise gift. I understand that unless you hear from me, I will receive 6 superb new titles every month for just £2.90 each, postage and packing free. I am under no obligation to purchase any books and may cancel my subscription at any time. The free books and gift will be mine to keep in any case.

E3ZEE

Ms/Mrs/Miss/Mr ....Initials......................................
BLOCK CAPITALS PLEASE

Surname ....

Address ....

....

....Postcode...................................

Send this whole page to:
UK: FREEPOST CN81, Croydon, CR9 3WZ
EIRE: PO Box 4546, Kilcock, County Kildare (stamp required)